SHADOWS IN DEEP BLUE

Suzanne Cass

S C
STORM CLOUD
PRESS

Shadows in Deep Blue

Storm Cloud Press, Perth Australia

Copyright © 2018 by Suzanne Cass

Cover by Vikncharlie

All rights reserved.

This is a work of fiction. Names, characters, places and incidents are products of the authors imagination or are used fictitiously. Any resemblance to actual events, locales, organisations, or persons, living or dead, is entirely coincidental.

Dedication

For the people of Margaret River and for my mum.

CHAPTER ONE

Ebony McAllister was drowning.

A wave broke over her face and filled her nostrils with burning saline water. Ebony's throat stung and her body shook with a fit of coughing. Glimpses of Redgate Beach over the tops of the steely gray waves showed the thin band of sand was a lot further away than she first thought.

Choppy waves kept crashing into her, the ocean rising up against her, determined not to let her pass. A larger wave broke over her head and this time she felt herself being driven down into the depths. She had to struggle hard to find the surface.

It took a few seconds for Ebony to shake free of the cascading water and take a gasping breath. Adrenaline coursed through her body, making her limbs shaky and increasingly ineffective.

The next wave—bigger than any before—loomed and smashed down on top of her, burying her deep beneath the iron-gray surface.

Ebony struggled upwards, but her flailing arms and legs seemed to take her nowhere. Her eyes sprang open in fright, but she was surprised to see that beneath the surface the water was no longer a bruised slate color; rather a haunting blue. And so much calmer. Down here she didn't have to battle through the senseless, smashing waves.

She stopped thrashing and let her gaze wander, seeing nothing but never-ending sapphire to the ends of her vision. It was peaceful and quiet and if she stopped pumping her legs, she floated effortlessly in the water. Like a rag doll. Without direction and without care.

A tiny voice whispered in her head that it was tranquil here; maybe she could stay for a while. It was easy to just float and glide with the currents, allowing the Indian Ocean carry her where it may.

Let the tide and the waves take her down, not fight and scramble and scream to get to the surface. Stay here, surrounded by this impassive beauty.

If she never came back from the ocean would she finally be liberated? Finally be absolved of the guilt? It was a tantalizing thought.

Bubbles rose like spheres of pure silver from her nose and she watched, fascinated, as the last breath left her body.

A dark shape cut through the surface above her. Something tugged at her hair. It hurt, and she winced at the intrusion into her guiltless world.

Then someone grabbed a handful of her hair, and this time she felt herself being lifted upwards.

A hand reached down and grasped her under the arm, then her head broke through the surface of the water and her lungs instinctively sucked in great gulps of life-giving air.

"You okay?" A deep voice broke through her numb mind, but she couldn't answer, she was coughing too hard, gasping for air.

"I saw you go down that last time and I didn't think I'd be able to find you in this god-awful murky water."

She tried to croak out an answer, but another spasm of coughing overtook her. Gentle hands pushed her upwards, maneuvring her onto a surfboard.

Lying on her stomach, she allowed her body to be guided shoreward by the strong paddling arms of the man behind her.

* * *

"We're on shore. You're safe. You can open your eyes now." Jay Connolly watched anxiously as the woman lying on the sand—who looked more like a drowned kitten than anything else right now—slowly unglued each salty eyelid. He pressed a hand into the wet sand beside her head as she stared up at the leaden clouds sulking unhurriedly across the sky above, ready to start first aid procedures if she didn't answer.

Her gaze flicked toward him and awareness dawned in her eyes. He could see she understood she was alive, thanks to him. But she still wasn't talking, and he hovered above her, scowling in consternation.

"How are you feeling? Shall I call an ambulance? Did you swallow any water?" His questions came thick and fast. He needed her to answer.

"No. No. Please no! I'm fine. Just give me a moment," she finally croaked.

Thank God. She was talking and she seemed coherent. His pounding heart began to slow its erratic beat as he watched faint color come back into her face. He'd seen her dark head —a black dot on the gray ocean surface—go under for the first time as he paddled powerfully against the rising swell. But when she'd disappeared the second time, he'd not been sure he would get there. Desperate to find her, he'd flung himself from the safety of the surfboard, diving deep and searching wildly in the murky water.

Finally, his fingers felt the swish of floating hair and he'd grabbed it and held on with all his might as he rose to the surface. Now he could see her hair was fairly short and it was just luck he'd been able to snatch a handful. Any shorter and he may not have got her. The relief when she'd taken that first, ragged breath, was still a palpable thing inside his chest.

"Are you sure? You nearly drowned."

The woman groaned at his words, as if she didn't want to hear them. Shaking her head, she tried to sit up, but her movements were slow and she almost fell back onto the sand. He curled his arm around her shoulders to steady her. Tears formed in her eyes and she shook her head again, as if to rid herself of them.

"It's okay, you're just in mild shock." He tried to make his voice gentle, but it came out harsher than he wanted as he battled against his own fear at her near-miss with death.

It was her lucky day that Jay was surfing Conti's Break that afternoon. Otherwise the outcome might've been disastrously different.

* * *

That was when Ebony remembered she was only dressed in her underwear. But it was more than just embarrassment making her want to curl into a tight ball to cover her nakedness. Had he seen them? Had he seen her scars?

He seemed to be doing a very good job of ignoring her attire, however, and if he had seen her scars, he gave no indication. She was more than just a little mortified she had to be rescued from the ocean, but to be salvaged in her underwear as well. She wanted the sand to swallow her whole and pretend this never happened.

To make things worse her teeth chose that particular moment to chatter together violently, as uncontrolled trembling took over her entire body.

"You're freezing," he said, concern again furrowing dark eyebrows. "Wait here, I've got a towel and some clothes up behind the sand dunes. I'll get them for you. Wait here," he repeated, as if she may just up and run away.

Perhaps if she had the strength she might indeed do that, but instead she only said, "Thanks," from between chattering teeth.

The man sprinted up the beach, his black wetsuit-covered form disappearing from view over the nearest dune.

An explosion of red and tan fur erupted from the shoreline, hitting Ebony with the weight of a cannon ball, sending her tumbling backward onto the sand.

"Chili Dog!" Ebony was nearly as pleased to see her dog as the dog was to see her. The dog's warm tongue frantically licked Ebony's face, unheeding of all the wet sand she was spreading around in her frenzy. Despite her bone-chilling shuddering, Ebony smiled at Chili's enthusiasm. The dog snuggled in close to her side, but her wet fur was no help at all in warming her up. Pushing Chili gently away, Ebony struggled to sit up again, hugging her knees to her chest in a vain attempt to hold onto her last remaining body heat.

The gusts blowing straight off the ocean froze her to the bone and she wondered why her perfectly good wetsuit was still hanging in her cupboard at home. Normally she would've been wearing it on a day like this. It was early summer, and the beach should've been warm and inviting, but a cold snap had driven the temperature back down so it felt almost like winter again. The south-west of Western Australia could be like that, four seasons in one day someone had once told her.

Then she remembered why her mind had been pre-occupied with other thoughts when she left the cottage this afternoon.

It was her birthday today. Turning another year older always rattled her.

Today had hit her like a brick wall. She was forty years old. But it wasn't her age bothering her.

Her daughter would be twenty-three by now.

Exactly twenty-two years since she'd last seen her. Since she left her behind.

For some reason, on this day, she felt more alone and lost than any other birthday she could remember.

She hadn't intended to go for a swim when she'd stumbled down to the beach. She'd just been looking for somewhere to escape from her thundering thoughts, the clamoring images that taunted her. Her mind, fogged by memories, had not been thinking clearly when she stripped down to her underwear and plunged into the water. It was the memories driving Ebony to find sanctuary on the beach, hoping the wind and the fresh briny water would cleanse her mind, wash away the reminders. Take away the gnawing guilt.

Memories of a cherub baby face. A little girl with wide blue eyes and downy blonde hair, reaching out a pudgy hand, entreaty in her cheeky smile. Until Ebony reached out her own hand and was rewarded with warm sticky fingers grasping firmly onto hers.

Never again would she look into those amazing blue eyes, or clasp that little hand in her own. Normally she could keep these feelings of loss and bereavement shut behind a heavy wall in her mind. She knew they were there, waiting for an unguarded moment to reappear and taunt her. But most days she was able to cope. Today, not so much. She just wanted to be free of remorse, free of the destitute sadness she kept so artfully hidden from the rest of the world.

Chili licked her face, breaking her reverie and Ebony shook her head to get rid of the dog's affectionate tongue.

Ebony rubbed her legs in a feeble attempt to bring some warmth back into them. She'd been bloody silly today and now after her freezing dip in the ocean, she couldn't believe she'd been feeling so desperately sorry for herself she'd walked out of her house so severely under-prepared. It was unlike her. In general, she kept up a cheery façade that had most people fooled. Except today, when that strong mental fortitude had slipped. And look what'd nearly happened. Time to put the façade firmly back in place.

A dry towel landed on her shoulders and then her rescuer appeared in front of her, wrapping her tightly in the fabric and rubbing her shoulders to force some warmth back into her body.

"Thank you," she said, chattering through her teeth.

"Not a problem." His tone was almost brusque and his movements capable, as if it was the norm to rescue a drowning woman every day of the week. "We need to get you warmed up, or you'll get hypothermia. And if that happens then I really will need to call an ambulance. Although it'd take a while for an ambulance to get here on these roads," he mused, lips puckered in thought. "You picked a pretty isolated spot to swim." With a skeptical quirk to his brow he asked, "What are you doing all the way out here anyway?"

The rough five-o-clock shadow gave his strong jawline a rugged appearance, as his piercing gaze bored into her while he waited for an answer.

"I live close by. I swim here all the time," she answered, still fighting her chattering teeth.

"You live close by here?" His voice contained a hint of disbelief. Instead of waiting for an answer he stopped his rubbing and dumped a backpack off his back and onto the sand. Rummaging around in its depths he finally pulled out a dark blue woolen sweater.

"This should do the trick," he said with a satisfied grunt. "Put this on and then wrap the towel around your legs."

Gratefully, she slipped the sweater on, glad of its soft warmth that helped cover her near-nakedness, making sure she kept her back partially turned away from him as she did so.

"Maybe I should light a fire, it might help," he said, already scouting around for dry driftwood.

"Oh no, you don't need to do that. I'm fine now, especially with your sweater." She plastered what she hoped was a winning smile on her frozen face. She was already uncomfortable this stranger had rescued her and lent her his clothes; he didn't need to go the bother of lighting a fire as well. What she really needed was to get home. To curl up in the fetal position on her couch so she could reconcile what this black mood had led her to do.

"Are you sure?" He still sounded doubtful.

"Yes, I'm positive. Like I said, I live close by, I'll just go home and warm up there." Thankful as she was to this man, she was silently wishing him away now. She stood up, clutching the soft sweater close. "Thank you again," she said and then paused. "I seem to be saying that a lot, but you have to know how truly grateful I am to you. Thank you just doesn't seem to be enough."

"Well it's enough for now." He stood alongside her. "Come on then, lead the way."

"What?" Confusion clouded her still-numb mind. "What do you mean?"

"I mean you don't think I'm going to go to all the trouble of pulling you out of that freezing ocean and then not see you safely home and dry, do you?"

Not what she wanted at all. She wanted to be rid of this man, so she could wallow in her own desperation and stupidity. "Oh, you don't need to do that. I—"

"Oh yes I do." The steely look in his dark blue eyes told her he'd brook no argument.

CHAPTER TWO

Ebony led the way in silence through the sandy track that wound away from the beach into the scrubby coastland. He followed wordlessly behind her. As usual, Chili Dog snuffled around in the bushes off to the side, popping back onto the track every now and then to make sure they were still following. Ebony picked up her clothes from the spot she'd left them in a sandy pile at the start of her beach track. As soon as she got back to her hut, she'd give him his sweater back.

"Don't you think we should introduce ourselves?" His voice sounded loud behind her.

Clenching her jaw, Ebony turned to face him, having to duck her head to evade some low hanging branches as she did so. Her name was the least she owed the man who'd risked his life to save her.

"Sorry, I've completely forgotten my manners. I'm Ebony."

"My name is Jason." He extended his hand toward her. "But my friends call me Jay." He smiled for the first time and Ebony noticed a row of very white, very straight teeth. The smile loosened the tight lines around his eyes, lighting up his face and Ebony was struck at once by his handsome features. Her foggy brain had registered that he was good-looking down at the beach, but now she was up close and a bit warmer, his chiseled cheekbones gave her goose-bumps all over.

"Nice to meet you, Jay." Reluctantly she let his hand enfold hers. It was warm and sturdy against her cold fingers. The contact caused an unexpected jolt up her arm and she almost flinched away from him.

She took a quick perusal of her savior. He was taller than her—although that wouldn't be hard given her petite stature —but not tall enough to tower over her. He had short dark hair, almost regimental, but left a little longer on top where it showed a tendency to curl. A strong, square jaw highlighted determined dark brows that hovered over the most brilliant dark-blue eyes she'd ever seen. The combination of dark hair and blue eyes wasn't one Ebony was accustomed to, especially here in Margaret River where the local surfers usually sported long blond locks and tanned skin. He looked to be in his early to mid-thirties and his proficient no-nonsense attitude suggested he wasn't so unused to rescuing people.

"It's not far to go now," she said, turning quickly to hide the confusion at her body's visceral reaction to him. Maybe she really did have hypothermia and it was blurring her mind, making her more receptive to the effect of a virile male so close to her. She crossed her arms tight over her chest in a vain attempt to quell the tiny shivers that were not all due to the cold.

Leading him deeper into the scrub, they walked up a small incline and she stopped at the top, so he could catch up with her.

"You live here?" He couldn't hide the incredulity in his voice.

"Yes I do. I know it's not much, but I like it." Her tone was defensive but she didn't care. She loved her little house in the bush. It was quaint, idyllic even. She loved the washed-out suntanned color of the rammed-earth walls and the weather-beaten corrugated iron roof, even if it was lifting up in a couple of places.

"No, you've got me wrong." He chuckled at the indignant rise of her eyebrow. "I was admiring the place, not condemning it. Not many people get to live in such a peaceful place as this."

"Really?"

"Really!" She followed his gaze as it slid appreciatively over the small cottage huddled into the stand of banksia trees in the small valley below.

"I honestly thought you'd made this up, that maybe you swallowed too much sea water or something. I've been coming to this beach for years now and I never knew this place existed."

"I haven't lived here long." Just shy of three months to be exact. But that wasn't unusual for her.

"It looks like it could do with a little bit of TLC."

She had to agree, the outside timber-work of the front porch desperately needed painting and the weeds that gamboled around the outskirts of the building were tall enough to hide a small child.

"It suits me fine," she said with a shrug.

"It's a fairly secluded little place, you don't live here alone do you?"

Her skin prickled at the veiled implication behind his question. Belatedly, she wondered how sensible it was to bring a strange man back to her isolated shack. If she screamed way out here no one would hear her.

No, intuition told her she could trust this man. There'd been genuine concern in his face when he'd first entreated her to open her eyes on the beach, and a resigned protectiveness in his air when he'd insisted on walking her home. She believed he was sincere when he said that all he wanted to do was to see her safely home. He was obviously a local, so why hadn't she met him before?

"Yes, I do. And that's the way I like it." Let him put whatever connotations into her lifestyle he liked. She was proud of her independence and happy with the fact she didn't have to answer to anyone else in this world besides herself. "Anyway, I have Chili Dog. She's better protection than any other person I know." *And a better companion*. At least her dog would never hit her. Or lock her, cowering and petrified in a room for hours on end.

At the mention of her name, the dog appeared beside them and proceeded to escort them down the hill, red tail waving happily through the long grass that edged the side of the track.

* * *

"Thanks for the loan of your sweater." Ebony handed Jay the warm woolen garment, giving it a last shake to get rid of any remaining stow-away sand from the beach.

"You're welcome," he replied, handing her a cup of tea in return.

He'd insisted on coming inside her little cottage and proceeded to make himself right at home in the kitchen while she went to have a shower to warm up, her repeated entreaties that she was fine completely lost on him. His concern was unwarranted, she was very used to fending for herself. But she had to admit a small part of her was touched by his matter-of-fact thoughtfulness. And as long as she was admitting to truths about herself, his presence in her house also lightened her mood. The urge to curl into that fetal ball on her couch and bathe in her own misery wasn't quite so strong anymore.

"It's not every day I get to lend my sweater to an attractive woman."

She frowned. Was that supposed to be a compliment? His façade never wavered from a solemn regard of her, even though she searched his eyes for any hint of false flattery. Heat flushed up Ebony's neck and she ducked her head. Was he flirting with her? Not possible. She was too old for anyone to want to flirt with her anymore.

"Thanks for the tea, it's great." A change of subject was in order. The mug of tea was hot in her hands, almost scalding, but she liked the heat.

"Warm, sweet liquids are always good after you've had a shock." Again, he sounded like he knew what he was talking about and again she found herself wondering exactly what it was he did for a living.

He stood in her small lounge room, still encased in his black wetsuit, appraising the tiny house with his blue gaze. Placing his own mug on the nearest table, he unexpectedly unzipped his wetsuit and proceeded to strip down to the waist. All of a sudden, Ebony was confronted with a view of a strong chest and a well-muscled stomach. Quick as she could, she dragged her glance away, not wanting to be caught staring. Was that a scar zigzagging its way down his stomach? There was another wound high up on his shoulder as well. She sucked her breath in over her teeth with a quiet hiss. What had this man done to deserve such scars? And there was also some kind of Celtic looking tattoo over his left pec, near his heart. Some kind of stylized tree. Ebony liked it, it gave him even more of a dangerous edge.

Scars to match her own. But hers were marks of shame. She'd bet a hundred dollars his were gained by nobler pursuits.

She couldn't remember the last time she'd had a half-naked man standing in her living room, especially not one that looked this good. He seemed completely unaware of her discomfort. As he reached into his backpack on the floor and pulled out a t-shirt, she took a few steps backward, too lost in the sight of his bulging bicep to have anything sensible to say.

He flashed another one of his devastating smiles her way. "I must admit, I am a little cold myself now. Hope you don't mind if I change into some warm clothes." He pulled the t-shirt over his head and then followed it with the woolen sweater she'd just returned. But when he started rolling the wetsuit further down, she was suddenly galvanized into action.

"I'll just go and wait outside while you finish." Backing out of the front door, she whistled Chili to follow her.

"Okay," he said without looking up. "I'll bring my cuppa out in a minute."

Closing the door smartly behind her, Ebony let out a small grunt of amusement. The wind ruffled her hair and she drew in a deep, calming breath of cool air.

Ebony raked her fingers through her damp hair. She tried to smooth it into some semblance of order, but as usual the unruly black curls that hung just below her chin wouldn't be tamed. Catching a glimpse of herself in the little decorative mirror hung from the edge of the porch, Ebony's gray eyes stared back at her, and not for the first time she wished they could've been a nice blue, or a fetching green, anything would've been better than the odd light gray reflected back at her. There were a few small wrinkles starting to show around her eyes, but genetics were on her side, and her high cheekbones and creamy skin kept a youthful look to her face. Irritably she pushed a curl behind her ear. In general, she didn't feel her age, so why had she let it bother her today? Forty was just another number, right?

The door creaked open and Jay came to stand next to her under the cover of her tiny porch.

"Sorry, I didn't mean to make you uncomfortable in your own house."

"No, that's quite all right, you didn't," she lied.

Chili got up from her resting spot in a huge patch of weeds and came over to sniff Jay's shoes. He bent down to pat her head. Without thinking, Ebony found her gaze tracing the outline of his broad shoulders as he bent over.

"She's a good-looking dog. Kelpie is she? Red Cloud?"

"Yes, she is." Ebony was impressed. "How did you know that?" Most people didn't even recognize that Chili was a Kelpie, a breed of renowned Australian sheepdog, let alone that her ochre red coat and light tan chest and feet marked her as special.

"I like dogs." He stood up again. "I have a German Shepherd cross called Axel. He likes to try and swim out to me when I'm surfing, but I'm worried he'll get taken by a shark or something, so I don't usually bring him along when I'm surfing." Jay chuckled and Ebony was struck by the deep richness of his laugh.

"Chili hates swimming in the sea, she just runs up and down the beach chasing the waves. It's the only place she won't follow me, otherwise she's like my little shadow wherever I go." She smiled down at her faithful dog.

"It was lucky she was on the beach today. It was her insane barking that alerted me to your troubles in the first place. If it hadn't been for her, I might've paddled back in and never even known you were there."

"Thank you again for saving me." There it was again, that awkward gratitude. She did owe him big time. What was she going to do about that? She plastered a grateful smile on her face.

"What were you doing out there?" The note of concern was back in his voice as he fixed a firm, inquiring gaze on her.

"Like I said, I often go swimming at the beach." She kept her tone breezy and light. It was true after all.

"You were a long way from shore," he said quietly.

"I know, and I don't understand how I got that far out." And that was also the truth. How she'd got that far out without noticing still shocked her. "I must've lost track of how long I'd been swimming."

"You sure you're okay then?" His blue eyes searched her face, deadly serious now.

It was on the tip of her tongue to tell him that it was her birthday. It might be nice to have one person wish her happy birthday just this once. It might take the sting out of the desperate loneliness she'd been feeling all day. But of course she couldn't tell him. She could tell no one. Because that might lead to the story of her baby. And no one could know about her.

"Of course I am. I'm fine. You don't need to worry about me anymore."

"Hmm." His non-committal reply made it obvious he didn't believe her. There was an uncomfortable silence and for once Ebony didn't race to fill it.

"You said you haven't lived here long, is that why I haven't seen you in town?" The implied question hovered in the air and her shoulders tensed as she let out an inaudible sigh. She hated having to answer the same questions over and over, and she hated the conclusions people usually jumped to.

"Yes, I only moved to Margaret River about three months ago."

He nodded, his gaze drifting out over the enclosing sand dunes. "Ah, I've been off on a business trip for the past two and a half months. Buying stock and checking out improvement strategies for my retail shop."

"Oh." He owned a business, was self-sufficient. She was sure he was going to say he worked in some kind of military capacity, a fire fighter, or security guard. It would've made more sense with his no-nonsense, cool, take-charge kind of personality.

"Do you travel around a lot then?" His question was more insightful than he realized.

"I guess you could say that." Concealing the wariness she always felt at questions like these, she hoped she sounded casual as she waved her arms in an all-encompassing gesture. "I like to get out there and experience the world. There are so many beautiful places to see here in Australia. I'd love to sample them all." If only that were the truth. The truth was, she'd like nothing more than to stay put in one place for more than a few months at a time. But that was a luxury for people with real lives, real families, real jobs, and real loves.

"Sounds like you lead a pretty carefree lifestyle." His voice sounded enthralled, but she noticed a slight tightening of his jaw. Had he guessed she was being intentionally vague?

"This is the first time I've been in the south of Western Australia though," she admitted. "It's just as wonderful as I've been told."

"Yeah it is that." Taking a last swig of his tea, he leaned back against the wooden pillar supporting the tiny porch, the move bringing his shoulder to within inches of hers. The urge to take a step back, away from his nearness, was strong but she stood her ground. "I came here a little over four years ago for a bit of a surfing holiday and look at me now, I'm still here." He flashed her a quick grin. "I found it pretty hard to go past the natural beauty of the superb beaches and those never-ending Karri forests. Toss in the laid-back lifestyle of the surfers and hippies in this area and you've got yourself an almost perfect little town."

"It does seem quite idyllic," she murmured in reply, her gaze tracing the outline of the undulating tree-covered hills rolling inland toward the horizon. When she returned her gaze, he was staring at her thoughtfully with those brilliant blue eyes.

Her stomach contracted, and curls of tension wended their way down her legs. His gaze trapped her like a rabbit in a snare. What was going on behind those unreadable eyes of his? She wished she knew. Her lack of experience when it came to reading male body language put her at a disadvantage and she felt somehow vulnerable. She licked her lips.

Still watching her intently he announced, "Anyway, I'd better be off before it gets dark. I just wanted to make sure you were okay after your dunking." He headed inside to grab his backpack. She took a few precious moments to reclaim her cool veneer, the smile firmly fixed back on her face when he returned.

"Will you be able to find your way back to the beach? Shall I go with you?"

"Nah, I'm pretty good at finding my way around, don't worry about me," he said, retrieving the surfboard he'd leant against the porch.

"Oh, as long as you're sure." She hesitated. Maybe she should go with him. He did seem to be more than competent, however. She watched him stride confidently up the little track toward the beach.

"Next time you're in town, stop by my place. It's called The Bottom Out Surf Shop," he called out over his shoulder as he walked away.

"You own a surf shop?" Why had that little tidbit not come up in conversation earlier?

"Yep, it's hard to miss, it's at the bottom of Main Street in town, hence the name."

"I might just do that," she called across the distance between them.

"Good, see you then," he yelled back just as he disappeared into the shrubbery at the top of the dune.

Alone once more, the cold breeze crept into the crevices of her warm woolen cardigan and nipped at her bare neck as it passed by. Fingering the blue-gray crystal that always hung on a chain in the hollow of her throat, she decided she could ignore the cold for a little while longer as she stood in her night time vigil, watching the last vestiges of the day slip from around her. Whenever she was able, she liked to watch the sun set over the horizon and drink in the luxury of this spot she'd been so privileged to find.

A stand of Karri trees crowded the rim of the valley behind her hut. Even now, after three months of living here, she couldn't stop marveling at how tall and straight they were, like sentinels of the bush, protecting all that their height encompassed. Most of them were of an age even beyond her comprehension, witness perhaps to the land before white man's domination.

When she stood beneath these trees—at the base of their massive trunks—her petty worries melted away, replaced by their calming presence. Even when the fierce ocean gales made their boughs thrash and dance, the tall trunks remained solid and unyielding, standing their ground forever.

Ebony wished for some of the trees' sense of situation. She longed to be able to stay in one place long enough to put down some firm roots. But she was destined to keep moving like a gypsy, forever.

She thought back to her near-drowning earlier in the day and her mind recoiled from what she'd nearly done. It was a stupid mistake, and of course there was no way she'd swum that far out on purpose. But the picture of the baby face kept returning, unbidden, to her mind. Out of habit her fingers reached up to trace the smooth oval pendant hanging around her neck. She'd bought it only a few days after abandoning her baby, from a local market place in one of the many towns she passed through. Had been drawn to it, almost as if by some kind of higher power. It'd cost her most of the cash she had in her purse, but she was unable to resist. In a way it reminded her of the daughter she'd left behind and she'd never taken it off, not once in the past twenty-two years. It also reminded her of the pink sapphire ring she'd entrusted to the old man's care. To give to her daughter when she was old enough. Had he done as she asked? Did her baby—now a grown woman—wear that ring? Or had it been relegated to the back of a drawer somewhere, forgotten. It hurt that she'd never know the answers to these questions.

Determined, Ebony forced the welling sadness back into a corner of her mind. She would conquer these feelings, she had no other choice.

In the end, it was the face of the man who had rescued her today that helped replace the images of her child. When she thought of Jay, warmth spread through her body and the cold wind seemed to suddenly have less effect as her cheeks heated with a rising blush. His presence felt somehow solid, as if he was a rock she could cling to. And when he'd looked at her, he gave his full attention, as if she mattered somehow. Had she seen a flicker of something else besides concern in his eyes? Had he been flirting just a little? *Don't be so stupid.* He was a lot younger than her. There was no way he'd be interested in a woman like her. A woman of her age.

And anyway, her life didn't allow for frivolous things such as romance.

* * *

The smile faded from Jay's lips as he strode purposefully up the dune, his brows lowered in deliberation. Shifting his surfboard, he tucked it under his arm so he could climb the dune more easily. His heart still pounded in his chest whenever his memory flicked back to the scene out in the ocean. Of Ebony nearly drowning. Thank God he looked up to see what that dog was going crazy about on the beach, just in time to catch the dark bob of her head before the crest of a wave swallowed her.

What in hell had she been thinking, swimming in such a treacherous ocean today?

He was the only surfer out there, everyone else had already gone home for the day. Perhaps he'd also been unwise to tackle such a large swell. Even with his skill on the surfboard, he'd eventually admitted defeat and come in from Conti's after only half an hour. He was a strong swimmer and a good surfer. He knew he could handle the conditions.

But she was way out of her depth. Another shiver ran down his spine as his imagination toyed with what might've happened if he hadn't spotted her when he did. He might very well be pulling her lifeless body out of the water right now.

Recognizing the old, deeply ingrained habit of needing to save-from-harm, it made him laugh out loud. *You will not die on my watch.* The old mantra echoed hollow and heavy in his head. That mantra no longer held true, he reminded himself. Lieutenant Tom Logan had died despite his best efforts. Jay had watched as the life ebbed from the young man's eyes, and there wasn't a damn thing he could've done about it.

Jay didn't need to turn his arm over to read the date tattooed underneath, it was ingrained in his memory. But he'd had the numbers etched into his skin anyway, as a reminder. A date four and a half years ago.

At least Ebony hadn't died today. At least he'd been able to save her. From the ocean. But there was something in her eyes, a haunted look. He'd seen that look before, in the eyes of Tom Logan's mother when he'd informed her of the terrible news. As if something was permanently broken inside of her.

And he'd bet anything those burn scars he'd glimpsed on her back had something to do with it. Burn marks from a cigarette held purposefully to her skin. Jay had seen them a few times before. Enough times to know exactly how they were caused. She'd been careful to keep her back turned away from him once she'd regained her composure after he pulled her from the ocean. He clenched his fist, wanting to lash out and pulverize the cowardly bastard who'd done that to her. They were old scars though, old enough to give him hope that she was no longer tormented by whomever caused them.

A silent but emphatic voice kept telling him Ebony wasn't really as okay as she kept insisting she was. That perhaps there was a reason she'd been out in the wild ocean all by herself. But she obviously didn't want to talk about it, was good at hiding it; whatever *it* was. He'd been reluctant to leave her alone, looking so vulnerable standing on her porch in the dusk. And as he walked away, he had to keep reminding himself she wasn't his problem. His well-used mantra wouldn't save anyone now, especially not from themselves. But he couldn't get those odd, light-gray eyes out of his head. Or the way her cheeks turned pink when one of her rare smiles emerged.

She wasn't his type at all, petite but with curves in all the right places and wild dark hair that fell over her face in waves. He preferred his women simple and straightforward, choosing young surfer girls to hang with—there were certainly plenty to be had in this town. No need for any deep commitments or drawn out romantic angst with those short-lived dalliances.

He tried to quash the reluctant admiration for a woman who lived on her own out here in the isolated bushland.

If she lives alone, does that mean there's no boyfriend around? The question burst into his head before he could stop it. No, it didn't matter, he wasn't going to get entangled with this woman. She was way too complex. Which wasn't the aim of his carefree lifestyle. Simplicity and good sex, that was about all he asked from any relationship. And the girls he chose were usually happy to offer that. He'd just have to ignore the ache in his gut that'd urged him to reach out and touch her creamy cheek when she'd smiled oh-so-hesitantly at him. And overlook the way the swell of her full breasts under the soft fabric of her cardigan caused a hot flash of craving to run rampant through his body.

He pushed on through the low scrub, following the little trail, nearly back at the beach now. How come he'd never seen this track before? He came to this beach a few times a week on average. Probably because he'd never bothered to look. And who would've guessed a little ramshackle cottage was hidden behind the dunes. Who owned that property? It obviously wasn't government land. He might make a few discreet enquiries around town. Just to assuage his curiosity.

The image of Ebony standing small and alone on her dilapidated porch kept re-surfacing until he gave his head a quick shake to rid himself of the impression. She obviously valued her independence and was more than used to fending for herself.

Except when she was drowning.

CHAPTER THREE

Jenna Simmonds was the picture of misery, as the frogs sang their welcome to the summer storm in a symphony of deafening croaks. Raindrops pattered onto the already saturated soil, turning the usually fine red dust into scarlet sticky mud. Sitting in the saddle atop her horse, she tried to look out through the mini waterfall of rain cascading off the front of her hat.

Her loyal dog, Dune, hunkered beneath a low salt bush a few feet away, peering up at her as if to say, *really, do we have to be out in this weather?* She gave a small laugh at his comical expression.

"Sorry, but this *is* the wet season," she told him. Both golden ears pricked forward at her words, his normally sandy colored fur turning a dark amber in the rain. He was of dingo descent, and the wild-dog blood ran strong in his veins. Everybody warned her he'd never make a good working dog, but she proved them all wrong. She had a gift with animals, a strong empathy with them, and she knew Dune would always obey her.

She returned her gaze to the sky, rain spilling on her face. Without the wet season, there would be no green grass covering the desert dunes to feed the cattle come the dry. But no matter how much she told herself the rain was an essential part of outback life, Jenna couldn't shake the cold depression that'd settled in her stomach with the coming of the wet.

She should've listened to Dan when he told her she was crazy going out in this weather to fix a stupid drainage ditch, but the compulsion to be on her own had driven her outdoors. Away from the station and the rest of the stock hands—her friends—and into the deluge. Tucking her chin right down, she hunched her shoulders and settled in to wait. The pelting rain would fade soon, it always did, and while she waited, she mulled over the emotions churning through her gut.

Her fingers found their way to the locket hanging around her neck and she ran her thumb over the smooth gold heart. Inside it held a miniature photo of her on one side, matched by a photo of Dan on the other. Her mind roamed back to the time, just over a month ago, when Dan had placed it around her neck.

"Happy Anniversary, babe." Dan grinned from ear to ear as he handed her an elegantly wrapped box. She was leaning up against the island bench in the large communal kitchen of the staff quarters, chatting with Linda, Mark and Cookie.

"Thanks." Jenna smiled back and reached out to catch his hand and pull him near. "I love you." Dan understood the significance those three words conveyed. She loved him more than life itself. He'd given her life meaning once more, given her back her freedom.

"I love you too, babe," he echoed, his beautiful amber eyes locking onto hers.

"Go on, open it," he whispered in her ear. She tore at the gold ribbon and the tissue paper until she finally found the small wooden box inside. Opening it, she pulled out the exquisite gold locket on a fine gold chain. She turned it over and on the back was engraved the number one, with *D & J*

Forever underneath. Surprising tears moistened her eyes, but she blinked them away, not wanting everyone to see her cry.

"Here, let me put it on." Dan's tanned fingers stole the jewelry from her hand, brushing her long blonde hair out of the way so he could fasten it around her neck.

"Oh God, is it here already? I'm sorry, I forgot!" Mark slapped his forehead and groaned. As he apologized he got up from his chair and gathered them both in an all-encompassing hug. "I can't believe it's been one whole year since you made me stand out in the middle of the West Australian desert in that bloody monkey suit and watch you get married!" He gave Dan an extra hard slap on the back. "Imagine that! One whole year. My, how time flies."

"Mark O'Brien, did you think Cookie was going to all this trouble making this wonderful meal just for your benefit?" Linda glowered at him from behind the kitchen bench, where she was helping Cookie mix up the last batch of scones. "The whole point of this dinner is to celebrate their first anniversary." Linda's scowl got even deeper. Jenna hid a private smile. Mark was never going to change, and the sooner Linda acknowledged that, the better.

"Oh, come on, darlin', you know my skills of observation are a little rusty at times." He flashed her one of his best, cheeky smiles, the freckles on his face dancing as he walked around the bench and gathered her up in his arms. Bending her over backward, he planted a resounding kiss on her lips. "But at least my skills of lovin' you are right up to scratch."

Linda only hesitated for a heartbeat before she grabbed him with her floury hands and returned his passionate kiss. Cookie's fat arms jiggled alarmingly as she threw them in the air in pretend disgust and turned her back on them both. Jenna continued watching with delight. They fitted each other to perfection, Mark with his big, happy-go-lucky personality and Linda with her warm smile and infectious enthusiasm.

In that instant, Jenna recognized with piercing clarity how lucky she was to have friends such as these. Friends who'd been willing to put their own lives on the line last year to help her defeat Liam, the man who'd murdered her step-father and then tried to hunt her down as well. Without their help who knew where she might be now. Doubtless dead, or maybe worse. Perhaps there were worse things than death, especially if Liam had got hold of her.

Liam, her half-brother, had pursued her on behalf of their sick and twisted biological father, Alexander. Jenna had never met Alexander, but from what she'd gathered in her conversations with Liam, Alexander was a rich and powerful man, who hated to lose. At anything. A vicious psychopath who thought he was above the law. And he was desperate to find his long-lost daughter, stolen from him by his wife when she was just a baby. But since Liam's death there'd been no sign of Alexander. Apart from the wedding card he'd sent, the card that'd scared the bejesus out of her. There was no hint he was still hunting her. Dan believed Alexander had been scared off by Liam's failure, and she clung to that belief. It was the only way to keep herself rational, otherwise she'd be driving herself insane at every shadow in the desert. It was now over twelve months since the fateful night in the desert when she killed Liam. Surely, Alexander wasn't coming after her anymore. She was safe now.

Jenna counted herself extremely lucky to have found mates such as these. She was happy here, building a life with Dan, busy returning Shiralee back to its former glory. Why then couldn't she shake this vague feeling of unease?

Recently, she'd found her mind wandering from the job at hand. Instead of concentrating on counting the number of tins of tomatoes they had left in the pantry during stock take, she'd suddenly find herself daydreaming of a white sandy beach, with small wavelets breaking gently in the background. Other times she'd come back to herself with a start, realizing she'd been staring out over the expanse of spiky desert spinifex grass instead of repainting the horse yard fence. The urge to take her horse, Chainsaw, and gallop him bareback over the desert was coming more frequently.

But now, a month later, Jenna's qualms remained, niggling and annoying. The rain had stopped, but Jenna was still miserable. Her stomach protested and roiled in a wave of nausea. She'd been feeling this way for a week or so now, but she put it down to her state of mind manifesting as physical symptoms. Her stomach was sympathizing with her wretched, traitorous soul.

Drawing out the other, long chain she kept ring kept around her neck, she held up the ring on the end. The large pink stone in the heavy white gold band was a star sapphire, and it was so opalescent it almost seemed to cast a faint pink glow onto her fingers. Jenna kept it around her neck most of the time, scared she'd damage it or lose it in the hard, daily grind of working on the station. She only wore it on her finger on special occasions, the rest of the time it stayed safe on its chain.

The ring had been left to her by her mother. The mother who'd abandoned her when she'd been too young to even remember.

Without her having to move a muscle, Chainsaw anticipated her need to head for home and started up a slow ground-eating jog, shaking her out of her reverie. Sitting comfortably in the saddle she let him choose his own path, his neck spread out long and ears pricked up high. She could sense he relished the thought of the biscuit of hay waiting for him back at Shiralee. Dune trotted along at Chainsaw's feet, nose wiffling as he picked out the interesting smells of passing rabbits and other small animals, but he never left the horse's side.

Lifting her gaze from the track in front of them, Jenna scanned the horizon. Spreading outwards as far as the eye could see was a rolling sea of red and orange sand dunes, gently marching one after the other. On top of the dunes floated another sea, green and brown clumps of spinifex, the hardy grass of the desert. The colors of the land were so vibrant and alive it almost hurt her eyes to look at them.

Large areas of shallow muddy water collected in the lower areas between the dunes, too big to be called puddles, but not quite a lake either. They wouldn't last long, soon the fine red dust would rise again to invade every nook and cranny, get up nostrils and into eyes, stain every piece of clothing ochre. The puddles would become small dried up salt pans, the red earth bleached white by the rising salt, crackling and writhing as if being tortured by humanity's misuse of the land.

It was all so familiar to her now, the landscape had become entrenched in her spirit. She knew most of this station like the back of her hand.

Again, a vision of a white sandy beach and crashing waves wavered in her mind's eye, clouding out the harsh reality of the desert.

Suddenly Jenna knew she needed to see that beach for herself. She needed to feel the sand beneath her toes and have the cool salt water swish past her calves.

Dan had been right after all, she did have a gypsy heart, and the urge to travel once more was striking hard. The thought made her even more miserable than before. She had everything she could ever want on Shiralee, why was her mind telling her she wanted more? Why couldn't she just accept the happy life she'd made for herself here? What was calling to her? It was more than just the need to curl her toes into the warm sand. There was something else unfathomable, something she couldn't put her finger on. It wasn't fear, not exactly.

Was it some kind of inner instinct? Warning her Alexander was still on the hunt for her? Is that what this disturbing, disquiet inside was telling her? That she needed to move because she was somehow in danger?

CHAPTER FOUR

"Mmm, your coffee really is to die for," mumbled Ebony appreciatively through the aromatic steam rising from her mug.

"I know, darl," chirped Viv from across the other side of the counter. "But all praise bestowed is still accepted graciously." Viv punctuated her sassy comment with a wave of the tea-towel in her hand. Ebony watched her friend from behind her mug. Viviane was the owner of The Gabardine Organic Café nestled at the top of Main Street. Locals and tourists alike loved to come and ensconce themselves in the café which was filled with gaudy cushions, large mismatched chairs, and the wonderful aromas of homemade cakes and freshly brewed coffee. Viv prided herself on her superb coffee and proudly declared to everyone who'd listen it was a secret recipe handed down by her grandfather.

"So, what are your plans for today, my darling?" Viv smiled questioningly as she laid a plate of Ebony's favorite, French toast with lots of cinnamon and strawberries in front of her.

"Well, after your delicious morning heart-starter kicks in, I've actually got a few patients coming into the clinic this morning." Ebony dragged a weary hand across her forehead. She hated to admit it, but even two days afterward, she hadn't fully recovered from her dunking in the cold ocean. Tiny shivers ran through her as nerve-endings remembered and reacted, even now, to the bone chilling water lapping over her head.

"Good for you." Viv's cheery voice echoed from where she had her arms buried to the elbows in sudsy sink water. "More customers means more money, and that's always a good thing."

"Amen to that." Ebony was more than used to the day-to-day struggle; getting by on the bare minimum was the norm for her. Which made her appreciate the rare kindness shown by people like Viv. She was always offering a coffee or left-over delicacy, dismissing the freebie with a wave of her hand.

"I hear you're getting quite a following. Word must be getting around, even the tourists are coming to see you now. That Reiki healing thing you do certainly works. My bung ankle is much better since you worked your magic on it."

Ebony winced inwardly. She hated it when anyone referred to what she did as magic. "And I've been telling anyone who'll listen what good stuff your Reiki is," Viv went on in a conspiratorial voice.

"Thanks, Viv." Ebony kept her sigh quiet. One of the things she loved about Viviane was her boundless optimism, but sometimes she was hard to keep up with. Ebony could imagine Viv telling all her customers to go and check out the Reiki Clinic two shops up. Yes, the extra money would be good, but Ebony liked things the way they were, a few customers here and there, just enough to pay her frugal bills.

This was the first time in her life Ebony had ever actually had a proper shop front from which to practice her healing. Normally she would either share a room with a local healer for a day or so, or ply her trade at the local markets. She made a point of never working from home. The less people knew where she lived, the better. Ebony was always careful to keep a low-profile, and shunned all versions of social media. All her work was gained through word-of-mouth.

It'd been Viviane who had suggested the vacant property in the first place, encouraging her to take up the lease in the small assortment of shops. The rent was incredibly cheap, just a token really. Margaret River was a town that relied heavily on tourism and surfing, and this fluctuating market made it hard to keep shops open for long periods of time. The owners would do just about anything to make it look as though their little mall was a thriving place, helping to attract the tourists. Ebony finally caved, mostly because Viv had been so insistent, but partly because a small voice told her it was time to stop hiding. Surely by now he would've forgotten all about her. This was her first hesitant step back into living as a real person, in the real world.

The bell above the café door gave a merry tinkle, announcing another customer. Ebony didn't turn around, taking a bite of the delicious toast, lost in thought about how she might improve her little clinic. Maybe she could find a few cheap second-hand rugs at the Sunday markets. If the colors were right, she could even hang them on the walls, to revitalize the drab gray, give it more of a cozy, restful feel. Hunkered down on her barstool at the end of the counter, she hardly registered as Viv dried her hands and turned to serve the person. But she couldn't miss the way Viv's face lit up with pleasure as she recognized her customer.

"Well hello there, welcome back. How was your business trip?" Viv leaned forward, eyes fixed on the new patron, her high cheekbones tinged pink as she smoothed her blonde flyaway hair into a semblance of order. Ebony was intrigued, Viv didn't normally greet a customer with that amount of interest. But even before she could turn around, a deep male voice made the hairs on the back of her neck stand up.

"Dull and boring, most of it. Meeting after meeting. I hardly got any surfing in. It's real good to be back." The voice was unmistakable.

"What can I get you today?"

"A piece of your date and chocolate gluten-free cake, thanks, Viv."

It was Jay.

Damn, what is he doing here? She hadn't anticipated meeting him again so soon. She tried to shrink into the corner of the counter. *Maybe he won't notice me.* But even without turning around, she could feel his presence as he moved to stand next to her.

"Hi. All recovered from your swim the other day?" His deep blue eyes were steady, regarding her with a directness that was unnerving. The corners of his mouth curved up in the hint a smile and for a split-second Ebony was mesmerized by his lips, so straight and masculine.

"Oh. Hi, Jay," she replied, hiding her apprehension behind a bright smile. He smelled clean and fresh as if he'd just stepped out of the shower. She found herself wanting to lean in a little closer for another whiff. "Yes, I'm all good now, as you can see." His black t-shirt stretched neatly over his broad chest, highlighting the breadth of his shoulders, fitting snugly around his muscled biceps. Suddenly a vision appeared in her mind's eye. An image of his half-naked chest standing in her lounge room, a sprinkling of black curling hair following the hardened planes down his stomach. Swallowing self-consciously, she lowered her gaze before he saw the guilty desire that was surely lurking behind her eyes.

"What swim?" asked a suspicious Viv, bustling down to their end of the counter and butting into the conversation.

Ebony's heart sank. She hadn't told Viv about her near-drowning. She didn't want her worrying needlessly. Actually, she'd hoped Jay might keep the rescue to himself. It'd been a stupid mistake. She'd just misjudged the water the other day, that was all.

"Nothing to speak of really," she said, jumping in before Jay could say anything more. "I got into a touch of bother while I was out swimming at Redgate. It was lucky Jay was there on his surfboard, but I would've been fine even without him." Ebony found Jay's gaze and held it, daring him to argue with her version of the rescue. She didn't need him blurting out to everyone about her mistake in the water and she didn't need Viv trying to dissect her motives or the outcomes of what'd happened on the beach. His eyes narrowed as he gazed judiciously at her. She gritted her teeth while maintaining her innocent smile, waiting for his decision.

It wasn't like her to flee a difficult situation, but the last thing she wanted right now was people delving into the whys and the wherefores of her swim. If he decided to blurt everything out to Viv, then she'd just get up and leave. The thoughts that'd been floating around her head while she'd been drowning were better left ignored, she didn't need anyone analyzing her ill-fated swim.

Ebony placed her hands on the bench, ready to lever herself off her stool, preparing for a hasty retreat, when Jay said, "Yeah, I guess that's what happened."

The tension in her shoulders relaxed, but she could read the amused disapproval in his profile as he turned toward the cake display.

"Why didn't you say anything?" Viv shot her a worried frown. When Ebony only shrugged in reply, she said with lowered eyebrows. "I'll get back to you in a minute, after I serve this man his cake." Viv moved off to the end of the counter where the cakes were all kept behind spotless glass covers. Jay didn't follow Viv as Ebony expected, instead he leaned against the counter staring at her. Why was he saying nothing, just standing there with a small, knowing smile playing across his face? Brushing an unruly coil of hair away from her forehead, she threw a glance toward Viv, hoping her friend would come back soon.

* * *

What was she thinking? Those enigmatic gray eyes regarded him with cool appraisal. Her short black hair wasn't nearly as wild and unruly as he remembered it from the beach. Now the dark curls fell in a nest of smooth waves, framing her face and setting off her pale skin. Not many women managed to keep such a flawless peaches-and-cream complexion, not when they lived in this harsh Australian climate. It was hard to tell exactly how old she was. Not that it was any of his business.

The air of vulnerability that'd surrounded her out on the porch the other day was gone. Replaced by a calm, no-nonsense exterior. Like she was used to being in charge of her life and of her emotions. She gave him a tight smile, obviously wondering why he was still standing next to her. His presence was a bother; he could hear that in the sound of her finger tapping a loud tattoo on the bench. And that was exactly why he stayed where he was. For some reason he wanted her off balance. She hadn't liked it when he broached the subject of the rescue with Viv. But why would she want to keep it a secret?

He was just about to ask her that very thing, when she beat him to it. "So, what are you up to today? Do you have anything interesting planned?"

He regarded her for a few more unsettling seconds before he replied. "You haven't heard then?"

"Sorry, heard what?"

"My surf shop is running a free clinic today." His team had been planning the event for months. They'd poured their hearts and souls into this thing, hoping it'd help increase visibility and sales with both locals and tourists alike. And perhaps give them the edge over the two other surf shops in town. He was more than a little worried it might all be a complete flop. He needed this to work. He really wanted to stay here in Margaret River, to become one of the locals, and his shop was a means to do it. The way back from the treacherous path his life had taken straight after he left the army. The way back to a normal life, where he was free to surf and enjoy the simple pleasures.

"Oh. Sorry I'm not into surfing."

That much had been evident the day he rescued her, she wasn't at all familiar with how to lie on a surfboard so it stayed balanced in the water.

"You really do live in an isolated little world sometimes, Ebony McAllister," Viv called out as she returned with a neatly folded brown paper bag. "The whole town has been talking about this for weeks. There are posters up all over town. There's even one on my café door." Viv gestured with a flick of her tea-towel toward the glass-fronted door. "There's going to be a free barbecue for everyone who wants to come down, and a bonfire afterward. I reckon the whole town is going to be there."

"I think that might be a slight exaggeration," Jay replied a little awkwardly. "Half the town maybe." He smiled at Viv's enthusiasm. It was good to know she was in his corner. Some of the locals hadn't been so generous. "I was hoping to get a bit of community spirit going."

"Well, I think it's great, what you're doing. We'll definitely be popping down for a few pointers."

Ebony let out a little grunt of surprise. She looked like she was about to open her mouth to say something, but a fierce glance on Viv's part quelled any argument.

"You're coming too, aren't you Ebony?' Viv crossed her arms and leveled her gaze at Ebony. Ebony stared right back, and a look passed between the two women that Jay didn't want to decipher. Better to stay well away from the undercurrent going on between them. A man was likely to get his head bitten off if he interfered in something like that. But it did look like Viv had taken Ebony under her wing, and the two women were friends, which was a good thing. At least Ebony wasn't completely on her own in this new town.

To change the subject, he said, "It's going to be at your beach anyway, so you'll find it hard to avoid."

"It's at Redgate Beach?"

He allowed himself a smug little grin. That was going to make it harder for her to come up with an excuse not to go. The thought brought him up short. When had he even started to care whether she was there or not? She was interesting, sure, tempting even. But just because he hadn't been with a woman in nearly six months, didn't mean he should let his libido run away with him. Physically, she wasn't his type. Long legs and pert breasts were the triggers for him these days, not round curves and luscious lips; not anymore. As different to Bryony as possible.

Today, Ebony was wearing a simple black button-up shirt over a knee length black skirt. A fairly innocuous outfit, except he found his eyes wanting to trace the hint of generous breast that showed in the cleavage revealed in the V of the shirt. And then run down over the curves of her hips to the tight backside encased in the body-hugging skirt.

He put a lid firmly back on the intriguing thrum of desire that curled deep in his gut. Time to distract himself.

"There should be more than enough people around to make sure you don't drift too far out to sea this time." His tone was light and teasing, but he could see her jaw work as she clenched her teeth.

"Like I said to Viv, I've got a few patients at my clinic today."

"They'll be well and truly gone by lunch time," retorted Viv.

"And I'm not much for surfing either, I prefer to watch," Ebony replied, shooting a look of exasperation toward her friend.

"The workshop is designed for beginners. There'll be young kids, all the way up to some golden oldies coming down." Why was he continuing to bait her, to find excuses for her to come, almost like it was a game he needed to win?

"What do you mean by *oldies*?" Her face was impassive as she waited for his answer, but there was a slight rise at the corner of one dark eyebrow. Her question was more than just trivial then. It mattered somehow. How should he answer it? With compassion or the truth? And who did he consider to be old anyway?

"Well, I have one lady who's signed up, Ethel is her name, she'll be eighty in a few weeks."

"Eighty years old," she said with a jerk. "And learning to surf?" He'd managed the correct answer, if he was reading the relief in her face properly. Ebony had nothing to worry about, she was beautiful, no one in their right mind would ever consider her old.

"Yep. Ethel tells me learning something new is a great tonic for keeping her young. She says she's out at that beach every morning for an early swim, wouldn't miss it for the world. And if she's that keen then who am I to stop her?" He lifted his chin as he described Ethel, respect for the wonderful old lady tightened like a spring contracting in his chest. He hoped he was that active and just plain *alive* when he was her age.

"It's settled then, we'll both be there this arvo, Jay," said Viv brightly. For a second it looked like Ebony might be about to argue again, but she kept her mouth shut.

"Great." That single word echoed around his head, as he wondered just what he was getting himself into. "I guess I'll see you there." He headed toward the door, brown paper bag tucked securely under one arm.

"Yep, see you there." Viv sounded enthusiastic, but Ebony was stony and silent. He could feel her gaze fixed on his back as he disappeared through the door, but he kept his gait relaxed as he sauntered out of the shop, fighting the urge to turn around.

* * *

Ebony's gaze roamed the street vista outside the café window. She was on her second cup of coffee, waiting for Viv to find a spare minute to join her at the table in the corner. She wasn't leaving until she had a stern word, or three, in Viv's ear. Her friend needed to know she'd overstepped the mark. Of course she would go to this damned surfing thing, but only because of her loyalty to Viv, nothing more. And Viv needed to know that.

The figure of a man wearing a long trench coat and a black fedora hat caught her eye. He had a straight-backed stance that seemed out of place in the street full of tourists. A younger male walked along beside him, shoulders hunched, a slouching teenager. She watched their retreating backs for a while and was about to shift her attention onto the next person walking up the street, when the man glanced sideways as a car suddenly tooted its horn. Her coffee stopped half-way to her lips, forgotten. Fear walked its cold fingers up her spine. Standing up in a rush, she craned her neck to get a better view, then the man turned to cross the road and the breath left Ebony's lungs in a rush of relief. She laughed at her own silliness. Of course it wasn't him. A long gray beard covered most of the man's face, but she was sure it wasn't Alexander.

She was being paranoid. Alexander would never find her here. Besides, he'd probably got tired of chasing her mere months after she left him. This thing she did, moving from town to town in an attempt to keep herself from being noticed was now more out of habit than necessity.

But the simple idea of her husband, Alexander, had the memories crowding back in. The look on Alexander's face the first time he caught her trying to leave. His features cold and still, like granite, no emotion existed in him at all. His eyes narrowed and dark, set with a terrible, cavernous anger. Terror turned her guts to jelly. Terror so strong it paralyzed her, making it impossible to move, or speak or even think.

The fear hadn't been for what he'd do to her when he got her home. It'd been for her baby daughter. Would he start taking out his anger on her as well?

Alexander had found her walking down the street, only two blocks from their house. That's as far as she'd managed to flee. She's done it all half-witted, hadn't planned her exit, took the first opportunity, just up and fled as soon as his back was turned.

Not a sound left her lips as she meekly let him take her by the arm—his vice-like grip biting into her flesh—and lead her away, her other arm cradling her baby tightly to her side. She'd known Alexander would never let them go. He said it was because he loved her so much. No one else would ever love her as much as he did. And he loved his daughter just as much, she had no right to try and take his daughter away from him. She'd wanted to scream for someone to help her. Instead, all she heard was a silent howl echoing inside her head.

That was the night he'd carved his mark into the soft mound of her belly. Got out his pocket knife and held her down, one hand over her mouth as he carved the letter A into her skin. He owned her and she needed to remember that.

Unconsciously, her hand reached down to cover the scar sitting just below her belly button. How she hated that scar. Because it reminded her of him. Which is exactly what he intended.

Running a shaky hand through her hair Ebony exhaled loudly. It couldn't possibly be him. Not here in Margaret River. Not after twenty years. There were plenty of other men who could easily resemble Alexander Pallan, even here in a small country town in Western Australia.

"That was a big sigh, darl," said Viv in her cheery voice, as she plumped down in the chair opposite Ebony. "The thought of going surfing with that hunk of a man this afternoon got you all hot and bothered?"

Ebony pushed the image of Alexander away.

"No, definitely not. And while we're on the subject, we need to have a chat about boundaries."

"Oh, really?" Viv wasn't the least bit fazed by Ebony's stern gaze.

"I thought you hated the beach." Ebony had often wondered why Viv lived in a coastal town, she never went near the beach as far as she could tell.

"Don't be silly, darl, I love the beach. Especially when it's filled with well-built men in tight black wetsuits!"

Ebony smothered a sigh.

* * *

The door closed with a muted swish behind her last patient for the day. Ebony turned and sank gratefully into one of the two overstuffed and well-used sofa chairs in her front waiting room. It was tiring, having to treat three people in a row, and she felt a little more lethargic than usual after the healing.

None of the sessions had been that taxing on their own. The first man had come in for relief from a sore shoulder, he'd wrenched it the day before when he'd been flung from his surfboard. He'd been to see her quite a few times before and loved to regale her with his surfing exploits. The waves got bigger every time he told his stories.

The second client, a local lady she hadn't treated before, came in for help with a twisted knee. The aura around this lady had been one of reluctance and doubt, but by the time she left half an hour later, there was the beginning of a hesitant smile on her lips. A smile because her knee did actually feel better. Much better. Ebony knew this because she'd felt the release of pain, like the slow ebb of an ocean tide receding.

Ebony was good at what she did. Very good.

The third person had come in to see if she could help him get over his severe exhaustion after suffering from a bad flu a couple of weeks before. The older gentleman told her he'd even ended up in hospital for one night because his wife had been scared he might have pneumonia. It seemed this was quite a bad flu season, the old man said he'd heard of many people being very sick with it lately. Ebony only half-listened to him as she began the healing, but she wasn't surprised.

No, the reason she was feeling washed out wasn't because of the seriousness of her patient's ailments, it was more to do with the thoughts that kept intruding as she worked. She needed to keep a clear head, a calm space inside to expedite the healing. But that space kept getting interrupted by snippets of the rest of the conversation she had with Viv this morning. A conversation about Jay.

Viv had been way too quick to disregard Ebony's outrage at being dragged along to some surfing thing she didn't want to go to and didn't even blink when Ebony threatened never to drink her coffee again. Viv knew she was bluffing.

Instead, she'd dived straight in, asking what the hell she'd been doing out swimming on her own. And more to the point, what had it felt like to be rescued by those amazing, strong arms. According to Viv, Ebony would now be the envy of every blond-haired, unattached woman in town. And all the brunette ones as well.

Being well tuned-in to all the small-town gossip, Viv was more than keen to tell Ebony all she knew about Jay. Ebony ignored the small twinge of shame at the fact she didn't even try to stop Viv as she gushed about him. Viv could put a name to almost all the blondes who'd passed over Jay's doorstep. It sounded like he certainly had his fair share of light-hearted flings. Ebony was a little worried about Viv's preoccupation with Jay's love life, guessing she might even have a secret desire to be one of those women Jay seemed to use and then discard. She couldn't really blame her, there weren't many good-looking, intelligent, single men to be had in Margaret River.

According to Viv, not once in the whole four years Jay had been in town had he ever hooked up with a woman for more than a few weeks at a time. He liked things free and easy, no commitment, no harm. There were plenty of women out there who'd love to tie Jay down, but he wouldn't have a bar of it. He chose girls who wouldn't take offense, who were either too shallow to truly care or were far too easily tempted to move on to the next surfer with long blonde locks and a laid-back smile.

Sighing, Ebony stood up and wandered back into the treatment room. She needed to wipe everything down, sterilize and tidy the room, ready for use next time. But her mind was still occupied with Jason Connolly. If Viv's information was to be trusted—and as the café was the central hub of much of the town gossip it usually was—it was rumored Jay had also been in the army, which explained a lot. But that piece of gossip had never been confirmed, he kept his cards close to his chest when it came to his past. A pang of compassion twisted through her gut. If he'd been caught in the terrible all-consuming war in Afghanistan, she felt wretched for him. Ebony could tie in Viv's suspicions with the story of the scars she'd seen on Jay's chest the other day. But she wasn't about to mention that to Viv.

War changed people. It either made them more, or less, of the person they once were. It might help to explain all those light-hearted flings with all of those young women. All the one-night-stands in the world would never free him from that kind of pain. It definitely proved he was brave, courageous even. But it was still only speculation. The man became more and more intriguing by the minute.

Her introspection was broken by an unexpected knock on the clinic door. Hurrying through to the front room, she heaved a great sigh when she saw the figure standing in front of the frosted glass door was dressed in bright clothing. Viv. No one else wore colors that bright, even in Margaret River. Ebony had forgotten all about Viv's threat. She'd been sure she wouldn't follow through with this crazy idea of hers, but it seemed she was actually going to Redgate beach and she was determined Ebony go with her.

As soon as Ebony opened the door, Viv grabbed her by the arm. "Come on, darl, it's time you had a little bit of fun in your life. You're much too morose sometimes you know." Ebony drew in a breath to argue, but Viv beat her to the punch. "All right, you're not morose, I take that back. But you do need to get out more and I'm not taking no for an answer. I am prepared to stand here all day if that's what it takes."

"Really. In that get-up?" Ebony's rebelliousness turned to amusement as she took in Viv's attire. She looked for the entire world like a bird of paradise standing in the waiting room, a long orange silk caftan floated over a cerise colored bikini that surprisingly showed off Viv's buxom figure quite well. A bright yellow straw hat and a pair of over-large sunglasses finished off the multihued picture.

"Come on, we can stop past your place on the way and grab your swimmers and a wetsuit. I've got mine in the bag." She held up a green polka dot bag, the arm of a wetsuit poking out the top.

"Is everything you own pink?" snorted Ebony in mock disgust at the brightly colored wetsuit.

"Well, I couldn't very well own a boring old black one, could I? Then I'd be just like everyone else."

Ebony picked up on Viv's infectious mood on the drive out to the beach. She even found herself looking forward to the afternoon as they pulled into the carpark. It seemed summer was back with a vengeance today at Redgate beach. Sinuous waves curled smoothly, raising high in a perfect curve and then breaking into a creamy foam as they rolled softly up the shoreline. Sunlight sparkled in pinprick diamonds of light as it reflected off the aqua blue ocean. And the equally blue sky stretched forever to the horizon. Heat rose in a smudged haze off the back of the sand dunes and Ebony felt her forehead prickle with sweat as soon as she stepped out of Viv's car. They'd dropped her battered old Subaru back at her house and driven the final leg to the carpark in Viv's cute little VW Beetle.

The almost unbearable heat of the sand burned into the soles of her bare feet, so she had to hop from foot to foot while putting on her flip-flops. Jay sure had a perfect day for his surf clinic.

The complete opposite to the weather from two days ago.

Normally, Redgate Beach curved away in a single swish of white sand and blue water, out toward the rocky headland that jutted into the ocean half a kilometer away. But Ebony hardly recognized the beach today, people swarmed across it like ants. All the way from the car park as far as the eye could see. Brightly colored clothing mixed with a flotilla of equally bright hats, bouncing beach balls, and the bare legs of running children. Ebony stood spell-bound, watching the unusual spectacle of her beach being overrun by locals and tourists alike.

Scattered in between the sun-baking adults and screaming kids, small groups of black, wetsuit-covered people, gathered in semi-circles with surf boards at their feet.

"Come on, slow poke." Viv grabbed her by the arm and started to drag her toward a group of people lying on surfboards, pretending to paddle while they were actually still stranded on the sand. Ebony was hauled along by Viv's sheer force of will, in danger of being smothered by her friend's long-flowing dress which billowed behind as she towed her along toward the first surf group.

"Hi, Viv. Hi, Ebony." Jay turned around to greet them, aiming one of his high-wattage smiles at them as they hurried toward the group across the hot sand. "Grab a couple of those spare boards over there and come and join us."

Ebony groaned inwardly. Of course they would have to pick the group Jay was teaching.

CHAPTER FIVE

She was standing up! She was standing up on a surfboard. Ebony could hardly believe her luck. It felt great, exhilarating. Granted, the waves were fairly small, *tame* Jay had called them, but she was being pushed along by the force of the wave quite nicely. She could almost understand the addiction that kept surfers going back for more, braving the cold water and threat of sharks for this adrenaline rush.

She *was* glad she'd made the effort to go back into the water. She hadn't realized how much her near-drowning had affected her until she tried to walk into the shallows carrying her board. The cool water had furled over her ankles, the touch sending unexpected shivers up her spine. For a millisecond she'd hesitated at the water's edge before Jay's gaze settled on her, a frown hovering behind his smile. Forcing herself forward, she turned an unwavering gaze out to sea and walked into the waves.

For the first few minutes, whenever a wave splashed her face, she had to fight the urge to run back toward the sand, but when she concentrated on Jay's instructions on how to paddle the board and keep it level at the same time, her fear slowly melted away. The best thing to do when you fell off a horse was to get straight back in the saddle, and that's what she was doing right now.

Arms held out to each side like an airplane taxiing on the runway, she took her gaze away from the shoreline for just a second and turned to shoot a grin of delight at Viv, who was lying glum and despondent on her board, watching. Viv had given up a few waves ago, refusing to try any more. Waves and beaches really weren't Viv's thing.

Jay gave Ebony the thumbs up from further over as he helped Ethel back onto her board. And just like that, her arms started to windmill in the air and her front foot slipped. Too late to correct her balance, she tumbled off into the foaming water. Laughing at herself she popped to the surface. The water wasn't deep and her feet found the sandy sea-bed while she ran her hands over her face, sluicing salt water out of her eyes. With her back turned and her vision blurred she didn't notice the next wave rise up behind until it dumped on top of her. It was only a small wave, but water still found its way up her nose and she struggled to breathe. Flashbacks from the other day in the ocean speared through her brain and she battled against the surging water, trying not to panic, telling herself to remain calm. Ebony finally rebounded toward the surface, but something hit her head. Hard. It must've been her board, anchored by the leg rope as it sprung back from the force of the tumbling wave.

Pain exploded in her head and the water went suddenly black. For uncounted seconds she floated just beneath the surface, pummeled by the surging waves. Finally, she dragged herself back from the brink of unconsciousness and started to fight the heaving water. Dizzy and unstable, her feet scrabbled to find a foothold again on the sand, her hands battled feebly against the waves. Full-blown panic bloomed inside her head. She was going to drown. Again.

Then her foot found solid sand and she drove herself forward and upwards. Then her other foot connected with the sea-bed and she emerged coughing and spluttering in shoulder deep water. Raising a hand, she gingerly touched the top of her forehead and saw it was covered in red.

"Ebony, are you okay?" Jay was paddling fast toward her on his board.

"I'm not sure." Her voice sounded thin and wobbly. "Yes. I think I'm alright," she qualified, holding her hand to her head again. She continued to make her way toward shore as Jay approached. Her board made an appearance near the shore, as it was driven onto the beach by the waves, it must've broken free of the ankle rope.

"Let me have a look," he said as he jumped off his board and stood next to her, his chest heaving from the exertion of his paddling sprint.

"No, it's fine really, I'll just go and sit on the beach for a while." She was acutely aware this was the second time he'd come to her rescue. And she didn't like it one little bit.

"Ebony, you're bleeding, let me have a look." He laid a hand on her shoulder to punctuate his request. She stopped reluctantly and turned her face to the side, so he could see the wound. Tender fingers brushed aside her straggling hair. "It's not too bad. I think the fin must have collected you when the board went over the top. You're lucky it wasn't the point of the board, that would've made a nice gouge in your lovely head."

"Oh, really?" Did he just say *lovely*? She was almost too weak to care.

"Let's go, I'll help you in." He took her elbow just as another wave of dizziness overwhelmed her and she stumbled against him, nearly disappearing back beneath the water.

"Right, that's it, I'm going to carry you." He reached down and swung her into his arms as easily as if she was a child.

"No, Jay, I can do it myself, please put me down." This was indeed unfair. The last thing she needed was to be held up in his arms for everyone to see. She didn't need rescuing. Not again. Viv would be apoplectic with delight, as she watched this scene unfold. She started to struggle, anger at herself and her stupidity forming a lump in her chest. Anger at him for being in the right place at the right time, *again*.

"Look, Ebony, you're a surfer in my group. You're under my care, and I'll be damned if I'm going to end up with you drowning or suing me because I didn't take due care. So I'm going to carry you in and you're going to let me do it," he growled in the voice of someone who was used to being obeyed.

She didn't like to be told what to do, to be controlled. Her time spent with Alexander made her super wary of any situation in which she wasn't in complete charge of her own destiny. Her instinct was to struggle, to fight against that authority in his voice. But that would make her look even more stupid in the eyes of everyone watching from the beach. And would make Jay look like a fool as well. So she squashed her urge to keep arguing. She'd just have to suffer the indignity of being removed from the water like a recalcitrant child.

At least she was decent today as he carried her to shore, wearing her trusty one-piece swimsuit and rash shirt to keep the sun away from her pale skin—and to hide her scars from any prying eyes. She remained rigid in his arms, however, not willing to surrender her body to his embrace, determined not to sag against him like the weak female everyone must now assume she was.

After a few seconds, she wondered if this was such a good idea. Every little twitch of his tall frame became magnified; her own tension highlighting his firm body. Anger was quickly replaced by embarrassment over her body's reaction to his proximity. Her face was now only inches away from his, her gaze drawn inexplicably to the vein in his neck thumping in time with his beating heart. She was mesmerized by the sight of the corded muscles of his tanned neck working to hold her above the water, and the solid warmth of his chest held hard against her side. She tried to quell a nervous twitching that started way down low in her stomach. My God, she was behaving like a teenager. She had to stop this foolish reaction before it took over her rational brain. She was old enough to know better. Old enough to at last acknowledge her physical attraction to this man, but definitely old enough to also be able to conquer the futile cravings.

Just because she was attracted to him didn't mean it was reciprocated.

He was good-looking enough to have his pick of women and he often did, if Viv was to be believed. Sure, he'd been nice to her, charming even, but as far as she could tell he was pleasant to every woman he met. And most women found him more than endearing as well, Viv's reaction to his charisma was a testament to that. She shouldn't read anything more into his beguiling demeanor than plain old chivalry. And she shouldn't be feeling exceptional, just because he was carrying her snug against his shoulder. He would've acted exactly the same way if it had been Ethel or Viv, or anyone else who happened to gash their head open. Tearing her gaze away from him, she searched the blinding whiteness of the beach instead, leaning back and away from the intimacy of his face so close to hers.

* * *

"I don't think we need to call the ambulance for this one, either." Jay knelt in front of Ebony on the sand peering at her forehead. She narrowed her eyes at him but said nothing at his reminder of the last time he'd dragged her out of the sea. He felt a small jolt of smugness as his comment dug home. She was so determined to be independent, but no one was an island and a small part of him was glad he could help her now. Even if she didn't want his help.

"Oh, thank God for that,' sighed Viv, who was kneeling next to him, concern for her friend written in the hunch of her shoulders.

"But I will need to put some steri-strips on the wound, it's a nasty gash, and they'll help it heal without too much scarring." He dug around in the small first aid kit in his lap until he came up with the packet of strips to hold the edges of the wound together.

"This might sting a bit." He tried to be gentle as he dabbed iodine over the cut. She winced but didn't pull away. Respect for her strength of will mounted, even as he continued to clean the wound. He'd treated his fair share of cuts and grazes in his time and most people shied away from pain. It was an automatic reaction. Not Ebony. She certainly liked to maintain that steely resolve of hers. Almost like a suit of armor. Today she had on a sensible swimsuit and a long-sleeved surf top. Why hadn't she been wearing those the other day when she went swimming?

He rested a hand against her temple to steady her face, so he could feel around the wound for any fractures or soft spots. Her skin felt as smooth as he'd imagined it would. He could hear people talking in the background, but their voices faded as he became increasingly aware of his hands on her face. The warmth of her skin sending tiny shock waves through his fingertips.

He leaned in even closer, ostensibly to get a better look at what he was doing, but it brought their faces so close together. She'd her eyes closed as he ran his fingers over the lump forming on her head. Her lashes fluttered dark and soft against her cheeks. Breathing in deeply, his mouth became inexplicably dry. She held very still as he prodded, but the tendons in her neck stretched tight, her jaw clenched. It didn't seem she was enjoying his ministrations as much as he was, her breath coming in short shallow puffs. She gave a slight wince as he prodded just a little too hard.

"Sorry." He pulled away and cleared his throat. What the hell had he been thinking? She was his patient. For the second time in three days. The irony wasn't lost on him. Although this magnetism had been there the first time he rescued her, it'd been easier to disregard. This time it couldn't be denied. The attraction was hot and heavy in his guts. "I think that should hold it. You'll do fine now."

She opened her eyes and lifted her hand to feel his handiwork. He noticed a pendant sitting snug in the hollow at her throat, just above the collar of the rash shirt.

"That's an interesting necklace." Before he could stop himself, his finger traced the thick silver necklace downwards to hover over the ornament. She started at his touch, and he pulled his hand away quickly. Was she afraid of him or just naturally jittery? She looked as if she was about to jump out of her skin. Almost as if she was scared of his touch. That'd be a first, not many women shied away from him. She was frowning at him like he'd gone a little mad. He realized he was still kneeling in front of her, and he staggered to his feet.

"Yes, it's made of something called Kyanite. I think it's only a semi-precious stone though, not worth anything really." Her hand strayed up as if out of habit to feel the smooth stone. A faraway look entered her eyes, the pendant seemingly triggering some kind of memory.

"It suits you," he said simply. And that was the truth. The color set off her gray eyes. It was made of polished stone, turquoise blue and light gray, with striations so dark they were almost purple running through it. Depending on which way it caught his eye, he could almost swear he saw the ocean in there, and the next second it was a blue sky dotted with wispy white clouds.

"Thanks," she muttered.

"Looks like I'll be walking you home again, Ms McAllister." He tensed as he anticipated her reply.

"Oh no, you don't have to do that."

And there it was, her denial that anything was wrong. Again.

Ebony stood up hastily. "What about the rest of your surfing class?"

"They'll be fine. We were just about finished anyway. And, yes, I do have to walk you home."

"You'd better listen to him," Viv's stern reply came from behind his back. "Someone needs to make sure you get home okay, and I need to get back to my café for the evening rush." Viv stood, hands on hips, orange caftan billowing around her like a sail. The look on Viv's face reminded him of being scolded by his mother. Ebony took the news about as gracefully as she had the first time he'd told her he was walking her home. With a frown and what could almost be called a pout. She glowered at her friend but didn't object.

"It's all settled, Ebony, and it is no use you arguing about it. You're my responsibility." He wanted to add, whether she liked it or not, but controlled himself.

Viv failed to hide the look of triumph hovering in her smile.

Ebony gave an audible groan, which set his teeth on edge. Was his company really that repugnant to her? Did she have to make it that obvious? Slamming the first aid kit into the backpack with more force than was necessary, he growled, "Come on then, let's get this over with."

* * *

Ebony stopped in front of Jay, one foot resting on the edge of her porch. He almost collided with her back. He'd been too busy watching her nicely shaped legs stepping out in front of him to notice what she was doing. But now she had his full attention.

"I don't remember leaving my door open." There was a slightly puzzled tone to her voice, but alarm bells started clanging loudly in his head. "No, I most definitely locked that door before I left this morning," she continued. Even though he couldn't see her face, he heard the shiver run through her voice.

"Wait. Don't go any further," he said, rough and commanding. He moved to position himself between her and the door. Ebony laid a hand on Chili's collar as the dog growled. Casting quick glances left and right, Jay returned his glare to the offending door, which stood slightly ajar.

"Are you sure?" He didn't mean for his question to sound annoying, but the adrenaline was pumping fast through his body now.

"Yes, I'm certain."

He had to quell the urge to reach around to his right hip, where his Browning pistol used to sit. He was merely an unarmed civilian now. He'd have to be extra careful. Slowing his breathing, he focused, taking resolute, silent steps toward the door.

"Stay right here while I check out the house. I'll call you if it's clear," he whispered, never taking his eyes away from the doorway, trusting she'd do what she was told.

The slit in the open door showed only murky gloom beyond. Small beads of sweat broke out on his forehead. Cursing, he steeled himself against the images that threatened to overtake him. This was no time to let the memories of his last tour in Afghanistan make his body go weak. The last time he'd stepped into a darkened room a grenade almost ended his life. He wasn't in a war zone now, there were no assault rifles or bombs here. But his heart hammered loud and hot in his chest.

Dragging in a slug of air, he pushed the door and it slid open, revealing shadowy furniture illuminated by the last rays of the setting sun. Nothing moved. Knowing his silhouette in the doorway would make a good target he moved swiftly inside. Groping for the light switch, he flicked it on and took in the living room, muscles tensed, ready to pounce.

No one was there.

He checked the bedroom and then the other rooms. They were all mercifully empty. Whoever had broken in was long gone now. But they'd left their mark. Things were swept off tables, drawers gaped open, papers and clothes were strewn all over the floor.

"It's safe, you can come in now," he called. Chili Dog bounded inside, hackles raised and sniffed suspiciously around the entrance. Ebony bustled in after the dog, the dark glower she shot him telling him she'd not been happy to be left standing outside.

"Oh, no!" Her hands flew to her mouth as she took in the mess.

"I'm sorry, Ebony." He tore his gaze away from her devastated face. She didn't deserve to come home to this. It was obvious she didn't have much in the way of material possessions. It'd take an exceptionally small-minded and petty thief to do this. Resentment and disgust boiled in his gut at the dregs of society who'd stoop low enough to burgle this little isolated shack, and he found himself wanting to lay his fists on whoever had done this. He'd not been this angry in a long, long time, and the ferocity of the emotion stunned him. He needed to calm down. When he was angry, all logical thought fled, his brain running on brutish adrenaline instead. This had served him well in the army, but not what Ebony needed from him right now. She needed composure and compassion to help her over this terrible fright.

And if he were honest, it was more than anger turning his veins molten. There was something else there too. Something caused by those spikes of memory piercing his brain. Not fear, exactly. Foreboding? Heartbreak? Or just plain neurosis? Whatever, it was the same thing that invaded his dreams, left him sweating and wide awake some nights.

Ebony was still in the doorway, aghast at the scene in front of her, a human statue, only her head moved as she scanned the chaos. Even though he wanted to reach out to her, to take her into his arms and try and soften the blow, he didn't. He barely knew this woman. The fact that he'd rescued her twice in nearly as many days didn't mean she'd count him as one of her friends and he wasn't sure she'd welcome his presence. Besides, in his current mood it wouldn't be such a good idea. He could still snap and say something he'd regret. Like how much he wanted to kill the low-life scum who did this.

Instead, he strode over to verify the door had been forced open. It was better to keep moving and keep thinking. Don't let the emotion overwhelm. The best thing he could do was to make sure she remained safe and then help her clean up this mess.

"You should go and check to see if anything's been stolen." He didn't mean for his voice to sound so dictatorial. He tried again. "I'm really sorry this happened, Ebony." Catching her eye, he held her gaze for long seconds until she nodded, then he bent to check the lock. Running his fingers over the latch, he noticed them shaking slightly, and scrunched his hand into a fist. It was just a reaction to the adrenaline, that was all. If he kept saying those words over and over, they would become truth. It'd worked before, it would work again. He would do Ebony no good like this, he was just as shaken as she was, and he silently cursed his failings. She deserved someone strong and fearless right now, both things he'd been once.

Now, he was more like damaged goods.

* * *

Ebony wasn't sure what to feel. This was the first time she'd ever been burgled. It left her vulnerable and exposed. And dirty somehow. Jay was kneeling down testing the lock on the door, his calm efficient attitude a stark contrast to the jumbled emotions running like a steam train through her belly.

Stumbling, she made her dazed way to the bedroom. Who would do this? This little cottage looked very run-down, it must be obvious there wasn't anything of real worth to be found inside. The serenity and isolation she'd treasured so much when she'd first seen this place now seemed to be a bad decision.

Entering her bedroom, she immediately saw the small wooden box lying face down on the floor. It was empty when she picked it up. They'd found her meagre stash of money and the few pieces of jewelry she kept there. None of the jewelry had any real sentimental value, but the money would be sorely missed. At least most of her money was still safe in the bank, but she'd been keeping a reserve aside with the vague idea she might buy a new, state-of-the-art couch for her Reiki clinic. Now it seemed like a silly idea; she wouldn't be staying here long enough to make use of it anyway.

"Anything missing?" Jay poked his head through the doorway.

"Yes, they got some money and a few pieces of jewelry," she replied, turning to face him, the empty wooden box held out for him to see.

"Bastards." Running a hand through his short hair, he mumbled a few stronger swear words under his breath as he looked around, taking in the ruin that was her bedroom. "The door was jimmied open, and they didn't use much finesse." His dark eyebrows drew together. "It looks like it may have been a crowbar or screw driver. Makes me think this might just be some kids wandering off the beach, nothing too sinister. I'll just go and check the back door to make sure it wasn't damaged as well." He stood for another few seconds in the doorway, as if trying to assess her frame of mind before finally turning on his heel and stalking down the corridor.

Returning to the living room, she collected clothing from the floor. The picture frames that'd once lived on the mantel piece were scattered underneath a tangle of books, broken glass littering the stone floor. Picking one up, she turned it over and was shocked to see that the photo was gone. The photo of herself and Chili Dog taken a few years back on a beach near Darwin was missing. Why would anyone take a photo of her? Ebony's eyes narrowed in contemplation. She searched through the debris on the floor. Perhaps it'd fallen out and was hidden in the piles of stuff scattered everywhere. But a serious search of the area turned up nothing. All the other photos, mainly of Chili Dog, an old pet cat, Aladdin, who'd since died, a beach sunset she'd taken up in Broome a few years ago, were still in their frames, even though the glass was broken. A chill settled like an enormous cold stone in the pit of her stomach.

Why would someone want a photo of her? There was only one person who'd be interested in that. But that was ridiculous. He couldn't still be following her after all this time. Could he? It had been over twenty years. The implications hit her abruptly and her mind swirled with various scenarios. No. She'd decided a long time ago that Alexander must have given up on finding her. She only moved from place to place out of force of habit now, not a need to stay one step ahead or to remain untraceable anymore. Surely no one could maintain the need for revenge for that long?

Alexander. The name whispered like an icy wind through her brain.

Nope. Jay was right, it was just some roguish kids with a misplaced sense of right and wrong.

But she had seen that man in the street. Was it just this morning? Who looked like Alexander.

Her head started to throb where the surfboard hit her, the pain of the headache making her squeeze her eyes shut tight. The sensation seemed to travel downwards until it constricted her heart, making it flutter unreliably. She felt light-headed and a lump formed in her throat. *Stop being silly, this is no time to be feeling sorry for yourself.* Taking a few deep breaths, she tried to center herself.

Unable to shake the sense of helplessness, she took the broken picture frame and headed outside onto the front porch to take a steadying lungful of seaside air. But the air didn't help either. In fact the enveloping darkness outside made her draw back in sudden panic. The wind had picked up now the sun was setting and was whipping the branches back and forth, making them dance like ghostly shadows. The noise of the rising gusts assaulted her senses, confusing her already distraught mind and putting her more on edge than ever. She was scared. She hadn't been this scared in a long time. Thoughts of Alexander made her insides turn to jelly. Even though her logical mind knew he wasn't here—couldn't possibly be here—just the idea of him dredged up those terrible old memories, where she had no control. Where she was weak and cowering and meaningless.

Turning away from the dark clamoring, she headed back into the warmth and light when she was stopped suddenly by Jay standing quiet and still in the kitchen doorway, studying her with kindness in his steel-blue eyes.

He never uttered a word, but there was sympathy in the creases around his eyes. A knowing concern in the set of his mouth. And his compassion was her undoing.

A tear emerged on her cheek before she could stop it. Surprisingly, another one followed as she tried to dash the first one away. She wasn't a cry-baby and certainly not in front of anyone else. Crying was a show of weakness, kept for when she was behind closed doors in the deep of the night and no one else could hear.

"Why—" The catch in her throat made her sound pathetic. Taking a deep breath, she tried again. "I'm sorry, I don't usually—" A sob cut through the rest of her declaration.

"It's okay, you've had a shock. Some bastard broke into your house."

She wanted to ask him why the thieves had taken a photo of her. But then again, she didn't really want the answer. If she opened that floodgate then she might find herself telling him of the terrible fear debilitating her these last twenty years. A fear of being found and dragged back. She'd never confided in another soul about her past, about her dread, or about the hole that lived in her heart in the place where her beautiful baby daughter once lived. The secret remained hers, and hers alone.

Another tear rolled down her face and she looked around, desperate for something to focus on, something to save her from these welling emotions. Brushing two more traitorous tears from her cheeks, she sucked in large gulps of air, but it didn't help. Her shoulders trembled with the effort of holding in her feelings.

He took two steps and strong arms encircled her, bringing her tightly into his chest and there wasn't a thing she could do to stop the sudden torrent of tears that erupted at his touch. Years of anxiety and loneliness combined in this moment to make her more defenseless than she'd ever been. She cried and cried, and he stood firm and unmoving for the many minutes it took for her desperate sobbing to abate. The warmth of his arms cradled her, and his solid chest became her haven in which to shelter. Her fist lay curled against his sternum, absorbing the strong thudding of his heart beneath. Sheltered. She felt sheltered and safe in his arms. It was an alien feeling. It'd been such a very long time since she'd felt this kind of sensation.

Finally, she lifted her head, her sobs reducing to sniffles. Keeping her enclosed within his arms, he raised a hand and wiped away the last of her tears. His touch on her face was a shock, his fingers gentle and tender, much like they had been down at the beach this afternoon. Her reaction was exactly the same, her pulse started hammering and her skin felt like tiny electric shocks were going off all over it. Was he even aware of the response he was triggering in her? Probably not, he was just comforting a scared and lonely woman, that was all.

Laying her hand flat against his chest, she steeled herself to push him away, to break the contact. His hand moved to cover hers, wrapping strong fingers around hers, and she halted. She stared at their hands together, his so strong and masculine, hers small and delicate. His thumb stroked across the quickening pulse at her wrist. Beneath her palm Ebony felt a small tremor run through his chest. The thrill of the tremor echoed in her own body. What was going on?

She raised her gaze to his. His pupils were large and dark, his blue eyes now nearly black. She held her breath, unable to look away. Chemistry. There was a definite chemistry flowing between them. Strong enough to make her knees want to buckle at the intensity. His embrace tightened.

"Ebony?" With that one word he asked the identical question ringing in her head. But she didn't know how to answer. She licked her lips and her gaze flickered between his mouth and his stunning blue eyes. The gap between them closed, his lips coming closer.

Chili's harsh barking made her jump and Jay tore his gaze away, his head snapping up to find the cause of the dog's distress. She followed his narrowed gaze toward the front window, where she could see lights bouncing crazily off the coastal shrub. He let her go and made his way to peer out of the window, leaving her swaying, unsteady on her feet. What had she been thinking? Whatever had just happened between them, she shouldn't let it happen again. She couldn't get involved with Jay. She closed her eyes and willed her rapid breathing to return to normal.

"There's someone coming," Jay said in his deep voice.

CHAPTER SIX

Cool water lapped at Jenna's toes. Pristine white beach spread out on either side of her, like two long arms drawing her in for a hug. The hot sun trickled down over her bare arms, bringing beads of sweat to her forehead.

A smile broke on her lips as Dan called to her from the water, where he was splashing around like an excited three-year old child. She hadn't seen him like this—completely relaxed and happy—for a while now. She laughed along with him, secretly smiling at his *cowboy* tan lines. Only his lower arms, neck and face were tanned by the harsh desert sun, the rest of his nicely muscled chest and legs remained untouched. His skin was a wonderful olive color, so the effect wasn't as dramatic as it was with her lily-white skin, but it still looked a little comical. It wouldn't take long for his skin to darken while they were on holiday and he was looking forward to going back with an all-over tan.

They'd arrived at this peninsula of land called Monkey Mia yesterday evening. It'd been too dark after they'd set up their tent and had their simple meal of macaroni cheese to see the beach. But this morning had been a revelation for them both. This place was paradise. Crystal clear azure water, cloudless blue skies and soft sandy beaches. And the best part were the dolphins which frequented the area. Wild dolphins that'd befriended humans and came in to the beach to be fed and petted every day.

But it wasn't the place she'd seen in her dreams. The one calling to her. Was this just her gypsy heart pushing her to move on, experience new places, keep moving? Or was this feeling something else entirely? The only way she was going to find out was to keep moving, for at least a little while longer. Keep traveling further south. She'd heard there were more beautiful beaches down there as well. And trees that towered so tall and straight they made you dizzy staring up into their branches.

Her stomach lurched, and she had to resist the urge to put her head between her knees. The nausea was getting worse. Coming in unexpected waves so that she couldn't predict when the next one would hit. She hadn't even tried to eat breakfast this morning, just fobbed Dan off with an excuse all she needed was a cup of tea to wake her up. But once the sweet tea had kicked in, she was refreshed and eager to get to the beach. The sick feeling slowly passed and she focused once more on the wondrous beach.

Thank God Dan had been as keen as her to go on this little road trip. Told her it was the honeymoon they never got to take. Once they'd decided to go and worked out all the logistics of leaving the station in the capable hands of the other staff, Dan had grown more and more enthusiastic about the idea. Never having traveled to the west coast of Australia before, he suggested places they could go, things they could see.

Dan knew as much, or as little, as she did about the reasons she needed to go. She told him everything now; about her fears and insecurities. He was her rock, he grounded her and made her feel safe. So Dan knew her constant worry about Alexander. The fact he was always at the back of her mind. Whether he had anything to do with this current feeling, Jenna couldn't say for sure.

Her mind flicked back to the day after she and Dan were married. Sitting, basking in the afterglow of the simple ceremony, surrounded by all their wonderful friends.

A small pile of envelopes sat on the kitchen table.

Jenna reached for the top one and opened it. Her fingers trailed over the raised filigree on the ivory face of the wedding card. It was a picture of a rose surrounded by trailing vines and tiny white doves. The detail was fantastic and the sheer beauty of the card enraptured her. There was no return address on the envelope.

"Are you just going to stare at that all day, or are you actually going to open it?" Dan's voice rumbled from across the room.

She could hardly believe it was only yesterday they'd gotten married. It felt surreal. Returning her attention back to the card, she opened it with a sigh.

"Oh, no!" The card dropped from her numb fingers.

"What? What's wrong, babe?" Dan was at her side immediately. He picked the card up from the floor and flipped it open. Then he gave a loud grunt and ripped it into a dozen pieces. Crushing them into a ball, he threw the offending paper into the waste paper bin and enfolded her in a fierce embrace.

The card said, *Congratulations to my daughter on her marriage to a jackaroo. What I feared was forever lost, is now found.*

"It has to be Alexander," she said, her voice small and tight. Nausea gripped her stomach and she had an overwhelming urge to run from the room. Her eyes flicked toward the bin where the pieces of card lay.

"You're just guessing." His voice sounded as frayed as hers.

"Maybe, but deep down you know I'm right." She lifted her head from where she'd buried it in his chest. "How did he find us—find me?"

"I don't know. Perhaps Liam told him after all. Or one of his imbecile henchmen." Dan's embrace tightened, his arms crushing her until she found it hard to breathe. "It doesn't matter, even if he does know where you are, you're safe out here. I'll protect you, Jenna. We'll never let him hurt you. We'll fight him off just like we did with Liam." He loosened his vice-like grip and held her out at arm's length. "You do believe that, don't you?"

Her heart beat wildly as she searched his eyes. Images crowded in. Images of Liam laughing at her while he pointed a gun at her head, images of her step-father hanging, lifeless in a tree, images of Dan's unwavering gaze as Liam held him captive. No, she wouldn't allow any of that to happen again. She'd fought Liam and won. She'd found the strength within to defeat him, and she'd do it once more if need be.

Liam was Alexander's self-declared right-hand man. Had tracked her down for the sole purpose of returning her to *her real father*, as he'd put it. But she had no intention of ever going near that psychopath who was her biological father. Especially not after what she learned about him from Liam. She'd never met him and never wanted to.

"Yes, I believe you. If Alexander shows up here, we'll be ready for him. And we will prevail."

She was determined not to be bowed down by fear or self-doubt ever again. And Dan's words remained true, they never had another sign, not an inkling or a hint that Alexander was coming for her. Over the past year her fears had slowly dulled as she and Dan carved out their fledgling life together. But he was always there, lurking in the shadows of her mind.

"Hey, babe, I think the dolphins are coming." Dan's voice drifted in, breaking through her memories. A gaggle of voices sounded from further up the beach as a crowd of tourists made their way down to the shore, eager to meet the friendly creatures.

Her feet turned toward the crowd before she even had time to think. She'd been looking forward to this for days now, as they'd traveled over the dusty red roads to get here. Would she be able to feel them too? Have a connection with them, like she did with horses and dogs?

Poor Dune, she had to leave him tied up by their car. Dogs weren't allowed on the beach. He would've been very curious to meet these wet animals.

Jenna let her mind wander, freed it of all other thoughts. Yes. There was definitely something there. A faint tickle of anticipation. Abstract images of bubbles and wheeling through blue water. She gave a little skip of delight. This was going to be fun.

Dan emerged from the water, droplets clinging to his skin, and grabbed her up in a big bear hug, making her squeal in delight.

"Come on, babe, let's go and have a chat with a dolphin."

"I love you," she said happily.

CHAPTER SEVEN

"Hush Chili Dog," Ebony commanded quietly. The dog stopped barking but continued to growl low and menacing at the front door.

The quiet drone of an engine reached her over the howling of the wind.

"Is that a car coming?" she asked Jay, incredulous. "Out here?"

Sure enough she caught the flash of brilliance as two headlights cut swathes across the stand of banksias beside her hut. *Who could it be?* Her mind, still reeling from the break-in and then what'd nearly happened between her and Jay, was finding it hard to come back to reality.

"Someone must have gotten lost." The dirt track leading to her house was tiny and un-signposted. "But no one ever comes out here," she added with a frown.

"Yes, we'll see about that." Jay's gaze never veered from the window. The taut lines of his body reminded her she'd just been burgled and she quickly grasped the gravity of the situation. What if it was the thieves coming back to finish the job? The thought made Ebony take an involuntary step backward. She was suddenly glad she had this masculine man standing as protector in her house.

She joined Jay at the window and they both watched a large four-wheel drive pull to a lurching halt right outside her front porch. The car looked vaguely familiar. A man stepped from the driver's seat and Ebony recognized him at once.

"It's okay, I know him, he's one of my regular clients," she told Jay in a relieved voice. But the tension in his shoulders didn't loosen, his eyes glittered dark and intimidating, and she was reminded of a Doberman standing guard, ready to pounce. It seemed Jay Connolly could be a dangerous man when the mood took him.

The man getting out of the car was Beau Neilson, but what was he doing out here at night? He'd been to her house once before, he'd offered to help her move the big old dining table she'd bought at the second-hand shop. Beau was harmless, with his heart in the right place, though just a tad annoying. Was she going to regret letting him know where she lived?

Opening the front door, she held it wide, allowing the cool night air to swirl inside. Beau stepped through the door carrying a bundle of blankets in his arms.

"Beau, what's going on?" she asked, forcing her voice to be steady and calm.

"I'm so sorry, Ebony. I couldn't think of where else to go." Lank blonde hair fell over the tall man's face, but it couldn't hide the desperate worry etched into the lines around his eyes.

He stopped in his tracks when he saw Jay hovering behind Ebony's shoulder.

Taking in the threatening look on Jay's face he said, "Sorry to come barging in like this. I didn't mean to alarm you."

"It's okay, Beau. This is Jay, he was helping me out with a little … situation." That was a major understatement, but Beau didn't need the details of her burglary right now, it was obvious he had a much bigger problem. "What have you got there?" she asked, pointing toward his arms.

Without answering, Beau walked toward the sofa and lay the bundle of blankets gently down on the soft cushions. She took a few steps across the tiny room, so she could see over the back of the couch as he tenderly pulled away folds of material to reveal a young boy's face. She didn't need to look around to know that Jay had followed close behind, his proximity still setting her nerve endings alight. But the anguish in Beau's eyes as he stared down at the boy almost made her forget about Jay.

She broke out in a cold sweat as she looked at the boy. Clenching her fists, she managed to steel herself enough to stay standing where she was. Fear and self-doubt warred for domination inside her chest. Fear won. Fear of what Beau was about to ask her.

"My son is sick," Beau said, never taking his gaze from the boy's pale face.

Yes, she could see that. She could feel the life-sucking pall that hung around the boy like an overcast shadow.

"He's running a dreadful fever and now he's getting harder and harder to wake. I didn't know what else to do." The grown man's eyes filled with tears as he looked up toward Ebony.

Fear turned to panic and an urge to run made her feet itch. The only thing stopping her was the knowledge that Jay stood between her and the door. Jay, strong and composed, his presence behind her a soothing balm.

"Umm. I don't think I can ..." She didn't know how to finish her sentence. She was completely out of her depth in the face of this man's terrible need.

"Please, you have to help us?" His entreaty was barely a whisper.

Her breath came in small, sharp gasps. She couldn't help him, but how could she say no to him; to this vulnerable, desperate man who knelt in front of her.

"What does he mean?" Jay's voice sounded low and intimate in her ear.

She knew he was only concerned for her, would be able to see her distress written all over her face as she battled to get control of herself. Ebony had treated Beau many times before, using her Reiki skills to heal his minor ailments and sore muscles. He'd always been more than grateful and as a joke had once suggested she had magical healing powers. He swore she never failed to cure him every single time. The Beau she knew was always carefree and confident, nothing at all like this anxious father who now knelt before her.

"Oh God!" She rubbed her hand over her face and tried to decide what to do. Jay still hovered solicitously behind her, and Beau's earnest stare impaled her. They both deserved an answer.

Without turning around she said, "I practice Reiki, it's a very old form of healing." Did Jay even know what Reiki was? Too bad if he didn't, she'd fill him in on the details later. "You know I only use my Reiki to cure small stuff, like headaches and bruises. This is too big for me, Beau." She gave him a dark frown.

"Why didn't you take him to the hospital in Margaret River?" Jay asked, echoing her exact thoughts.

She turned her head just enough to see his face in profile. There was reproof in the jut of his chin and she couldn't blame him. She felt the same way. Why bring a terribly sick child to her? He should be in the hospital. She cringed inwardly as she envisaged how Jay must be interpreting this situation. A crazy man bringing his sick child to be healed by an equally crazy woman. Great! Just what she needed. First he had to fix up her head, then he had to pick up the mess of her house being burgled and now there was a nightmare scenario playing out in front of him. Three strikes in one day was surely enough to scare any decent man and make him run for the hills.

Beau stood up, startling her. "I did! But they're next to useless!" The sudden venom in his voice was unmistakable. "They made me wait in the emergency for over four hours and then they just gave him some paracetamol and told me to take him home and monitor him. The nurse spouted some bullshit about the hospital already being overloaded with people with the flu." Beau realized he'd raised his voice and shot a concerned look toward his son, but the boy hadn't stirred.

"I did what they told me to and now look at him, he's much worse. You have magic hands Ebony. Every time you heal me, I can feel the magic flowing. I know you can help my boy. Please!"

Ebony flinched. If there'd been any doubt in Jay's mind she was a crazy woman, Beau calling her *magic* would just have confirmed the title in his head forever.

"Beau." The word was an exasperated sigh.

"All right, not magic then," he replied. "But I know you can do something special." The man looked her squarely in the face, his pale blue eyes daring her to disagree with him. She let out a sigh that was half groan. She couldn't believe she was even entertaining the thought, there was no way she was prepared to take that risk again.

"Please, Ebony," he implored again.

"Just give me a second to think." Turning around, she paced toward her little kitchen, away from both men's stares. She was grateful Jay didn't follow her and demand answers, as he had every right to. He seemed to respect her need for space.

The boy was very sick, she could feel it pulsing within him, even from this distance. And she knew she could help him, but did she dare? Was it her place to try and do something that most people had decided was impossible? What if she failed again! Needing something to busy her hands, she filled the kettle with water and plugged it in to boil. A cup of tea might help her think straight. A quick glance showed Jay had moved to lean against the doorway to her bedroom. She couldn't read anything in his carefully schooled expression. One thing was obvious, he wasn't about to leave anytime soon. She wasn't sure if she was grateful or irritated.

"I didn't even know you had a son." She was stating the obvious but she needed to buy herself some time.

"His name is Laken," Beau replied. "His mum and I have never really been together. It was all a bit of a mistake really, and he stays with his mum most of the time." Beau continued to stroke his son's hair. "I don't tend to tell most people I have a child." There was a hint of defensiveness about his tone.

"I'm very flattered you brought your son to me, Beau, but I'm not sure I'm the right person to be helping him. I agree with Jay, you should take him back to the hospital."

"I'm not going back there!" Beau didn't raise his voice, but there was an ice-cold edge of certainty in his words. She poured out three cups of tea, watching the steam rise in petite tendrils toward the ceiling. She couldn't take the risk of trying something this meaningful again. Could she? She already knew too well what happened when the healing didn't work. It'd only happened once, but that was once too often.

Walking slowly, so she didn't spill the tea, she handed a warm mug to Jay.

"I'm not sure what's going on here," he said in a low voice, "but if you need a hand to convince this guy to take his son to the hospital then just ask." He raised his chin in the direction of the sofa, his gaze steely blue.

Ebony's heart twitched in her chest at this man, so concerned for her, protective. It was something she'd never had from any other man.

"I don't know what to do," she answered candidly, running a hand through her hair.

"Can you actually help his son?" There was that directness again, no sign of how irrational this must all seem to him. Just cool and composed. What was he thinking? Beau looked over at them, his hand resting on his son's feverish forehead. He didn't speak, he didn't need to, the beseeching look said it all.

"Yes, I believe I can." And that was the truth. She could do this. If she wanted to. She was surprised at how easily the decision was made after all. She hoped it was more to do with the compassion evident in Jay's eyes, rather than wanting to prove his misgivings wrong.

"You may as well go home," she said to Jay, the tired resignation in her voice rebounding back to her from the corners of the cottage. "Thanks for getting me home in one piece. Again." She was giving him an out. His presence would be unsettling if he stayed and she needed to have her full faculties if she was to do this. She was sure he'd take the excuse and leave. What sane man wouldn't? She started toward the door to let him out.

"I'll stay, if that's okay with you."

Did she want him to stay? And why would he stay? To make sure she was okay? Was he worried about her safety? Or the boy's? Or to see if what she just declared she could do was actually true? His gaze was inscrutable, the answer not evident in the depths of his blue eyes. Fine, if he wanted to stay then she'd make the most of it.

"All right then, if you're going to stay then make yourself useful. Could you please light the fire to warm this place up? The wood pile is just outside the back door."

"Good idea," was all he said, and then he was out the back door before her bemused frown had time to deepen to a scowl. This situation wasn't ideal to say the least, and doubts circled her mind like blackbirds on the wing.

Padding back toward her bedroom to put on some warm socks and a cardigan, she tried not to look down at the bundle of needy humanity lying on her couch.

Returning to the living room a few minutes later, Ebony saw that Jay was coaxing the kindling into a bright, hungry warmth.

"You'll have to promise to be quiet while I work." She nudged Beau out of the way, taking a cushion and placing it on the floor next to the couch as she knelt down.

"Thank you, Ebony. From the bottom of my heart." There was a light, fleeting touch on her shoulder as Beau moved out of her way. "Of course I'll be quiet," he continued in a wounded tone. "I know how this works."

"Yes, I know you do, but I really mean it. You have to just sit over there," she indicted the dilapidated old arm chair in the corner, "and not move a muscle once I've started. Even if your son calls out or makes a noise. Do you promise? I can't have you breaking my link to him, not at any time, do you understand?"

"Yes, I promise." Beau sat down in the worn chair, his mouth set in a thin line of determination, hope alight in his eyes.

"You too, Jay, it's very important you don't interrupt me." She found his gaze as he knelt in the hearth behind her, still tending the fire. His face was thrown into sharp profile, lit from behind by the orange glow of the flames.

"You can trust me, Ebony," was all he said. That would have to do.

As gently as she could, she unwrapped the boy from his blankets. Slight shivers racked his small body, but he didn't move or make a noise as she continued to remove his covers.

"How old is Laken?" she asked as she closed her eyes to compose herself.

"He's six years old," Beau replied, pride lingering in his voice. "I only get to see him every second weekend. His mum has custody the rest of the time." Although Ebony didn't open her eyes, she could imagine the tall man brushing his long hair away from his forehead in his usual habit as he spoke.

"That's sad for you," she murmured in support.

"Yeah it is." His voice took on a softer note. "It's funny, you know, when we first had Laken, I was almost happy I didn't have the responsibility of looking after a kid. I didn't want him cramping my style. You know, all that surfing and hanging out with me mates and stuff."

Eyes still closed, she only half heard him as she drew in a deep breath and laid her hands on Laken's small chest.

"But lately things have been different. I actually want to spend more time with him, and he wants to see me too. He's such a determined little bloke, you know. A bit of a handful for his mother now. He needs me to show him what's right and what's wrong in this world."

Ebony gave a muted grunt as a reply.

"Oh God, Sally is going to kill me if she ever finds out about this. She won't let me see him again, I just know it. This has to work, Ebony, you have to help him!" Beau's last plea was almost lost on her as her concentration lay solely on the boy now.

Ebony summoned silence into her mind. She'd learned everything there was to know about Reiki, done years of study and training and was a certified Reiki Master. So that was how she knew what she did, the way she healed people, was completely different to Reiki. What she was doing now was far more complex and powerful. She used Reiki as a facade, an excuse for what she was really doing.

The practice of Reiki taught her a life force flowed within the physical body though pathways called chakras, as well as around the body in an aura. Her Reiki teachers showed her how to re-direct energy through the affected parts of the physical body and in doing so clear and heal the energy pathways, allowing the life force to flow in a healthy way once more. She'd been a very quick learner. Eventually her teachers had paled with fear when Ebony had revealed even a small part of the power she had available to her as she wielded the energies. Very soon she'd learned to hide her abilities. No one knew how strong she was.

Letting her mind empty itself was often the one thing Ebony found hardest to do. Especially tonight, with Jay here, watching her. Her mind had to be clear and sharp as a tack for her to make a healing connection. Her awareness became absolute, nothing could break her concentration now. She could feel the energy flowing from her hands, which hovered mere millimeters off the child's chest. She let the energy course into Laken's body, and her mind flow with it, until she could hear each beat of his heart pulsing, experience the immense fever burning him up, feel the terrible lethargy sucking his very bones dry.

She became one with this tiny person, linked to him mind and body. That was the reason it was vital she not be interrupted, the link should not be broken. Last time she'd delved this deeply, the link had been broken too soon. She'd only just managed to withdraw in time. What might've happened if she hadn't disconnected fully? Would it leave traces of herself behind in the other person forever? Or would that person remain in her mind instead? Perhaps nothing would've happened, but Ebony wasn't prepared to take that risk.

Her mind followed the threads of energy into his body, directed them toward the areas of intense darkness where her presence was needed most. It was a delicate procedure. The only way Ebony could possibly describe it to someone else was like trying to unpick numerous knots in the finest thread of pure silk. It was time consuming and tedious and her physical body tired the longer she spent with the boy. There were so many knots needing to be undone, but she would stay until they were all loose. Until it was all done.

* * *

Jay stood in a darkened corner of the room, watching. At first, he'd wanted to scoff at Beau's insistence Ebony could heal his sick boy, and he had to hide his disapproval behind his question as to why the man hadn't just taken his son back to the hospital. The boy was very ill, even Jay could see that by the pallor of his skin and his limp, unresponsive form. Surely the man had to be two-parts crazy. Yes, he'd heard of Reiki, even heard rumors of good things from people who'd been to see Ebony in her new clinic since he'd come back from his business trip. But cure a dangerously high fever? Really?

He'd watched Ebony struggle with some kind of internal decision, waiting for her to tell Beau to return to the hospital with his sick son. It'd come as a complete surprise when she'd agreed to treat him. Admittedly, he hadn't known Ebony for very long, but the persona she emitted was one of calm control, reasonable and rational—for the most part. Why then was she making this seemingly unwise choice? It was an interesting situation, but he was prepared to sit back and play along—trust Ebony knew what she was doing. For now. He was prepared to step in and stop it if need be.

So, he'd backed into the shadows, to watch and wait. A task he'd become very good at while deployed in

Afghanistan. There was a lot of watching and waiting before any decision was made over there. Those decisions could potentially be life-changing. Perhaps the same could be said of what was happening here tonight.

Because his mind had conjured up Afghanistan, the memories came. It wasn't because of anything dangerous or fear-provoking in the scene unfolding in front of him. No explosions of sound or bright flashes of searing light. Nothing at all that resembled the cacophony of war. But the flashbacks clamored at the door, demanding to be heard. Ebony, with her head bowed as if in prayer was outwardly as still and serene as the surface of a deep mill pond. But he was the exact opposite, muscles wound tighter than a steel trap, a band of iron constricting his chest. He took in deep, slow breaths, and tried to unclench his fists just a fraction. But it was no good.

The boy's pale features were replaced with images of Tom Logan's face, the young Lieutenant who'd been his platoon leader. The dim room became full of smoke and settling dust. Loud spurts of gunfire rent the air, sounding just outside the shattered wooden doorway. In his arms he cradled the young man. Tom had dark brown eyes but today they were glazed with fear, pleading. His mouth moved, but no words escaped through dry, cracked lips. Jay screamed for a medic but wasn't sure if he'd been heard over the incessant gunfire. He tried to cover the gaping hole in the Lieutenant's chest with his jacket, but blood seeped like a crimson tide, to join the growing pool on the floor. Pain shot through his abdomen as he moved, a wicked burning sensation he ignored.

The medic came at last, too late. Jay watched Tom Logan's eyes go wide with pain, then fade to blank and staring. The rasping, croaking breath in his throat stopped.

Tom Logan was part of the hand-picked squad of six men he'd chosen to complete a job. A reconnaissance mission. To scout through a deserted industrial area on the extreme outskirts of Jalalabad to make sure the abandoned buildings were clear. A fairly easy job from all accounts.

But the area hadn't been empty, as they'd been led to believe. Instead they'd been ambushed. Jay was wounded, but two of his men died that day. And now he couldn't rid himself of the specter of Tom's eyes.

Jay shook his head. The flashbacks were getting harder to ignore, coming at odd times, never predictable, but always the same. Closing his eyes, he ground his teeth together. He would rid himself of this demon, he just had to try harder, not allow those memories to take control of him any longer.

Filaments of the moon's rays penetrated the curtains. The room lightened, casting eerie shadows. How long had he been standing here? He rolled a shoulder, trying to ease the ache in his back. Ebony hadn't moved, but Beau was slumped over in the armchair in a fitful sleep. Maybe he should do the same, who knew how long this might take. He didn't move, however, afraid of interrupting Ebony's concentration.

His gaze followed the curve of her neck as she knelt, bowed over the boy. The skin exposed, warm in the glow of the fire, as her dark hair curled around her ears. He couldn't see her face, hidden as it was behind the curtain of curls, but he could imagine her lips, soft and relaxed as her concentration floated far away. Lips which were plump and luxurious, especially when she quirked up one corner in a curious smile. Sensuous lips. He'd liked it when she licked them in unconscious reaction as he'd held her close today. When they'd almost kissed. What would she have tasted like if they *had* actually kissed?

Why had he stayed here really? Not a question he could easily answer. His ready excuse was Ebony needed someone to protect her in case Beau became angry or troublesome if things didn't go according to plan. Or moral support even, but that was only scratching the surface of his conflicting thoughts. Ebony … Well, she intrigued him. That didn't happen often in this small town. A woman who was both astute and compassionate. And capable of captivating him. A woman with secrets, that much was also obvious. She had many complex facets to her personality, with new aspects revealed every time they met. Up until now he'd actively shied away from intelligent women. Once bitten twice shy, was that how the saying went? In his experience, women who were exceptionally smart were also very adept at cold, calculated indifference. The women he was fond of dating had simple needs and were more than easy to please. He didn't need secrets in his life and had more than enough of his share of complications.

So why had he stayed?

* * *

Shuddering, Ebony could feel her reserve was now spent. She had nothing left to give the boy. Little by little she withdrew from him, careful to recall every fiber of herself, not daring to leave even one tiny bit behind. Exhausted as she was, she took her time to check everything was as it should be, spending laborious minutes re-checking all the pathways were clear. Her physical body was shaking with fatigue now, and it was only sheer force of will holding her erect.

Taking in a huge breath, Ebony withdrew her hands from where they hovered above the boy, her shoulders slumping, her chest caving inwards as she struggled to drag in enough oxygen to replenish her lungs.

"Ebony, are you all right?" Beau had half-risen from the chair before he stopped, unsure whether he could speak, terrified he might break her concentration.

"I've done what I can," she croaked, pushing against the couch, trying to raise herself up.

"Here, let me help you." Gentle hands lifted her under the arms and guided her toward the other chair. It was Jay who'd rushed to her aid, Beau was still looking at Laken from his chair with a dazed expression. "God, you look terrible," Jay said as he peered into her face.

"I'll be fine soon." Her voice was just above a whisper, it was all she could summon for now. "How is he?" Ebony indicated the boy with a tilt of her chin.

Beau took two enormous strides and knelt down by his son's side and laid a tender hand on his forehead. A frown appeared as his eyes narrowed in deliberation.

"He's still really hot." Ebony felt despair descend, she'd not been able to help after all. Mixing with her body's weariness, the despair was going to crush her under its weight.

"But ..."

But what? A flicker of hope lifted her head. Jay still knelt beside her chair, dark eyebrows lowered, but he twisted toward Beau as he spoke.

"He's also drenched in sweat. He's sweating so much the blankets are soaked." A grin broke on Beau's serious face.

"That's good, isn't it?" Ebony asked, exhaustion making her wonder if it really was good.

"I think it might be," Beau replied, the grin spreading to light up his eyes. "I think it means the fever is breaking."

"Yes, a sweat usually means the fever has broken," Jay confirmed in a low voice.

Was that surprise in the curl of his mouth? Did he think what she did was just some mumbo-jumbo? It didn't really matter, she reminded herself. Actually, it'd be better if he did think that. She didn't want anyone knowing her true powers, she'd end up becoming just another freak, someone who was hounded or accused of being a fraud. No, it was better to keep what she'd done in the shadows, off everyone's radar.

Jay glanced at his watch and she had to ask, "What is the time?" How long had the healing taken? She had no idea whether it'd been hours or minutes.

"It's after one am," he replied.

Jesus, she'd been at it for nearly five hours. Could that even be possible? No wonder she was completely washed out. And no wonder both men looked tired and rumpled.

Gorgeously rumpled, when it came to Jay. Dark hair spiked and ruffled, the sleeves of his sweater pulled up to his elbows.

"Let me get you something hot to drink," Jay said into her ear, his voice gentle. Well, even if he did think she was crazy, he was still acting like a complete gentleman.

"A cup of tea, white with two sugars would be lovely," she replied with a tight smile.

"Coming right up." He stood, but as he turned toward the kitchen, Ebony placed a hand on his arm.

"Can I ask both of you a big favor?" Jay swung curious blue eyes back toward her. She locked onto his gaze. "Can I ask you don't tell anyone else what happened here tonight?"

There was only a millisecond of hesitation before Jay said, "Sure."

Beau echoed his comment.

"This kind of thing will only make people talk," she went on. "You know what small towns are like. People get hold of some piece of gossip, and the next thing you know, it's all be blown out of proportion."

"I know exactly what you mean," said Beau, and gave her a conspiratorial wink. "This will be our little secret."

Ebony was pretty sure he'd keep his word. After all, he didn't want the boy's mother to find out how sick he'd been. But what about Jay? He was looking down on her, inscrutable.

"This will remain between you and me. Unless you tell me otherwise," he promised.

Ebony believed him, there was something about the man that spoke of sincerity. But she could tell he was curious as to why she'd want to keep such a secret.

CHAPTER EIGHT

"Thanks for staying. It was nice to know you were here," Ebony said, her figure silhouetted in the light spilling from her doorway as he stood on her front porch.

"Not a problem," Jay replied, stifling a yawn. Poor Ebony, she must be exhausted. He knew he was about ready to drop where he stood, and he hadn't been the one doing all that … well, whatever it was she was doing. Especially after she'd had that nasty knock to the head as well.

It was just after two am and they'd finally packed Beau and his son off into his 4WD and sent them home, Laken sleeping peacefully. Jay would still have to walk back along the beach to the carpark where he'd left his car. Not too far, but far enough on a dark night like this one. Ebony offered to drive him around in her battered old Subaru, but it was only a five-minute walk and he knew she needed to get to bed. The walk in the brisk night air would help to clear his head.

"I'm sorry it's so late, do you have to work tomorrow?" she asked, sounding contrite.

"Nah, Dave and Stu will open the shop for me tomorrow. It's Sunday and I like to have one day off a week. So I can sleep in." Thank God he'd arranged that yesterday with his two full-time staff. He knew he could rely on them to do a good job on his days off. He caught flash from her white teeth as she gave a smile of relief. "The only thing I've got on tomorrow is VFRS training in the evening, but I'll be fine by then."

"VFRS?" she repeated, turning the letters over slowly on her tongue.

"Yes, I'm a member of Volunteer Fire and Rescue Service."

Ebony shook her head as if to rid it of weariness and said, "Oh, of course, they help fight bushfires as well as rescue road crash victims. Country communities depend on them."

Right at this very moment VFRS training was the last thing he wanted to do tomorrow. But after a few hours' sleep that feeling would fade. Normally he loved the training. It was his way of giving back to the community, of being able to help people. Of finding some of the camaraderie he'd shared in the army again. Sometimes it came a little too close for comfort to what he'd experienced in Afghanistan, if they were fighting a fire and lives were at stake. But most of the time he loved the little adrenaline kicks he got from rushing to put out a fire, as well as the community spirit surrounding everyone involved.

"I've often thought about joining the VFRS." Ebony's words broke through his thoughts, but then a stricken expression crossed her face, as if she hadn't meant to say it.

He gave her a broad smile. "We're always looking for new members," he replied. "Why don't you come along and take a look at what we do?" It was true, the small brigades often struggled to fill their quota of members. They were down a few volunteers this year, and even though she was petite, with proper training she'd still do well.

"Oh, I … um." It seemed like he'd caught her unprepared. She was going to say no, it was there in her eyes. A whole raft of emotions crossed her face in the dimness of the porch.

"No pressure. Just pop along, meet a few people. We always have a few drinks with some crackers and cheese afterward." He tried to keep his voice encouraging, with a strong dose of understanding. It was scary for some people, the thought of doing something selfless for someone else. Not that this should bother her, after what he'd just seen her do. Perhaps it might even be of help. It seemed to him that Ebony was missing something from her life. A deep connection, a link to one place. She was a drifter, never settling for very long before moving on. There would be no harm in her coming along for one night ... He stopped his train of thought. Why was he suddenly so keen for her to come? Did he have an ulterior motive? Was it an excuse to spend a few more hours with her, before she disappeared from his life once more?

"Yeah, sure, I'll come along. Where is it and what time?"

He could hardly believe she was uttering the words and his heart skipped a beat. He told her where to meet him and to wear loose-fitting long clothes and covered shoes.

"I'd better get going, Axel will be wondering where I am." He'd left his dog home alone all day. It wasn't the first time, and Axel was a very patient, well-behaved dog, but he would be glad to see Jay. And even gladder to get his much-belated dinner.

Ebony's eyes widened in surprise and then she reached down to give Chili a quick pat on the head. "Oh, your poor dog. Yes, yes, you'd better go. Give him a hug from me. The dog that is," she added, sounding a little flustered.

"Ebony, that was a very fine thing you did tonight." He allowed his hand to rest on her shoulder and gave it a quick squeeze. The instant he touched her, he was reminded of how he'd looked into her gray eyes earlier tonight and wanted to kiss her. Desperately. He withdrew his hand slowly. When she didn't answer, he asked, "Are you going to be alright?" Should he be leaving her alone tonight? She'd been pretty shaken up by the break-in, and her place was still in disarray. Even though he assumed it was just some blasted kids looking for mischief, she didn't seem so sure. He hesitated, about to ask her if she wanted him to stay.

"I'm fine, I just need some sleep now. You go, you've done more than enough for me for one day," she replied. Yes, she was right. She'd be fine, and he needed to get back to his dog.

"Make sure you jam the chair under your front door handle, like I showed you. And report the break-in to the police tomorrow, too."

"I will. I'll call the locksmith first thing in the morning to come and fix the door," she replied.

"See you tomorrow then. And look after that gash in your head, we don't want it getting infected."

"Yes, Dad," she replied sarcastically. "See you at training." She was already backing into her house. Jay cast one last look over his shoulder as he wound up the track toward the beach, and the tiny house disappeared into the inky blackness of the night.

* * *

"God, you have beautiful eyes." *Shit*. Did she really say that out loud? Well the old adage, *a person's eyes are the window to the soul* was definitely true when it came to Jay. "Sorry." Ebony gave a light laugh and shrugged off the comment. "Did I say that out loud?" Damn, if only she hadn't been caught staring at him. She might blame it on the half glass of white wine she'd just downed, but that wouldn't be the truth. If pressed, she would've classified his eyes as dark blue, but they were more than that. There were flecks of gold and amber and even green hidden in the irises. His tanned face only highlighted the colors even more. Framed by long, dark lashes, the same color as his hair, the complete picture was captivating. And now she was swooning like some ardent teenager.

"Yes, you did just say that out loud," he chuckled. "Perhaps you need some more cheese and crackers." He stared pointedly at her nearly-empty glass.

"Right," she said, making a big pretense of turning around and snagging two cubes of cheese and a few crackers from the table nearby, while at the same time hoping she was hiding the growing blush suffusing her cheeks. Double damn. Why couldn't she keep her thoughts to herself?

At least no one else seemed to have heard her blunder. They were inside the Fire Brigade Building, in a large, open room set aside for VFRS training. All the rest of the VFRS volunteers were huddled around one of the young guys, Neil, who held his phone up so they could all watch a video of him doing some kind of amazing surfing maneuver.

She'd enjoyed watching their training tonight, even found some of it fascinating. But now it was time to leave, before she said something else incriminating.

"I hope you weren't bored to death. The Captain is certainly a stickler for his PPE training." Jay was enough of a gentleman to change the subject and she silently thanked him.

"Not at all, it was kind of fascinating. I never really thought about how much gear you guys have to wear to a fire before. It must weigh a ton." The training tonight had been all about the merits of Personal Protective Equipment. The Captain, Mike Edgewood, made them all spread out their equipment on the large gravel courtyard out the back of the Fire Brigade building and then name each piece, what it did and why it was important. Ebony learned their orange jacket and pants were called the outer shell. And the structural firefighting helmet provided protection against penetration and impact, thermal protection, and face and eye protection. Mike chastised one of the older women volunteers, Julie, for not wearing her helmet properly with ear flaps down and chin strap affixed. It could be the difference between life and death, he said, staring at her with steely eyes until she lowered her gaze and apologized. Then there was the heavy-duty footwear, safety goggles, gloves and even breathing apparatus. It was a hell of a rig. And Mike made them put it on and take it off again four times in all, timing them as they went, haranguing them to do it faster and better, each time.

"Yep, it does weigh you down, but I wouldn't be without it in the middle of a fire, that's for sure."

"I'm not sure I'd even be able to move in all that getup," she replied, turning around so she could look at the group of other volunteers still engrossed in the phone, her shoulder nearly touching Jay's arm. An arm covered by a snug-fitting dark blue knit top, which left nothing to the imagination when it came to just how nicely defined his biceps were. Ebony drew in a few deep breaths and let them out again. How could a man who'd spent most of last night helping her with a sick child come to a training night looking so wonderfully delicious in his relaxed chinos and long-sleeved sweater. It wasn't fair. She was sure she looked like the Wicked Witch of the West with huge dark shadows under her eyes, her face pale with lack of sleep and worry.

"You do get used to it after the first few times," he said quietly.

"Hmm." She wasn't convinced. But a little voice insisted she needed to try it out before she disregarded it out of hand. This group had a kind of relaxed camaraderie that she envied. Something she'd like to be part of. And there was also the serious undertone. That they were doing something special here, something that mattered. Saving their own community from the demon that was a bushfire, the scourge of country areas.

Could she do what these people were doing? They were just everyday people after all. People with a common cause and a need to help their fellow man. Wasn't that what she did as well? Helped people? Her skills might even come in handy under certain circumstances. But of course she couldn't join up. She wasn't going to stay here long enough.

It was true, she'd always been fascinated with people who volunteered, their selflessness and community spirit. But she never stayed long enough in one place to ever consider joining. Perhaps that's why she admired those people, they had something she'd never have. A place within society. A unity, a reason to feel like they belonged.

"Do you think you'll join?" His question made her give a guilty twitch. What, was he a mind reader now? "You don't get thrown in the deep end straight away. You'd do an induction course first and then work through the various training modules, before you're put under a three-month probationary period. And you can change your mind at any time."

"I did enjoy it. And I'll definitely think about it," she said. "But I won't promise anything."

"Fair enough." A friendly silence descended between them as they listened to the rest of the crew joking and laughing.

"I should go now," she said. It was getting late and she still wasn't properly recovered from her late-night emergency last night.

"I'll walk you to your car," he said, placing his half-empty beer glass on the table and waiting while she collected her handbag from beneath the table and thanked The Captain for letting her watch tonight.

He held the door open for her as they went out onto the street where her car was parked a little way down. The VFRS building looked fairly new, they obviously took their volunteers seriously here. Directly opposite was the old-fashioned police office and court house, which looked to have been built back in the seventies.

"How was Axel when you got home? I bet he was pleased to see you."

"Yes, he was." Jay smiled and in the light of the single street lamp Ebony could see how much he loved that dog. Her heart did a tiny flip-flop. Whose heart wouldn't soften at the sight of a grown man who treasured his animal? It struck her to the core, what a good man he was. She smiled back at him, then kept walking.

"Ebony?"

"Hmm," she replied, only half-concentrating as she fished around in her bag for her car keys.

"I'd like to cook you dinner one night."

"What?" Where had that come from? She hadn't been expecting it. "Oh … Ah …" she dithered, not coming up with any real answer.

"What about Tuesday night, are you free then?"

She stared up at him, speechless. What should she say? The look on his face said he was possibly as shocked by his invitation as she was. When she didn't answer, he looked down at his feet, uncomfortable. Double damn, for the second time tonight.

"Sure. Okay, what time?" And she was as shocked by her answer as he seemed to be. Ebony drew in a breath and let it out on a sigh. Why was she letting this man affect her? She didn't know exactly, but he must be at least six or seven years younger than her for a start. Viv thought he may be early thirties, which put him well below her batting average. There was no way he would be interested in a forty-year-old woman. And there was no way she was ever going to consider a younger man, even if her lifestyle allowed for romance. Sooner or later, he'd want kids, the whole package, and she just couldn't give that to him.

What was she doing? This couldn't go anywhere, so why was she saying yes? Probably because he had beautiful eyes she thought miserably. And she was a sucker for beautiful eyes.

CHAPTER NINE

Damn these fiddly bloody things. What'd made him think he could cook cannelloni anyway? Jay let the pasta shell drop onto the bench with a disgusted grunt. The recipe looked so easy, just stuff the spinach and ricotta mixture into the long, round pasta shells, but the bloody stuff was going everywhere except into the shells. Globs of white and green dotted the bench, the chopping board and the pasta dish. There were even bits of it on the wall. He thought he'd do the right thing and cook Ebony a vegetarian meal, but it was backfiring on him in a big way.

If only he could've cooked a nice big beef vindaloo curry instead. His favorite. And now he was on the topic, why had he asked her to dinner anyway? Because the link between his brain and his mouth had failed, that's why. With a frustrated sigh he went to the sink to wash the gloop off his fingers. Ebony wasn't his type of woman. Well, not anymore.

Axel sat on the other side of the kitchen bench and stared at him with those liquid-amber, perceptive eyes. Jay had banned the dog from the kitchen, he was too big and prone to getting under Jay's feet. But it didn't stop him watching his every move from his chosen spot near the small dining table.

"How am I going to salvage this?" he asked the dog.

"Woof."

"Yeah, thanks mate, very helpful." Jay winced as he glanced over at the mess he'd made of the kitchen.

He grabbed a tea-towel to dry his hands and stared out the kitchen window. During the day the view from the window took him over his back fence and through a large stand of Karri trees, down a slight slope that disappeared into thick bushland. He'd love to buy a place with a view of the ocean, but this little cottage was all he'd been able to afford when he'd first moved to Margaret River. It was on the main road about halfway between the township of Margaret River and the river mouth and was completely surrounded by bushland. The white hardy-plank walls and the corrugated tin roof lent it a quaint, almost colonial look. But the best bit about the cottage was the privacy. His nearest neighbors were a couple of hundred meters away, hidden by the thick bush between.

Tonight, all he could see through the window was the dark silhouettes of the large trees swaying in the breeze caught in the glow of the full moon, and his own reflection staring back at him. Jesus, was that a gray hair? He was only thirty-two, surely not. He grunted in self-deprecation. If he took into account all he'd done with his life up till now, it was no wonder he was going gray.

Like his time spent in Afghanistan. That was enough to send any man gray. The face of Tom Logan appeared in the glass in front of Jay and he clenched his fists tight. The loss of a good man, it wasn't something you got over quickly. If at all.

Tom's features morphed and changed in the glass, replaced by three cherubic faces. Aasif, Noor, and Roshan. Three innocent children caught up in that terrible war and its after-effects. At least now they might have a chance of a better life.

Jay grunted and shifted his bare feet on the linoleum floor. He just wished he could do more for them. Sending them money and gifts just didn't seem enough. Fariba, their mother, was grateful for the money. He'd met her one morning while she was out getting water for her family. Saved her life. Jay and his team had been tasked with clearing mines from an area surrounding a local mosque in Kandahar, when she'd unwittingly walked right into the dusty area. Jay had yelled at her in Farsi to *stop, don't take another step*. He and another of his team-mates had skirted around the zone until they were opposite her and then cleared a path back toward safe ground. Poor Fariba was sobbing and shaking so hard she had to sit down once she was safe. Jay took pity on her and walked her back to her home—if it could be called a home—it'd been more like a lean-to shack, constructed from the three walls of the building they'd once called home, with sheets of metal situated precariously on top for a roof.

Jay learned Fariba's husband had been killed by the Taliban. Rounded up and shot on the street, for no apparent reason, leaving her to fend for three children on her own. The children hadn't said a word, as he towered in the doorway to their hut. Just stared at him with terrified, hungry gazes. Right then, Jay decided he was going to help this family. He couldn't just leave them there to a fate worse than death—starvation. It would be either that or death at the hands of the volatile Taliban. The very next day, Jay organized for the family to move into a UN facilitated housing estate, which was more of a refugee camp than anything else, but it had facilities such as clean water and food and a proper roof over their heads. Fariba was embarrassingly grateful.

Since then, Jay had been trying his level best to get Fariba and her family to be declared refugees and granted asylum here in Australia. No one else knew he sent money to them every couple of weeks, or the lengths he'd already gone to, to try and cut through the reams and reams of paperwork to save them. God, the amount of red-tape and paperwork he'd had to wade though, and even after all that it seemed to make no difference. The wheels of the government turned excruciatingly slowly. It'd been months now since he'd heard anything on their case. For some reason he felt it was his duty to save this family. His one little ray of hope in that otherwise terrible debacle of a war.

"Moof." Axel's gentle reminder broke through Jay's musing. There wasn't enough action going on in the kitchen for his dog and he was getting bored with watching Jay stare out the window. Jay laughed and went over and ruffled the big dog's ears, which had him leaping about like a puppy, lapping his big tongue out to slobber on Jay's fingers.

"Yeah, yeah, settle down, you big lug."

From his spot in the dining room, Jay had a good view out the front window. A glint from something metallic in the moonlight caught his eye. A car, parked out front of his place. At the same time, Axel must've spotted it too, because his hackles rose up. It must be Ebony, here already. She was early. Damn, now he definitely wasn't going to get dinner finished on time. He stood and stared through the low bushes lining his front garden. She was sitting in the car, unmoving. Why wasn't she getting out? Hands on the steering wheel, she stared straight ahead through the windscreen. Contemplating. If he didn't know better, he might've guessed she was thinking about changing her mind and going home. Then the low muffled growl of a car engine drifted through the front window pane.

She *was* going to leave. In two strides he was at the front door. He unlocked it and stood on the front porch, flicking the outside light on so he was illuminated. She couldn't help but notice him now. The pale oval of her face turned toward him in the interior of the car, her eyes wide. He gave a friendly wave. Was it his imagination, or did her shoulders just slump?

Axel whined from the other side of the screen door. Jay left him there, he was liable to get too excited and rush out and scare Ebony. He could wait his turn and greet her like a gentleman when she came inside.

The car engine cut out. Why would she take all the trouble to come out here, if she was just going to turn around and go home again? Complicated didn't begin to describe this woman. He still wasn't sure exactly what he'd witnessed the other night at her house, when she'd supposedly healed that kid. Whatever it was, it should've scared the bejesus out of him, sent him running for the hills. For the second time that night he wondered why he'd asked her over for dinner.

Then she got out of the car and walked toward him, hips swaying beneath a long skirt that brushed the ground and his question was answered. The clench low down in his gut was unmistakable. He was attracted to her in a big way. Petite and curvy, she was just plain gorgeous to look at. With those big limpid eyes and high cheek bones, she reminded him of some old-fashioned French actress. And truth be known, the fact she was so complicated was also a draw card. She tested his intelligence, didn't let him get away with anything. Unlike most of the other women he chose to date.

"Good evening, Ebony," he said and extended a hand to help her up the three steps onto the porch. Her fingers were warm and small inside his.

"Hi," she said, a little breathless.

Now she was close up he could see the pink glow on her cheeks. He kept hold of her hand.

"I was wondering if you were going to come in, or just sit out there all night?"

"Ah. Um sorry about that." The pink rose higher on her cheeks as embarrassment claimed her. "I brought some mango sorbet," she said, holding the tub of ice-cream up for him to see. Fair enough, she wanted to change the subject.

"Lucky you did, because I completely forgot about desert. Come and meet Axel." He led her inside by the hand, saying, "Sit," to Axel in case he forgot his manners. But he was perfectly behaved and sniffed her hand when she held it out to him and then let her stroke his head, half-closing his eyes in enjoyment.

"He's beautiful," she breathed, obviously more enamored by the dog. "And so well behaved."

"Yes, well. I believe animals thrive on discipline and boundaries as much as kids do."

"So, the rumors are true then. You must've been in the army with convictions like that, Jay." She gave him a charming smile to cut the sting of her words. "I've tried to get Chili Dog to behave, but she's her own person."

"She's a great dog, and much better trained than most others I've met," he replied. "And yes, the rumors are correct. I was a corporal in the army. But I've moved on from that. I hope." It was the first time he'd told anyone but his closest friends and workmates what he used to do. He wanted to move on from that life, not be reminded about it constantly. But she deserved to know the truth.

"How's the head by the way?" he asked, taking the sorbet from her hand.

"Healing well." She lifted a curl of dark hair off her forehead to show him the wound. He bent in closer to get a good look at the red welt. It'd leave a scar, but not a bad one and it could've been a whole lot worse. The hairs on the back of his neck stood up when he thought about just how much worse. She could've lost an eye, if the fin had gouged lower, or it could've ripped open half her cheek. That pretty face would've been scarred for life. And it was a very pretty face. His eyes flicked to hers and they widened as she stepped back.

"Yep, all looks good to me," he said brusquely, straightening up and heading toward the kitchen. She followed him through the dining room and then stopped just before the kitchen as she took in the mess he'd made.

"Do you need a hand with anything?" she asked politely.

Now it was his turn to look sheepish. "Are you any good at spinach and ricotta cannelloni?"

"I'm an expert. Why don't you make us a green salad to go with it, and I'll ... um, tidy this up a bit."

* * *

Ebony had never seen such a mess. Even the walls were splattered with spinach. What had he been doing? It was sweet though, him trying to cook her a vegetarian meal.

"Don't spend a lot of time in the kitchen?" she said conversationally as she picked up the half-stuffed pasta shell from the granite bench-top.

"Ah, well ... I can cook," he replied with a grin, sapphire blue eyes flashing. "But I'm much better at steak and chips, or a nice Vindaloo curry. You know, meals with meat in them."

She giggled, an almost girlish sound that brought her up sharp. She wasn't a teenager on her first date, she reminded herself. If only her heart would stop skittering around like a cat on a polished floor, she might be able to control her impulses. And she didn't really consider this as a date, either. It was just two friends having dinner and getting to know each other better.

Axel was so well behaved that he just lay in the dining room, head on his paws, watching everything going on in the kitchen with bright, interested eyes. Chili Dog would love to meet Axel. He was such a gentleman, he'd probably even let her sniff his butt first. Might even teach her a thing or two about manners.

"I'm too used to army rations, I'm afraid. Ten years in the military kind of killed any cooking instinct I may've had." He leaned up against the bench to consider her as he spoke, long, jean-clad legs stretched out at an angle. No shoes, which gave him a casual, relaxed look. But then relaxed might be his middle name, nothing seemed to faze him. Even leaning over, he was still much taller than her and she had to tip her head up to talk to him. Tonight, he had on a dark polo shirt, open at the neck, the short sleeves tight around his large biceps.

She swallowed and glanced away. Sexy was the word hovering in her mind. He looked so sexy, the dark blue of the shirt almost the same as his eyes, a five o'clock shadow highlighting his square jaw. It made him look dark and mysterious. A totally charming package.

"Can you handle making a salad?'

"Sure, I can do that." But he didn't move from his spot against the bench, and she had to fight the urge not to squirm under his penetrating gaze.

"While you're doing that, I'd love to hear a little about your time in the army," she said and took a deliberate step away from him, toward the sink where she found a sponge and started to wipe up some of the mess.

"Not much to tell, really." His voice was muffled by the refrigerator door and she got a good view of his very nice butt as he bent in to pull out the salad veggies. Busying herself with stuffing the rest of the cannelloni, she pretended she hadn't been watching him. Taking a look around, she decided it was a nice, modern kitchen, the cupboards painted in a pale cream, set off with a dark gray tiled splash-back and granite counter top. There was a large coffee machine taking up one whole corner—he must love a good coffee—and a large wooden knife block bristling with sharp knives. A little austere, it could do with a few splashes of color here and there to make it look more homey, perhaps a vase of flowers, but in general not bad at all.

"I joined up straight out of school. It just felt right, you know. I thought I'd be helping people. My dad didn't like it." He gave a wry laugh. "That was as good a reason as any to join. Then I did two tours in Afghanistan before I finally realized enough was enough."

She glanced over at him. With his back to her, he pulled out a chopping board and one of the vicious looking knives and started to slice a tomato.

"Is that where you got those scars?" Oh damn, her mouth had run away with her again. "Ah … I mean … I saw them the other day when you took off your wetsuit." Now she was embarrassed. Why had she asked that question? It was stupid, because hadn't she just opened the door for him to ask the same question of her? She was sure he'd seen the burn marks on her back the day he'd pulled her out of the water. It was the one time she'd let her guard down enough to let anyone else see them. Normally she was so careful about what she wore.

His hand stilled and the knife hung, suspended.

"Sorry, I didn't mean to pry." Her bottom lip caught between her teeth as she tried to gauge his reaction to her question.

He turned around to look at her.

"Yeah. It was." The knife twirled, forgotten, in his hand. "It was during my last tour. My platoon was ambushed on a reconnaissance mission. The area was supposed to be clear, but someone got their intel wrong." Jay's face grew hard, his mouth a tense line and she was suddenly sorry she'd brought it up.

"I'm glad you survived." It was the first thing that came to mind. But surprisingly, it was true. She was very glad this man was alive and standing here in front of her, vibrant and charismatic. "I mean, it must've been horrible," she amended.

His indigo eyes came up to meet hers, serious and somewhat troubled. But then they cleared and the deep lines in his forehead were wiped away.

"I guess I'm glad too," he replied and twirled the knife vigorously, the rogue grin back in place.

"Okay, I'm just about finished here. Where's the tomato paste and cheese to go over the top?" She forced her voice to cheeriness, changing the subject as soon as she was able.

It took them another ten minutes, but they finally had the cannelloni in the oven. Jay poured them a glass of wonderful Margaret River shiraz and he led her out onto the back deck. This house was so cute. Must be quite old, she surmised, but Jay had refurbished it nicely. From what she could make out in the pale light cast by the fairy lights surrounding the porch, the wooden deck had been freshly varnished, with a couple of pot plants sprouting succulents in the corner as decoration. Jay indicated she take a seat on the wicker lounge, the bright red cushions soft and comfy against her back. But he didn't take one of the other two wicker chairs as she expected him to, instead he stood next to the railing, staring out into the darkness. Axel came with them and bounded off the porch to disappear into the dim shapes of bushes at the back of the garden somewhere. His happy snuffling drifted up to where she sat.

"This is lovely out here." Tucked away in the bush, it almost reminded her of her own shack. It was just missing the soft boom of the waves breaking on the beach in the background. Although the wind was a little cool. Even though it was the start of summer, she was finding out the weather was quite fickle here in the south. It could still get cool at night, and even downright cold, as she'd experienced on her birthday when that storm came in. She pulled her cardigan a little closer around herself.

"Are you cold? We can go back inside if you like." He came over and sat next to her on the two-seater chair.

"Not too bad at the moment. I like it out here." She lifted her glass to his and they toasted each other. "Margaret River is a wonderful place to live," she sighed. "I wish I could stay here." Oops, where had that come from? Her spine stiffened and she clasped the wine glass tighter. Why was she saying all this stuff she didn't mean to speak out loud tonight?

"Why don't you?" He moved a little closer, so his thigh was now touching hers. "Stay here, I mean." That thigh was hard, the muscles like steel from all his surfing, bulging through the fabric of his jeans. She took a large swallow of her wine. A tingle made its way up her leg where it was touching Jay's, into her belly and lodged there. Heat spread outwards from that spot low in her abdomen.

"I ... might," she replied with a breezy wave of her hand. If she pretended his nearness was having no effect, then it might become reality. There was no use telling him she couldn't stay here. Not for long anyway. Six months, tops. The longest she'd ever stayed in one place had been eleven months, and five days. But who was counting? Her heart flipped over at the idea of being able to stay here, in this beautiful part of Australia. Wouldn't it be lovely? To stay. Perhaps even get to know this intriguing man a little better.

But that wasn't going to happen. She couldn't afford the entanglement. Sure, she'd had a fling or two with other men in other towns. They'd always been men who'd shown no taste for commitment. They'd been happy enough to spend time with her, but happy enough when she said she was moving on.

"If you stay you could join the VFRS," he said, voice low and very near her ear.

"Yes." It came out more as a squeak. "I enjoyed watching you all at training the other night. Thanks again for inviting me." Would he take her hint and change the topic?

"Why do you move around so much?"

Obviously not. His question came out of left field and caught her off-guard. With a light clink, he put his wine down on the table next to the chair and turned to face her.

"I'm a free spirit," she said and put on her faux smile for him. "I love moving around, seeing new places, that kind of thing. A gypsy at heart." She giggled.

"But if you stayed, we could get to know each other better." His finger reached up and tucked a stray curl being blown about by the breeze behind her ear. His gaze met hers and locked on to it. She couldn't look away.

Then his eyes flicked to her lips. It was only for a split second, but it was long enough for her to understand what he was about to do. They'd almost kissed the night when Beau had brought his son out to her. That kiss was interrupted at the very last second. But there was nothing to save her here. It was just him and her. Alone. And perhaps that fact had been behind her sudden reticence to come in from the car. She'd already parked outside his house before she'd changed her mind. If he hadn't come out and seen her, she would've driven away again. Because if someone didn't stop her, she was going to let him kiss her. Wanted him to kiss her. Wanted to find out what those serious, sensuous lips tasted like.

His hand came up and cupped her chin and she couldn't have looked away from his gaze if her life depended on it. Slowly, Jay leaned toward her, tilted her chin until his lips found hers. Soft, tender, exploring. He kissed her gently, as if he didn't want to break her, or scare her. Oh, sweet Jesus. He tasted better than she'd imagined. Much, much better. His mouth became more confident, more insistent. There was no conscious effort involved, she parted her lips for him and invited him in. His tongue darted along her bottom lip, teased at the corner and then delved deeper. She could hardly breathe, taking small gasping breaths in between his deluge of kisses. The effect made her dizzy and unbalanced. He made her dizzy.

Oh, this was bad. Very bad. She hadn't wanted a man this badly since—

Jay's phone rang. Strains of the song Light my Fire by The Doors sounded loudly from Jay's back pocket.

"Damn. I'm sorry, I have to answer this. It's the boss from the VFRS."

She sucked in a lungful of life-giving air as he stood up and walked away.

Saved by the bell. Again.

CHAPTER TEN

Jenna's hand rested protectively over her belly. They were driving into town from the little cabin they'd rented on the outskirts of Margaret River.

"You okay?" Dan's eyes crinkled with a mixture of worry and joy as he glanced over at her from the driver's seat.

"I'm fine. Stop worrying about me. I'm not about to sprout horns and projectile vomit while my head spins around and around," she said with a grin. He was so funny, the way he was treating her with kid gloves. She'd let him get away with it for a few more days, then it would have to stop.

She was still getting over the shock of finding out she was pregnant.

The sickness had been getting worse with every day they spent on the road, until Dan finally demanded she go and see a doctor when they'd reached Perth. And for once she hadn't argued with him. For a while she'd explained the nausea away as being stress-related. She was just worried about Alexander and this strange feeling she needed to be somewhere. But after they left Monkey Mia, it'd become obvious it was a lot more than that, and she suspected she was either pregnant or dying. Thank God it'd been the former.

Dan was over the moon, of course. And at least she and Dan had this trip together. She was loving the countryside around here. So green and verdant and populated. The complete opposite to the station. The coastline was so wild, the sheer beauty of the long stretches of sandy beaches, broken by tall cliffs where the waves smashed themselves to pieces had found a place in her heart. Now she understood why some people couldn't live anywhere but near the ocean. It was an elemental force of its own.

After the surprising news in Perth, they'd continued their pilgrimage south and a few days ago they'd arrived in this country town called Margaret River. Was this the place that'd been calling to her, from all the way up in the desert? It was just another unplanned stop on their wandering itinerary. But now she was here, the pulling, tugging sensation, which had forced her to go south in the first place had died right off. At first, it'd just been a vague feeling of restlessness, which had soon grown into an irresistible nag, constantly there at the back of her mind, until she and Dan had taken off in the ute. But even while traveling, the lure of the south kept calling her onwards. This was the first time in over two months the lingering feeling wasn't there.

Which was good, because Dan was starting to make noises about turning around and heading home. He was worried about her, said she was losing too much weight. Which was probably true, she could hardly keep anything down at the moment. The doctor warned her there was something called hyperemesis gravidarum, which was morning sickness so severe women who got it needed to be hospitalized. But she wasn't that bad. Not yet at least. Dan insisted they rent a proper cabin with a proper bed instead of sleeping in the tent, so she could get some good rest. Their days had been spent taking it easy, with her often staying in bed until lunch time, until the nausea subsided. Then they explored the wild, windy beaches, where Dune chased the seagulls and she sat watching the surfers ride in on the curling waves.

Today, while they'd been filling the ute at the gas station, Jenna had got talking to the guy behind the counter. Suddenly a wave of nausea struck and she had to bend over double while apologizing to the man, Jacko. When he asked what was wrong, she told him, and he extolled the virtues of the new Reiki healer in town. Said he knew quite a few people who'd seen her already and even he, Jacko, had given her a try. Right nice-looking bird too, if you asked Jacko. He asserted that Ebony McAllister would be able to heal her morning sickness. Jenna was getting so desperate she decided to give it a go. The only appointment available was for tomorrow at three o'clock, so she booked it.

The people in Margaret River were all so nice. They reminded her of their hometown community of Smokey Creek. Willing to lend a hand, give a smile—especially when it became obvious she and Dan were also from the country.

Like the day Dan and Jenna arrived in Margaret River. They'd been sitting on the beach, watching the sun set over the darkening ocean and pondering the best place to stay for the night. A couple had walked by and Dan took a chance.

"Hello," he called out and stood up, brushing the sand from his backside.

"Hey there," a guy with a lop-sided grin had answered back.

"Are you guys locals? We just rocked into town and were wondering if you could recommend any good places to stay." Dan stuck out a hand and gave the guy an answering grin. "I'm Dan, and this is my wife, Jenna."

"Oh, sure, hi there. I'm Beau, and this is Heather." He indicated the lithe woman walking a step behind him. Or rather the girl walking behind him. She looked to be a lot younger than Beau.

"Yeah, I can give you a few pointers on some good places to stay. Cheap too, if that's what you're looking for."

"Definitely, cheap is good," Dan replied.

They sat and talked to the couple until the sun disappeared and the wind grew surprisingly cold after what'd been a nice summer's day. Beau seemed to be the exact stereotype of a hippie surfer dude and Jenna had to hide her smile. He was friendly and a little flaky, but on the whole a decent bloke. He directed them to the cabins they were now staying at, which were nice, clean and cheap.

Beau had taken to them so much, he'd invited them to join him and Heather for a beer in the local pub. Which is where they were headed right now. Jenna wasn't sure she would be able to handle a noisy bar, but Beau assured her there was a little courtyard where they could sit and order a meal and he and Dan could down a few beers. It should be fun.

CHAPTER ELEVEN

The phone buzzed again in Jay's pocket. Hell, he had to answer this call. It was the Incident Controller from the VFRS, he recognized it by the ring tone, and that meant there was an emergency somewhere.

He let his palm linger a second more on Ebony's face, let the feel of her soft skin seep into his hand.

"Sorry." He got up and moved over by the railing to take the call. Out of the corner of his eye he caught Ebony sit back and wrap her cardigan tighter around herself. Then she touched a finger to her lips, almost as if she couldn't believe what'd happened. He knew exactly how she felt.

"Connolly here," he said brusquely, then listened as instructions were relayed by the controller.

"Right, I'm on my way." He hit the End button and rammed the phone back into his pocket. "Bloody hell," he muttered softly to himself. Luckily, he'd only had half a glass of wine, which meant he was good to drive.

"Trouble?" There was a pink tinge high on Ebony's cheekbones and her lips still looked swollen from his kiss. All he wanted was to sit back down on that chair and kiss her again. Instead he remained leaning against the railing.

"Yes, that was the incident controller from the VFRS."

"Uh oh, that doesn't sound good." Her face became serious.

"No, it's not. There's been a crash, out on Caves Road."

A frown creased her beautiful forehead. "Oh God, is anyone hurt?"

"Four people were in the car. They all survived, but we're not sure how bad the injuries might be." The crash was out near the intersection with Carters Road, right near a nasty sharp bend and it was so bad the road was now closed in both directions. Mentally, he evaluated the site. The boundary to Leeuwin-Naturaliste National Park was right across the road from the intersection. Caves Road was one of the main thoroughfares down the coastline toward Margaret River, and while it wouldn't be busy at this time of night, they would still need to divert traffic.

"But that's not the only reason they're calling us out. It seems the impact of the crash has started a small scrub fire. They need us out there to contain the fire before it spreads. I'm really sorry to break up our dinner, but I have to go." She'd never know just how sorry he was. But his mind was already shifting gear, planning, calculating, running scenarios. This was something he was good at, one of the reasons he'd joined the army. Ted and Neil would take the firetruck out, as they both lived close by the firehouse, and he'd drive out in his Land Cruiser to meet them at the crash site to save time. And time was of the essence. If they could stop the small scrub fire spreading, they could avert a possible major bushfire. Bushfires were damaging and dangerous. Lives and properties could be lost in a bushfire. He needed to get out there, now. Sam and Julie, two other VFRS volunteers, would also meet him there. The local police had also been called in and would probably get there first. His foot started tapping a rhythm on the wood of the porch as he scrolled through the options but it wasn't until Ebony cast him a curious glance that he even realized what he was doing.

"I'm really sorry, I'm going to have to cut our night short. Perhaps we can do this again, soon?" He did feel bad. Worse than bad, at having this night, that'd been so full of potential, end so suddenly. His feet were already moving forward of their own accord, taking him inside to dig out his fire-fighting go-bag, when Ebony rose and came over to stand directly in front of him.

She crossed her arms and something akin to determination settled on her face. "I'm coming with you."

"What? No, I don't think that's a good idea." A really bad idea, actually, the last thing he needed was one more person tagging along to gawk at things, one more person who'd need looking after. And God help him, he didn't want to have to rescue her for a third time. He was smart enough not to voice that thought, however.

"I can help with the crash victims. I'm good with all aspects of healing, I've got great first aid skills."

She did have a point there. He'd seen her in action, even if he wasn't quite prepared to accept what she'd done yet. And if her first aid skills were up to speed like she said.

"I won't get in your way, Jay, I promise."

"You're not accredited with VFRS, I'm not sure they'll appreciate me bringing a civilian along."

She gave a scoffing laugh. "A civilian? Jay, you're not in the army now."

Well, technically that was true, but he often resorted to his army training in high-stress situations. His foot started its tapping again and he knew he needed to get moving. He couldn't afford to waste any more time. It was going against his better judgment, but he didn't have time to stand here and argue with her. And perhaps she might be able to help if there really were four badly wounded victims.

"Fine. But you need to stay out of the way," he said as he barreled past her into the kitchen. Now he'd have to find her some protective gear as well.

"Even though that skirt is very fetching, it's no good for what we're about to do, so put these on instead." He tossed her a pair of his well-worn jeans. "I know they'll be too big for you," he said before she even had a chance to speak, "but they'll be a damn site less flammable than what you're wearing at the moment." He knew he sounded like the army corporal of old, barking orders and telling her what to do, but that was his fall-back mode in times of crisis. And to her credit, she did everything she was told without complaint. She'd already seen this side of him before anyway, at the beach when he'd rescued her and then again after the surfboard hit her. If she didn't like it, well, there wasn't a lot he could do about it. This was a part of his personality, take it, or leave it.

Less than two minutes later, they clambered into his 4WD and Jay expertly backed it out of the driveway. Slamming it into first gear, he glanced quickly into the rear-view mirror and was surprised to see a dark sedan parked down the road. Strange for another car to be parked there, as there were no other houses for a hundred meters either way. Still it was a suburban road that anyone could use, they could've just stopped to check their phone. Jay didn't give the car another thought as he sped up, his head full of the coming scenario.

The crash site was less than fifteen minutes' drive from Jay's place, and while he stuck to the legal speed, he certainly pushed it to the limit around the corners. Caves Road, even though it was technically considered to be a highway, was winding and narrow and often downright dangerous, with tall trees towering close to the edge on each side.

Ebony sat in the passenger seat and hung on, not saying a word. But her face had gone quite pale when he finally slowed down to navigate the last corner before they came upon the crash. His jeans were far too big for her, and even with a belt cinched tight at the waist they made her look like a kid wearing her father's clothes. She was also wearing his official VFRS bushfire jacket, because her cardigan would've been no protection from ash or sparks if the fire did become a problem. He still had his orange outer shell that he'd wear. She certainly had some guts, he had to give her that much. Not too many women would volunteer to come out and help at a dangerous site, with a potential fire hazard, half-way through a date. He allowed himself a small, private smile.

The crash was as much of a nightmare as he'd been expecting. One of the two Margaret River police cruisers was already there, parked well down from the smashed car, red and blue lights flashing a warning. At least five or six cars had pulled over to the side of the road, all the drivers out and gawking at the scene. One of the police officers was trying to shoo them back to their cars so he could clear the area. The other police officer was striding down the road, toward the crash site.

Jay pulled his car onto the side of the road and turned it off.

A dark-colored older style 4WD lay on its side near the embankment on the right-hand side of the road, with open pastures of dry grass behind it. Something tugged at Jay's memory. The car looked familiar. But he couldn't pin-point why, so he let the idea drop. He was acquainted with at least half the population of Margaret River, he'd probably seen the car countless times driving through the main street.

Flames licked at the rear of the car, a grass fire started by leaking gas. Was anyone trapped in the car? Jay could see a huddle of bystanders further down the road, well away from the growing fire. There were people crouched down over several inert bodies. He needed to get that fire out while it was small and fairly harmless. If the fire made it to that small stand of eucalyptus trees fifty meters or so inside the fence line, it'd be much, much harder to control. Although it was only the start of summer—not toward the end when the forest was one huge pile of tinder just waiting to go up—the fuel load was still high enough to be dangerous.

"You okay?" He turned toward Ebony, gathering his orange jacket off the front bench seat as he spoke. She didn't answer, simply stared straight ahead as if transfixed.

"Ebony," he said, louder this time. Damn, had it been a mistake to bring her after all?

"Jesus, that's Beau's car," Ebony breathed.

"What?" He swiveled around to get a better look. So that's why it looked familiar. It was indeed the same car Beau had been driving the night he pulled into Ebony's drive. "Shit. We need to get up there and help. Are you sure you're okay?" A nod was all he got in return. He jumped out of the car, and she slipped out of the passenger side, then came and met him around the back where he was pulling out his breathing apparatus, the rest of his PPE, and a large first aid kit.

"I'll go and see what I can do," she said, taking the first aid kit firmly from his hand.

"Tell the police officer, Gil, that you're with me if he tries to stop you." Again another nod of agreement was all he got. "And tell everyone the paramedics are on their way. Should only be another ten minutes or so. They were held up with a heart-attack victim earlier."

"Will do." Her serious face mimicked his own, but he couldn't help notice how pale she was in the headlights of the police car. She took the first aid kit and set off up the road, determination in every step. His gaze followed her, watching the flames glint off her black curls, her petite figure almost totally engulfed by his enormous clothes.

Then Ted and Neil arrived in the fire truck, siren wailing and lights flashing, Mike and Julie in the accompanying smaller truck right behind. Jay dragged his attention away from Ebony's slim form and went to help the police officer clear the remaining cars out of the way, to let the truck through. His main priority was getting that fire out as fast as possible. He'd just have stop worrying about Ebony, she could take care of herself.

* * *

The jacket smelled of Jay. Masculine and musky. She found herself wanting to pull it closer around her shoulders, as if it were actually him draped around her.

Smoke drifted across the darkened road and she quickened her step to a jog. The flames were getting bigger even as she watched them. Gil, the police officer had retrieved a small fire extinguisher from the cruiser and was now attempting to put out the flames nearest the upturned car. The last thing they needed was the gas tank to explode. One thing the flames did provide was much-needed light on the crash scene.

She tried to discern who was doing what in the huddle of human forms further up the road. There were definitely people lying on the road, others bending over them.

She ran harder.

Arriving at the gathering, she gently pushed her way through until she could see who was lying on the ground at their feet. It was Beau. He was conscious. She knelt down next to him, trying to catch her breath enough to speak normally.

"How can I help?" she gasped to the older woman, who had Beau's head cradled in her lap.

"Are you a doctor?" the lady asked, hope swimming in her eyes.

"No, sorry. But I've got a first aid kit and I'm pretty good with this kind of thing. The ambulance will be here soon," she said as she remembered what Jay had said.

"Ebony," Beau croaked through half-open eyes. His face was white as a sheet, a sheen of sweat covering his forehead. There were two large gashes running down his cheek and blood smeared all over the left side of his face, giving him a ghoulish, cadaver-like look. "I'm sorry. Tell them I'm so sorry. It was all my fault." He tried to grab her arm with his hand and his face twisted into a grimace.

"Don't worry about any of that now, Beau," she soothed.

"I think he's possibly got a broken arm," said the old lady. The woman, who might be in her seventies, with neatly coiffured gray hair and white slacks—which were quickly turning red—was also going a nasty shade of green. Probably from the shock of it all. "We saw it all happen. My husband and I were following behind them in our car," the woman confided quietly. "It was horrible to watch. We saw the car swerve violently and then it over-corrected, and then … it rolled over and over and there wasn't a thing we could do about it." The woman's voice wavered, and Ebony laid a comforting hand on her shoulder.

"You did a great job to get them all out of the car and away from that fire," she said, making her voice sound more confident than she actually felt. "Can everyone just stand back a bit, let him have some space?" Ebony requested of the others gathered around. She needed to assess his injuries and move on to the other casualties. Rank them in priority so the paramedics knew who to look at first.

"Do you think he's got any other broken bones?" she asked the woman supporting Beau's head.

"I'm not sure, we dragged him this far away from the car, and the only thing he complained about was his arm," she said apologetically.

"That's good." Ebony gave the woman a reassuring glance. "I'm just going to check for internal injuries," she said gently to Beau. "Let me know if anything hurts." Her fingers probed softly over his abdomen and ribs. She didn't really need him to tell her if it hurt, she was using her own powers, sending in shards of energy to scan his body and gather the information she needed. After around thirty seconds she was happy there were no internal injuries. There were a few scrapes and another possible fracture low down in one of his legs. He was in a lot of pain and was slipping in and out of consciousness. "Does it hurt anywhere else?" she asked, face bent low over Beau's to catch his words.

"My ankle," he admitted huskily, swallowing a groan. "But Ebony, you have to tell them. Tell them I'm sorry. I wasn't paying attention, and that roo came from nowhere."

Ah, so they'd hit a kangaroo. That would make sense, explain why there weren't more cars involved. Kangaroos were a well-known danger on Australian roads after dark.

"I will, Beau, don't worry." She tried to keep the worried frown from showing on her face when he groaned again loudly. Even though he was badly injured, he wasn't going to die of his wounds and she needed to move on, check the other casualties. She'd have to leave him in the capable hands of the older lady for a little while.

She tried to loosen her hold on his hand. "Ebony." His grip was surprisingly strong, he wasn't letting go, even though he groaned again, and clenched his eyes shut. "I'm really sorry … I was the one. I told him … where … lived."

What was he talking about? Told who where who lived? But this was no time to ask as Beau's eyes rolled back in his head. Mercifully he'd passed out, so at least he was feeling no pain. Most probably he was just garbling pain-induced nonsense.

"You're doing a superb job," she said to the lady still cradling Beau's head in her lap. "He's passed out, but he's going to be okay." She took Beau's head and gently placed him into the recovery position. "Just keep monitoring him to make sure he's breathing. I'm going to have a look at the other victims and make sure they're okay. Call me if anything changes. Are you alright to stay here with Beau until the ambulance gets here?"

"Yes." The woman still looked green around the eyes, but thankfully she was made of sterner stuff than most and gave Ebony a determined glance.

"You there," Ebony said, pointing at one of the three young men she had shooed further back when she'd first arrived. "Can you come and help ... Ah I'm sorry, I didn't catch your name," Ebony said to the woman.

"Bertha."

"Can you come and help Bertha keep Beau calm if he wakes up? He needs to be kept as still as possible until the ambulance gets here."

"Yeah man." The young guy gave her a cocky smile, but there was a flash of fear in his eyes. She didn't care, if he was prepared to stand and gawp at an accident scene then he could damn well lend a hand at the same time. His two mates slapped him on the back as he came over and knelt on the ground next to Beau's prone body. Yep, she'd find jobs for those two as well, just to take some wind out of their sails.

"I'll be back in a few minutes to check on him again," she promised as she rose up off the bitumen road.

The next huddle of people were another twenty meters down the road, further away from the crashed car. As Ebony walked toward them, she took the chance to glance back over her shoulder. The scene was like something out of a disaster movie. Everything was cast in dancing shadows and flickering light, the bright glow of the fire turning everything into indistinct black shapes. The square form of the fire truck was parked right next to Beau's toppled 4WD. There were now three figures, bulky in their firefighting equipment, surrounding the fire, one of them aiming a hose directly at the heart of the flames, the other two holding up the hose, moving it to go with him as they were directed. The cop had left the fire and was now directing oncoming traffic away from the scene. Ebony couldn't tell which of the three figures was Jay, they all looked the same in the heat and glow of the fire. Perhaps he was the one holding the hose? The figure was taller than the other two and stood straight, with shoulders squared, his stance reminiscent of Jay's military background. As long as he was safe, that's all that mattered to her at the moment.

She could hear the groans before she even broke through the next crowd of people. That didn't sound good. There were two more people lying on the roadway. One of them—a woman—was in the recovery position. At least someone had known what to do. An older man knelt by the unconscious woman's head, checking her breathing and pulse. Bertha's husband perhaps?

The groans were coming from a young male who lay writhing on the ground. Which patient to check first?

"Is she breathing?" she said loudly to the old man crouched next to the unconscious lady.

"Aye," he replied in a heavy Scottish brogue. "And got a strong pulse, too. I think she got a nasty knock to the head, though."

"You seem to know what you're doing," she replied with a grateful smile. "If you're okay with her for a while, I'll just check on this gentleman here."

"Aye, lassie, we're good. You go right ahead."

The bitumen was cool beneath her knees and small stones dug in through the fabric of Jay's jeans, but she ignored the discomfort. The young victim had his eyes squeezed tightly shut and was thrashing around so much no one could get near him. Everyone stood around in a semi-circle looking bemused and scared.

"Does anyone know this guy's name," she enquired of the general group. They all shook their heads. She'd have to calm him down before she could find out what was wrong with him, which was going to be harder than it seemed.

"Sir," she said loudly, trying to sound calm and authoritative. "Sir, you need to lay still, so I can examine you." That just elicited more loud groans from the man. But he did crack open an eye to stare up at her, before he continued his thrashing. That sideways look had her suspicions roused.

More entreating on her part did nothing to make the slightest difference to the man. Surely he must be hurting himself with all that rolling around on the ground. Finally, she made a decision and reached in and grabbed him by the wrist.

"No, no, don't touch me. It hurts," he moaned.

"Where does it hurt, sir?" she asked loudly. But she didn't need to ask, now she had hold of him, she could feel where his injuries were. And they were all minor.

"My back, my back. I think my back's broken," he groaned through gritted teeth.

"I'm quite sure your back's not broken, sir," she replied, trying to restrain him by the wrist she now had hold of. "But if you calm down, I can have a proper look at it for you." He slowed his erratic movements at her words but didn't stop rocking back and forth on the ground. There was something else going on inside this young man. But she couldn't put a finger on it. It wasn't a physical injury, more like a mental … a mental impairment of some kind. No, not an impairment, more like an impression or a suggestion had been planted in his brain.

With a gasp she dropped his wrist like it was a hot coal. What did it mean?

"What happened?" one of the bystanders asked in a panicky voice. "Is he really bad? Is he going to die?"

"What?" she snapped. But at least his question had brought her back to reality. "No. Of course he's not going to die. He's fine." Let the paramedics deal with this one, she wasn't about to touch him again. Not after that. The urge to wipe her hand down the length of Jay's jeans was strong, such was the impression of a greasy, sinister feeling left behind by the young man's touch. She stood up and stared down at him. Both eyes were squeezed shut again, but at least his thrashing was reduced to rolling and moaning. There was something else going on with this boy that she didn't completely understand. He was obviously convinced he was in pain, that he had in fact been injured. But why?

She turned and made her way to the unconscious girl. After checking all her vitals, she decided the Scotsman knew what he was doing and after a few words with him to make sure he was fine to stay with her a while longer, she moved on to the last victim. A quick glance over her shoulder as she walked told her the fire was now under control and hopefully wouldn't be causing them any more problems tonight, thanks to Jay and his VFRS mates.

It was another young woman, with messy blonde hair and a sun-kissed face. Conscious and sitting up with her back braced against the wheel of one the passer-by's cars. But she was pale and hunched over, taking small gasping breaths. A middle-aged woman sat on the ground beside her, holding her hand.

"Hi, I'm Ebony, I'm a first aid responder," she said, crouching down next to the girl, giving the woman a nod of acknowledgement as she did so. "Can you tell me your name?"

"Heather," the middle-aged women replied. "And I'm Narelle, I'm a midwife." Ebony was grateful at least one other person knew what she was doing. "I think Heather may have a fractured rib and perhaps a punctured lung, but no other injuries as far as I can tell." Hence the reason she had Heather in a sitting position, it opened up the lung cavity to reduce the pain and help her breathe.

"Okay, the ambulance is on the way. They can assess the patients themselves, but they'll want to take the unconscious woman and Heather first."

"Sandy," gasped Heather through short intakes of breath.

"Sorry?" Ebony asked.

"Sandy, is the other girl's name." She turned sky blue eyes toward Ebony. "She's my best friend. And that's Bryce over there."

"Oh, that's good information, thanks."

"And Beau, he's my boyfriend. He was driving." Heather tried to raise an arm to point down the road, but then gasped and lowered it quickly as pain from her cracked rib shot through her. Ebony digested that interesting tidbit of information. The girl looked much younger than Beau, but then who was Ebony to pass judgement? Here she was fantasizing about a man nearly eight years her junior. Heather did fit with the image Beau projected, a bit of a Peter Pan figure, someone who refused to grow up. Ebony hoped that for his son's sake, Beau changed his ways sooner rather than later.

"It's okay. I saw Beau on the way up here. He's got a few bumps and maybe a broken arm, but he's going to be fine," she replied, hoping to keep the girl calm and as relaxed as possible.

"Thank God," the girl puffed through her pain. Then to Ebony's surprise she kept on talking. "We were coming back from Redgate Beach, just doing a bit of beach fishing. We had such a lovely afternoon."

Ebony startled as the girl named her beach, but then there was nothing peculiar about that, it was a popular fishing spot. The girl's blue eyes filled with tears and she struggled to get the words out through her rasping breaths. "We were all laughing and joking and having a good time. And then … Oh Christ, are they really going to be okay?"

"Yes, everyone's going to be fine," Ebony soothed.

Narelle took Heather's hand and patted it in a motherly way. "Everything's going to be fine, dear. You should try and conserve your strength, don't talk too much."

"But when we got back to the carpark something weird happened, you know?" A small chill ran up Ebony's spine at the girl's words. She just wouldn't stop talking, like she needed to tell someone, to unload whatever it was that was bothering her. "We were all mucking around by the car, and there was this older man with his son, they came up to us. But they didn't look like they'd been fishing or swimming or stuff, you know?" The girl liked that phrase, but Ebony ignored it and prompted her with a nod of her head to go on.

"The man said hi to Beau, as if he knew him or something. But I know everyone Beau knows and this wasn't the sort of guy he'd ever hang out with. Too fancy, like he had a stick up his butt. They asked Beau some weird questions. Like did he ever pick up hitchhikers? And had we seen a young couple around the town lately. Beau just laughed and said, yes, he picked up hitchhikers all the time and he'd seen heaps of young couples. 'Cause you know how much of a tourist town Margaret River is, full of all those backpackers and everything. And you know how Beau is, he always likes to help anyone he can. Well anyway, the old man didn't much like Beau talking like that, and he got all pissed off and fluffed up like an angry rooster, you know? And then he muttered something to Beau, like, don't take your eyes off the road, accidents happen if you do that." The chill up Ebony's spine turned decidedly colder. The girl's words had an ominous ring to them. By now Heather's words were coming in short, static punches of breath, as she struggled to breathe against the pain.

"And then Beau crashed the car and it rolled. It was so scary. I've never been in a car crash before." This time the tears spilled over and ran down Heather's cheeks. Narelle handed her a tissue and continued to pat her hand sympathetically.

"I know, crashes can be bloody scary," Ebony said. "But you're alive and you're all going to be fine in a few days. And it wasn't Beau's fault you know. Kangaroos cause some terrible accidents around here."

Heather's features screwed up in consternation. "There wasn't any kangaroo. Beau just started swerving all over the road, for no reason at all." What was the girl saying? She obviously just didn't see the roo, was probably too busy chatting or looking at her phone.

"Oh, okay, whatever happened, you're all going to survive and that's the main thing," she said soothingly.

"Okay, that's really enough talking now. You can tell the police what happened later." Narelle's features sharpened into what Ebony thought of as her I'm-a-midwife-don't-mess-with-me look. But she agreed with Narelle, even if she did want to hear more. The girl's face had gone pasty white and tiny pain-wracked creases ran downward from her mouth.

"Yes, you should stop talking. I'm going to find those paramedics and bring them here. I think I can hear the sirens now." It was true, a far-away wail could be heard in the background, sending up eerie echoes as it reverberated through the forest.

She and Narelle exchanged a look before Ebony levered herself off the ground and made her way back toward the crashed car where Beau still lay on the road. She found herself unconsciously searching for Jay's tall, limber figure. The flames had just about died now, leaving only glowing embers, which a lone figure was still dousing with the water hose. Jay, she suspected. Smoke and steam billowed from the blackened area of grassland, filling the dark space between the tall trees and the roadway with fluorescent smoke wraiths. Without the flames the roadway was almost completely dark, only the headlights from a few of the cars casting their bright beams to show her where to go. Sometimes she forgot just how dark it got out here, away from the big city. So dark that all the stars were made bright and the milky way shone like a beacon above them.

She wanted to go up to Jay, to hear his voice, make sure he was fine. Perhaps feel his strong arm around her. Let him know she was okay. But she had one more thing to do before she could go to him. She needed to go back and touch Beau. She had to know. If the same kind of ... influences that ran through the other man were also in Beau. Perhaps she'd missed it the first time she'd laid her hands on him, because she was only concentrating on his physical pain, which was considerable and which'd probably deflected the threads of any mental polarity.

One paramedic hurried toward them, with a heavy black bag in hand, while the other was already opening the back doors to the ambulance and retrieving the trolley. She needed to do this quickly.

"Hi, Beau," she said as she dropped to the ground beside him. "The paramedics are here, they'll help you with that pain in just a few seconds." But he didn't hear her, he was still mercifully unconscious. Her hand dropped to his undamaged shoulder as she spoke, her fingers rested against the bare skin of his bicep, below the sleeve of his t-shirt.

She let tendrils of energy snake through Beau's body, probing, investigating. And she felt it. Threads of coercion. Remnants that were fading fast, but she could still feel the overtones. The same as she'd felt in the other young man. Almost as if Beau had been hypnotized somehow. The hairs rose on the back of her neck. Who would hypnotize him? And why?

The dark-green clad form of a paramedic dropped down next to her on the bitumen, breaking her train of thought. He was a young man, with a mop of dark unruly hair.

"Hold this will you," he said to Ebony, passing her a large, heavy-duty torch. She flicked it on and Bertha had the presence of mind to shade Beau's eyes from the bright glare, as the ambulance guy started checking him out.

An idea occurred to her. "Bertha, did you see what caused Beau to swerve? Was there a kangaroo, or anything else on the road?"

"No, dear. That's why it was all so strange. The road was perfectly clear. I know because I was looking straight at them when they just suddenly veered into the middle of the road."

"Okay, thanks, Bertha, you've done a stellar job here." She thanked the older woman and stood up, glad to let the paramedic take over. Ebony allowed her mind to drift. She needed to talk to Beau, as soon as he was able. Find out what else he knew. Find out who'd been talking to him in the carpark. And what his cryptic apology was all about. She'd make sure she paid him a special visit in hospital tomorrow morning. Early.

She lifted her head and saw three indistinct figures gathered around the fire truck. They'd turned off the flashing lights now, which made it even harder to see what was going on. As if he could feel her gaze on him, one of the figures raised a hand and waved, then started toward her.

Jay. Thank God.

CHAPTER TWELVE

The 4WD headlights lit up the driveway as he swung into the garage. It was just after midnight, but it felt like they'd been gone for hours. Ebony sat in the passenger seat beside him, quiet and introspective. They'd hardly talked on the way home from the crash. Ebony seemed jumpy somehow, distracted. He couldn't put a finger on it, but it bothered him. She assured him she was fine, and it wasn't shock or any other after-effect of being at the crash scene. Still, he was beginning to wish he hadn't taken her along. Because something was definitely up with her. Nevertheless, he'd been ultra-aware of her, sitting there in the seat next to him, so close. At one stage he had to stop himself from reaching over and taking up her small hand in his.

He hopped out of the car and went around to open her door, helping her out with a flourish.

"Shall we go and finish our dinner of cold cannelloni and warm wine?"

"I am starving," she admitted, but without much enthusiasm. "I should just go home, though. It is getting late."

"Come on, the least I can do after dragging you out to help at a dangerous crash site, is make sure you're fed before you go." He took a step away from the car and closed the door behind her. She stood on the driveway, in his ridiculously large jeans and jacket, looking lost and undecided. "At least come in and change," he entreated.

"Okay, that's a good idea."

"Whew, I stink," he said lifting his arm to his nose. At last that comment brought a smile to Ebony's face. He'd stripped off his fire-fighting uniform, and thrown it in the back of the car, but the clothes underneath still reeked of smoke. As did his hair and skin. She leaned in and sniffed at him.

"You do smell a little like you've just rolled in the ashes of hell," she replied. He wanted to lean in and smell her, as she'd done to him. When he'd carried her out of the water the other day, she'd smelled fresh, of salt and sand, with a hint of coconut. And when he'd held her in his arms after her house had been ransacked, her soft hair tickled his nose, wafting hints of lavender and silk into his senses. What would she smell like tonight?

"But it's not altogether bad," she added with a small sideways grin. "It's kind of manly. You were out there saving lives, after all. I'm glad I was there to see it. Your team did a great job. You did a great job."

He was a little taken aback at her sudden compliment.

"All in a day's work," he said modestly and turned to lead her up the pathway to his front door.

"Yes, well, I shouldn't be all that surprised. You seem to be a very competent man all around. A born leader, even. And I should know, you've rescued me … twice I believe, from the ocean. I think this laid-back, surf-dude persona you portray is a bit of a cover-up. You did extremely well tonight."

"And so did you." He returned the favor. And he meant it. She'd definitely earned his respect tonight. She hadn't baulked at the sight of a car overturned, four people injured, and a mini bushfire blazing. There was a tough inner core of strength in this woman. But he already knew that, he just had to look at where she chose to live and her gypsy lifestyle, to realize that.

"To borrow your phrase, it's all in a day's work." This time she gave him a genuine smile as he held the door open for her and she walked through. The corners of her gray eyes crinkled in the porch light and an arrow of attraction speared through his belly at the flirtation he saw there. Goddamn, she was sexy. Even in his oversized clothes. When he'd asked her here for dinner tonight, he hadn't been sure of his agenda. It'd been a spur of the moment thing. But now he knew without a doubt why. He wanted her. Wanted to take her to his bed.

"After you." He gestured for her to precede him down the corridor, hoping the few seconds it took to reach the kitchen would be enough to tame the growing bulge in his pants.

He went to drop his keys on the hallway table and that's when he noticed it. The bowl he used to keep his keys in had moved. Only slightly. But just enough for him to notice. He was a little obsessive when it came to his things, a hangover from his army days. He always kept everything neat and tidy, everything had its place. Jay flicked on the hallway light and stood staring at the table. Beside the bowl with the keys, there was a stack of bills he needed to pay and two books he was going to return to Doug. The stack of bills looked like it was still in the same spot, unmoved, as did the books. But the bill on top of the stack was different. He always kept them in order of the date they needed to be paid. The electricity bill should be on top. Instead, he was staring at the phone bill. What the ...? What was going on here? Was he going crazy?

"I'll just be a sec," Jay called to Ebony.

He needed to check the rest of the house, see if anything else had been touched. He strode into his bedroom, opened the cupboard and checked the small safe he'd had installed in the floor. It was untouched, and he breathed a sigh of relief. It housed his Glock handgun, along with all his passports, a couple of thousand in spare cash and other important papers. Swiveling his head, he checked his laptop computer and Rolex watch were still sitting on his bedside table. Nothing had been taken. It wasn't a burglary. Was he imagining the stuff on the hall table?

"Shall I let Axel in?" Ebony called from the living room.

"What? Oh, sure," he replied, still staring at his cupboard.

Axel was waiting at the back door, Jay could hear him whining. He strode to the bedroom door and watched as Ebony opened the fly-screen and was immediately caught up in a licking, wagging whirlwind of fur and slobber. Ebony couldn't stop laughing as she tried to stay away from Axel's wandering tongue. It was a light carefree sound and it helped loosen the band that'd tightened around Jay's chest at the thought someone had been in his house.

She stood upright to look at him, face flushed with amusement at the dog's antics, teeth flashing white as she smiled.

"Can I get changed in your bedroom," she asked a little breathlessly, walking toward him. Axel had stopped gallivanting around like an untrained puppy and instead was now rushing around, nose to the ground as if following some sort of scent.

"Sure—" Axel swept past and knocked Ebony's feet out from under her. Jay lunged forward and caught her around the waist, and spun her toward him, clutching her tight to his chest.

"Jesus, Axel," he growled, and the dog slunk away through the living room.

"It wasn't really his fault," she said, looking up at him. Her hand came up to rest on his shoulder. Innocently. His arms were wrapped tightly around her back, holding her to him. Stopping her from falling. Only now she was safe. But he didn't want to let her go. The soft dip of her lower back rested beneath his palm. The slight ridges of her spine ran beneath the fingertips of his other hand.

Head tipped back so she could see him, she suddenly stilled in his arms. The laughter died on her lips. His gaze locked onto hers and her pupils dilated, filling up the gray irises, turning them dark and smoky. His mind raced back to earlier this evening, when he'd tasted her lips for the first time. When she'd answered his surge in desire with an enthusiasm to match his own. Then they'd been interrupted, right when things were getting interesting.

But there was no one to interrupt them now.

The idea that someone might have been in his house took a back seat. He'd ponder that later. Now his heart was thumping so erratically in his chest, he couldn't think straight. She was so warm and supple against him, melting into him. So small. He'd have to duck his head to meet her lips.

"Jay, I ..." Her lips parted as if to say more, but no words came out. Her gaze locked onto his mouth, her delectable lips, soft and pouty.

He lowered his head and rested his lips against hers, asking permission. She gave a tiny moan and took his mouth, opening to him, inviting him in. She tasted as good as he remembered and he wanted to inhale her. Tiny shocks of sensation buzzed from his lips straight to his groin. He dropped one hand to her buttocks and pulled her tighter in toward him. There was no way she could miss his reaction to her now; what she did to him.

At last she broke the kiss, gasping for air and he could feel her heart hammering in her chest where it rested against his. But he didn't want to stop. Wanted to keep savoring her.

He dropped his head lower, feathering kisses along her jawline, down the side of her neck. Slowly, she tilted her head back, accepting his mouth on her skin, softening against him, so they were fused from hip to shoulder, pressing her breasts into his ribcage.

"You feel so …" she moaned from deep in her throat. "I haven't felt this way in a long, long time."

He could sympathize with that sentiment. Sure, he'd had plenty of women. The last date had only been two or three months ago, with Honey, if he remembered her name correctly. But none of the women, not even Honey, made his heart race like this, as if he were a thoroughbred running in a one-horse race.

"Come to bed with me," he murmured into her ear.

* * *

Yes. Yes. Please, yes. At least that's what her body was saying. Take me to bed, right now. But a tiny rational part of her brain was nagging, telling her not to do this. It was dangerous. Getting to know him. Even if this man only wanted a one-night fling, which was what he had a reputation for, it was still dangerous. But, oh God, it'd been so long since she'd had sex. And she desperately wanted it. With Jay. She didn't think she'd ever been this hot for any man before.

Looking deep into her eyes, he obviously found the answer he wanted, the one she couldn't articulate, because he took her by the hand to lead her into his bedroom, flicking off the harsh bright light and flicking on a soft bedside lamp instead.

"You stay out there," Jay said imperiously, pointing a finger in Axel's direction. The dog lay down with a small huff on the rug in the dining room, dejected eyes following them through the doorway. She wanted to smile at the begrudging dog but was too caught up with Jay. And only Jay.

She got a quick glimpse of his bedroom—warm browns and deep ochres—before she'd backed him up against the bed and forced him down. What the hell had taken hold of her? She wasn't usually the aggressive one in bed. Actually, she'd never been the instigator before. And certainly not with a man so much younger than her. Why was she suddenly acting like the dominant woman?

Because she wanted to see Jay naked, that's why. Ever since he'd stripped off his wetsuit in her house and she'd seen those hardened abs and muscled chest, even though she'd tried to deny it, her subconscious had concocted fantasies of what the rest of him would look like. And because he wanted her, too. Apart from his very obvious physical desire for her, which was now pressing into her belly, it was in the reverent way he held her hand, the explosive way he kissed her, the dark depths of desire that flared in his eyes.

"I'm sorry, I should've had a shower first," he apologized.

"I like the way you smell," she said, in a surprisingly husky voice. "Besides, I'm probably not coming across roses either."

He grinned at that, sharp white teeth flashing against his bronzed skin. There were black smudges on his forehead, where he'd obviously wiped a sooty hand. The effect was endearing, just more tangible evidence of how hard he'd worked tonight.

"Maybe I should take you out to crash sites more often," he joked. "It must be a turn on for you."

At his mention of the crash, Beau's words came back to her. But the horrible premonition raising the hairs at the back of her neck was a mere tickle now. Dampened by her need for physical gratification. Besides, there was nothing else she could do about finding out what Beau had meant by his cryptic words until tomorrow. She may as well just bloody well enjoy herself tonight.

"Shh," she commanded, straddling him with her legs, pushing him back onto the bed. Then proceeded to pull at the hem of his black t-shirt. He sat up for her, so she could tug it over his head, revealing his wonderful torso, in all its glory. She devoured all that hot, bare skin with her eyes.

Oh yes, it was just as spectacular as she remembered. The hard planes of his chest, sprinkled with curling black hairs, tapered down to washboard flat stomach and abs so ripped they ran like waves over his abdomen. The tattoo of the tree stood out on his left pec and she feathered her fingers over it, tracing the Celtic swirls. It suited him somehow. The scars were there too, reminding her of his courage and sacrifice, but she chose to ignore them tonight. There would be other nights to ask him about them. Her fingers danced down to circle his belly-button, then to the waistband of his jeans. They needed to come off. Again, he helped her by taking over when her fingers seemed incapable of undoing the buttons, and then he slipped them all the way off and lay back down, hands behind his head. Happy to let her just look at him. Long legs with powerful thighs tapered to well-proportioned calves, just as she imagined. She lifted her gaze to his face once she'd drunk her fill and dark sapphire eyes stared back at her.

"You certainly are …" She wanted to say beautiful, but that wasn't right. A work of art? Magnificent? They all encompassed him, but it sounded corny and not really what she was trying to say at all.

"You've had your fun, now it's my turn," he said with a grin. With an expert move, he flipped her over in one simple motion, so she was now beneath him, his long body laid hard up against hers. "You have way too many clothes on." But they weren't on for much longer, as he deftly got rid of his old pair of jeans and then her t-shirt, bra and panties before she knew it. And then it was his turn to skim his gaze down her naked body. A shiver of self-consciousness ran over her. Oh Jesus, she'd forgotten all about her scar in the heat of the moment. She tensed, stopped breathing. Saw his eyes register the small letter A carved into her abdomen—a brand of ownership. But they only stayed for a second before they moved on, devouring her with his gaze. She released her breath. His eyes had turned dark and hungry, letting her know he liked what he saw. There would be questions tomorrow, of that she had no doubt, but tonight it seemed he had more urgent matters to explore.

"I want to touch you everywhere," he murmured. "I want to run my hands all over your body and never take them off." She wanted to giggle at his words, but then his large, square hands took ownership of her hips and there was no more laughter left in her. Like a man sampling a sweet treat, his lips trailed softly behind his roving hands, running over her sensitive skin. Electric jolts exploded everywhere he touched, sending streams of desire pulsing through her. The palms of his hand were calloused from hard work, but he used them with such skill she didn't mind at all. Found she craved his slightly rough touch.

Everything inside her was ripe and ready, and she yearned for the promise of release. They moved together, body to body, skin to skin, and she rose up to welcome him against her hips. She could hear his rasping breath in her ear, the sound filling her with desire.

Suddenly he broke free, rolled away over the bed.

"What ...?"

But he was back in the space of a heartbeat, covering himself as he moved toward to her, and her skin welcomed his heat once more. At least he had enough mastery over himself to remember a condom. She'd completely forgotten about protection. Enveloping her beneath him, he lay along her length, a question hovering in his eyes.

Oh yes. Her answer was yes.

* * *

His blood was made of fire, it bubbled and charged a heated shaft of lust straight through him. She made him lose himself. He ached all over for release, his heart, his loins, his mind. She was driving him crazy. Those soft, creamy curves, that wild, dark hair like silk on the pillow around her head.

Her smoke-gray eyes gave him the permission he needed, and he slid between her legs. She cried out as he entered her, hips rocking beneath his, one of her hands came up to frame his face as they moved together. Slowly at first, but the rhythm soon increased till he was trembling with the need to let go. She made small panting noises, and he thrust harder as she moved with him and he guided her up and up, toward the peak. Until at last she cried out, closed her eyes and shuddered, long and slow, and delicious. He'd never seen such beauty before in a woman's face, never felt so tethered to a woman, both in the flesh and in his mind.

Then he finally let go with a cry.

Jay's heart still thundered as he held her beneath him, unable to move. He should roll off her, let her breathe, let her relax. But he couldn't, not just yet.

"We never did eat that cannelloni," she whispered into his ear. He let out a surprised grunt.

"Is that all you're worried about? Your stomach?" It was the sign he needed to lever himself up and off her, and he lay on his back staring up at the ceiling.

"No." She laughed. "I was trying to distract myself." The smile faded from her lips. "Because if I actually thought about how goddamned perfect I feel right now, I might just never leave," she countered.

Stretching out his arm, he pulled her in against his body and she curled into a sleepy ball next to him and let out a contented yawn, head resting on his bicep. He liked the way she looked, all mussed up and face flushed. It set his heart beating a tattoo all over again.

"Yeah, I was pretty awesome," he admitted.

"Oh, you …" She hit him with a closed fist, but it was only a half-hearted attempt at violence and she giggled softly, then yawned again. Eyes closed, her hand resting over his heart, her breathing slowed.

Should he let her go to sleep? He didn't often let women stay the night. Unease tickled the base of his spine. It'd be fine. He'd just stay awake and watch her sleep. She was so beautiful.

Before he knew it, his eyes had drifted closed.

Something touched his shoulder. But he was pinned down, he couldn't move. Helpless, he was helpless. Gunfire cracked close to his head and a bullet whizzed past. Then another, the sound almost deafening him. A low muffled boom of mortar fire vibrated through the ground. There was smoke, so thick he couldn't see through it. Could hardly breathe.

Tom, he needed to get to Tom, to help him. He'd been hit by sniper fire. He was bleeding out. Jay was the only person who could save him. The weight still pressed against his shoulder, stopping him from getting up. He needed to get up and help Tom.

He flinched. There was a voice, loud through the smoke. But he couldn't see who it was. Was it the Taliban? Come to kill him and finish off poor Tom Logan.

Kill, before he was killed. The Taliban would kill him if he let them. Murder him where he lay.

He lunged forward with a roar, slashing through smoke toward his unseen enemy.

Flesh beneath his fingers, he had them by the throat. All he needed to do was squeeze until they no longer posed a threat.

"Jay!" The pleading voice tickled at his memory. Was it familiar?

"Jay, stop!" Rasping now, like someone was gasping for breath, that voice continued to plead. "You're hurting me, Jay. Stop!"

Jay opened his eyes.

He was on top of Ebony, straddling her, holding her down, his hands around her throat.

"Holy fuck!" He let go of her like she was made of white-hot steel and jumped off the bed.

* * *

Ebony gasped for air, sucked gallons of it into her aching lungs. She sat up in bed and her fingers floated up to her neck. It was okay, she was going to be okay.

"Holy fuck," Jay shouted from the other side of the room.

She hardly heard him through the roaring in her ears.

"Ebony, I'm so sorry."

Her gaze drifted toward him, standing naked on the rug, eyes as round as golf balls, hands twisted into knots at his sides.

Images of Alexander, his face twisted with rage as he hovered over her, blazed in front of her eyes. Alexander hitting her as she lay curled up against the cushions of the couch. Hurling words like stones at her, making her feel small and ashamed. She hadn't had these flashbacks for years now. Damn. Why had she stayed? Why had she let her body's cravings get the better of her?

"I didn't realize ... Oh fuck," he said again.

"I'm okay," she managed to croak through a windpipe that still threatened to close up on her.

PTSD. The letters floated through her brain. Jay must be suffering PTSD from his time in the army. Either that or some god-awful bad dreams. Jay pulled on his jeans and came and sat on the edge of the bed, scrubbing his hand through his short hair.

"I'm so sorry. I don't usually let women stay over. For this exact reason." The fear and sorrow in his eyes pulled at her heartstrings. "I should've sent you home, or slept on the couch."

"I'm okay," she placated.

"I get ... bad dreams sometimes."

There was an understatement, if ever she'd heard one.

"From my time in the army. But, oh God, Ebony, I never meant to hurt you."

He leaned toward her, as if to put a hand on her leg and she instinctively flinched away from him. Shit, she hadn't meant to do that, and the expression in his shuttered eyes told her it was the completely wrong thing to do. She'd just confirmed in his mind that he was a horrible monster, one who had no right to expect her forgiveness, let alone her sympathy. She had to make this right. But she still wasn't sure if she was up to touching him yet. The ache in her throat was fading, but there would be bruises. How would she explain it?

"I'll be fine, you stopped before you did any real damage," she said. "And I know you didn't mean it." She wanted to ask him if he'd ever received help for his problem, but was that too personal? The thought uppermost in her mind right now, was to get as far away from here as she could. Space and time to dissect what'd just happened, that's what she needed. Those images of Alexander kept threatening to come back and overwhelm her, as if Jay's attack had opened a set of floodgates.

He didn't answer, but he got up and moved further away from the bed, the look in his eyes reminded her of someone who'd just been punched in the guts.

"I should go home, I didn't really mean to stay anyway. I need to get back to Chili Dog. What's the time?" She knew she was babbling and sounded way too cheery, blatantly ignoring the seriousness of what'd just happened, but she couldn't deal with it right now. It was only by the merest thread she managed to hold herself together, she needed to get out of here. Alexander had wrapped his hands around her throat once, too. His hot breath had hissed over her face as she'd cried out for him to stop. The image of his superior, reptilian smile, even as he calmly pressed his thumbs to her windpipe, wouldn't leave her mind.

"I'll just get dressed." She hoped he got the hint and left the room, so she could gather up her clothes in peace. Gaze roaming over the floor, searching for her wayward underwear, it wasn't until she heard the soft click of the door that she knew he'd gone. A loud gushing sigh left her lips and her hands flew to her throat. Oh, sweet Jesus. A sob threatened to break free, but she forced it back down. Get out of here and get home, then she could fall apart. She couldn't let Jay see her cry, it would destroy him even more than he was already destroying himself.

Forgoing the underwear, she went straight for the skirt, which was hanging over the back of the chair where she'd left it before changing into Jay's jeans. Oh Lord, that felt like a lifetime ago. Then she tugged the t-shirt over her head and dragged on her cardigan, stuffing the underwear in the pocket as she did so.

This wasn't Jay's fault, he was sick. He hadn't been in his right mind when he'd attacked her.

She could help him.

The thought brought her up short. He needed healing. And she was a healer. Mental scars were exponentially harder to heal than physical ones, but she had done it before, once or twice. He may not even accept it.

But the tiny voice in her head that kept telling her Jay was just like her ex, wouldn't go away. Jay was just as capable of violence as Alexander had been.

CHAPTER THIRTEEN

Ebony sat in one of the overstuffed couches in her clinic, deep in thought. It was after two thirty and a patient was due in less than twenty minutes, but she couldn't seem to concentrate. She should get up and ready the Reiki room, light the scented candles, turn on the soft background music she used to help the patient relax and make sure the aura in the room was calm and serene.

Instead she sat there, gnawing on a fingernail, worrying over the scene at Jay's place last night. Embarrassment at how she'd practically run out of his house—well, it was early this morning if the truth be told—trickled hot and thick down her spine. He hadn't tried to stop her. Just stared at her with hardened eyes, like blue steel. Face set in a stone mask. She knew he was probably filled with self-loathing, and was even now blaming himself for scaring her, for hurting her. But for the life of her, she couldn't have stayed to make it right with him. She just needed to get out of there, as if there wasn't enough air to breathe in that house anymore.

Then when she arrived home and glanced up at the mantle-piece, the missing photo frame triggered the memory of the break in, which left her even more jittery and jumpy than she thought possible. She hadn't even felt safe in her own house. Everything seemed to be going wrong lately.

Perhaps this town was trying to tell her something. It was time to move on.

Chili Dog had welcomed her home with such enthusiasm, she felt guilty at leaving her for so long. Chili gave her the complete once-over and Ebony could almost read the disapproval in the dog's eyes. She'd been *with* another dog. A very interesting smelling dog, Ebony could tell by the way Chili wouldn't stop sniffing at her clothes.

Jay had revealed so much of himself to her last night. Much more than she'd bargained for. She'd thought he was courageous and intriguing before. Now he was downright fascinating. She'd learned he was sweet enough to try and cook for her. Even if it hadn't quite worked out the way he wanted. He was dedicated, and valiant when it came to helping other people in danger. Determined to protect them, put his own body on the line when it came to fighting fires or rescuing crash victims. And tender. He'd been oh-so-tender with her when they'd made love. Had reacted to her touch with delicious abandon, and she'd responded with equal impulsiveness. Almost as if he'd touched her soul.

He was also damaged. Ebony could now confirm to Viv that her theories were correct, Jay had indeed been in the army. Had been to Afghanistan. And yes, he had been affected by that terrible war. Left with an invisible scar, that no one—except her—knew he had.

In the cold light of day, and with twenty-twenty hindsight, Ebony understood her running out on Jay was the worst thing she could possibly have done. She'd probably cemented in his mind he was a complete bastard, that he'd hurt her; he was completely untrustworthy. But she couldn't get rid of that nagging voice in her head that said he was capable of violence. And if left unchecked, his violence was likely to re-appear.

Ebony knew it wasn't fair to tar Jay with the same brush as her ex-husband. Her logical mind knew PTSD did horrible things to a person's psyche. As a healer she understood this. Had even read about some of the symptoms. Sufferers often blamed themselves for what happened and felt guilty or ashamed because they couldn't control their reactions.

So, if she understood this, then why couldn't she rid herself of the unease whenever she thought of Jay? The idea she might be able to stay here longer was evaporating before her eyes. It wasn't safe. She could pack up her life into her old Subaru and be back on the road by this time tomorrow. No one would be worse for wear. No one would really miss her. Nothing lost.

A car horn sounded in the street outside and Ebony was pulled from her introspection back to her Reiki room. She stared out the window and saw a pedestrian waving their hands in the air at a car. Tourists. They were a necessary evil in this town.

She checked her watch then leaped up and busied herself in the Reiki room. She'd meant to go and visit Beau in hospital first thing this morning, but she'd slept in and her morning got away from her. But it was the first thing on her list to do once she'd finished for the afternoon. At least his injuries weren't too bad, which meant they'd given him a bed in the small Margaret River hospital and she didn't need to travel to Busselton to see him.

Suddenly, there was a knock and a figure appeared in front of the frosted glass door.

"Come in," she yelled, running a hand through her wayward curls. No amount of smoothing was going to tame them today, so she brushed a curl out of her eye and put on her brightest welcoming smile.

A young woman stepped through the door. Petite, very close to Ebony's height, with long blonde hair drawn back into a braid, and a battered Akubra hat held in one hand. She had on well-worn jeans and cowboy boots and smiled broadly back at Ebony.

"Hi, I'm Jenna. Nice to meet you," she said, and extended her hand in greeting. There was a translucency to the girl's skin, and dark bruises under her eyes, as if she wasn't sleeping well. And the skin stretched tight over her bones where they jutted out, a little angular. Had she lost weight recently?

"It's a pleasure to meet you as well." Ebony took her hand but was shocked at the sudden jolt of energy she got from the young woman and yanked back in surprise.

"Oh, did you feel that too?" Jenna asked with a laugh. "That was some wicked static electricity. Wow, your carpet must be nylon or something." The girl glanced down and then frowned at the bare floorboards. They both looked up and caught each other's eyes and chuckled. The girl's eyes were a light blue, reminiscent of a pale watercolor, but fixed on her with an intense seriousness that belied the humor in her laugh.

Familiar. The young woman looked familiar for some reason.

"Come and sit over here and tell me how I can help you." Ebony indicated one of the antiquated couches, then took a seat on the other one, facing Jenna.

"Oh, ah …" Jenna's cheeks colored slightly, and she gave a small cough.

"It's okay, I get plenty of first-timers here," Ebony said gently. That niggle at the back of her neck was still there, telling her she knew this girl somehow. But for the life of her, Ebony couldn't place her.

"I'm not a first-timer," Jenna replied. "I've had Reiki a few times before. I was just talking to Jacko, over at the servo down the street." Jenna waved a vague hand in the direction of the local gas station. "My husband and I were filling up the ute. And when I told him about my bad morning sickness, he said you might be able to help me. And because Reiki's worked for me before, I thought I'd give it a go again."

"Yes, that's great." She'd have to remember to thank Jacko for his referral. And it certainly explained the girl's condition. If she was that sick and couldn't keep much food down, then she was probably losing precious weight as the baby drew all its energy from her. This was an unusual request, but she didn't let that show on her face. "I've treated morning sickness a few times before. But first of all, congratulations. How far along are you?" Obviously not too far, as the girl wasn't showing at all. Ebony racked her brain as to how she'd treated this kind of thing before. She'd have to be extra careful, now there were two souls involved in the healing.

"I'm just nine weeks. I only really confirmed it a week ago, that's when the morning sickness got really bad and Dan made me go and see a doctor."

Ebony assumed Dan was the husband, mainly because of the way Jenna's face lit up when she spoke his name. She looked a little young to be married, but who was Ebony to judge? If she was that much in love with the young man, then good for her.

"But I don't like taking drugs or anything like that. So when I heard about you, I thought I'd give it a try."

"Yes, well, like I said, I can definitely help you. How long will you be in town? This kind of thing can take a couple of sessions." Or more, but Ebony didn't want to go there just yet.

"We're not sure yet." The girl's eyes wandered to the window, searching for something outside. "This is kind of … our belated honeymoon, I guess you could call it. We're just touring around down south for a couple of weeks, before we head back to the station." Well that accounted for the hat and boots. "But our trip has kinda been eclipsed a little by my morning sickness. It's been so bad, sometimes I can't function until around lunch time. And even then, it often takes me until dinner before I can actually keep any food down. We've been here for close to a week now. We should move on, but Dan says I need to take it easy for a while. So we stayed. It's nice here."

"Yes, it is an easy place to stay. I haven't been here that long myself, but I feel this town's pull," Ebony said with a half-smile.

"That's an interesting necklace." Jenna pointed to the blue-flecked stone around Ebony's neck.

"Yes, it's a semi-precious stone, called Kyanite. It helps with my healing energy."

"Oh.' Jenna gave her an odd look and touched something hanging on a long chain around her neck, but Ebony couldn't see exactly what it was she had hidden beneath her shirt.

"Come on over to the table." She indicated with a nudge of her chin toward the back room. "I'd love to hear more about your travels while I get ready."

"Okay." Jenna rose, but something in her faltering step told Ebony she was still unsure.

"Don't worry, you'll be fine. Your baby will be fine. I know you've probably heard this before, but the main theme of Reiki is to do no harm." This seemed to mollify the girl, as she fell into step behind Ebony and followed her into the smaller back room. Ebony got Jenna to lay down on her table, after first removing her boots and then bustled around the room, readying a relaxing essential oil mix that wouldn't harm the baby to put in the burner, and prompting the other woman with questions. Ebony found out she was twenty-three, had only been married for just over a year, had met her wonderful husband on Shiralee cattle station, where she now lived and worked, and they were driving around the southern end of Western Australia in their battered old ute with Jenna's dog in the back. It was the wet season up north, and not a lot happened during the wet season on a cattle farm, supposedly.

While the girl talked, Ebony gently sensed the aura around her, sending out calming signals, but also making sure she wasn't hit with that electric shock that'd happened the first time they touched. If she made psychic contact first, before she started the healing, it usually worked better. There was something strange about the energy that radiated from her. All people had a life force that ran through them, which is how Reiki worked, the healer tapped into that life force and directed it where you wanted it to go. But Jenna seemed to have an awful lot of energy running through her, more than Ebony had felt in anyone for a long, long time.

It was time to start, Ebony couldn't put it off anymore. She explained to Jenna what she was going to do and what Jenna could expect to feel. Then she asked her to clear her mind of all wayward thoughts and concentrate her thoughts internally. Ebony found she got a better connection if she could have skin touching skin when treating a patient. When she asked Jenna if this would be okay, she said it was fine with her.

Ebony stood over the girl lying on the table and cleared her mind. Let it drift until there was only blank grayness in front of her eyes. She hovered her hands above Jenna's flat belly and sent her energy probes into the girl's body gently, softly, covertly, so as not to startle her.

Yes, there was the baby, growing strong, a bright, effervescent entity. Too young yet to be aware of Ebony, but still animated enough for her to recognize it as a separate creature. If Ebony probed a little deeper, she'd be able to find out whether the baby was a boy or a girl, but she shied away from that. She would never do that without the patient's explicit instructions. Instead, she pulled her focus back a little and sent her tendrils down into the stomach region of Jenna's body, flowing through the intestines, soothing the rippling waves of distress in the stomach and up the oesophagus.

It was a woman's high levels of hormones which caused morning sickness, and even though Ebony could manipulate those, she wasn't about to play with something that may affect the growth of the baby.

Wow, this girl had some powerful energy radiating through her. Ebony had to go carefully, almost as if she were pushing her way through an unseen barrier. The girl's energy wasn't trying to hinder her, in fact, if she'd let it, Ebony got the distinct feeling she might even be able to meld with the energy, to increase her own power. But that would just be plain ridiculous, it'd never happened before. Shying away from the whole idea, Ebony narrowed her focus, blocking the girl's energy from her own, so it became peripheral, and concentrated solely on stopping those waves of nausea from becoming overpowering.

* * *

Jenna lay still and silent. Part of her agreement with Ebony was that she wouldn't try and talk or communicate with her in any way. It might break her contact and then the healing wouldn't work as well.

But she could feel Ebony's power running through her. It was stronger than anything she expected. Surely normal Reiki wasn't this ... dynamic. On the few occasions Jenna had experienced it previously, it'd always been a soft, gentle style of healing, where the patient never felt anything. But this was like Ebony was burning a pathway through her veins with her power.

Should she say something? Jenna cracked one eyelid open. She didn't want to break the healer's obvious concentration.

It was almost as if she were in a trance. God, she'd never felt anything like this before.

And there was something vaguely familiar about the older woman. She was gorgeous, in an English rose, wild, and windswept kind of way. Almost the same build as Jenna, slight and petite, with far-away gray eyes. And she had a lovely calming air around her, Jenna wasn't nervous at all. That blue stone nestling in the curve of Ebony's neck caught Jenna's eye again. It was beautiful and unusual. Jenna thought about the pink ring she always carried around her neck. The pink star sapphire. She always kept it on a long chain tucked inside her shirt, out of sight, wearing it next to the golden locket Dan gave her for their anniversary. As her thoughts went to the ring, it was as if a pulse of heat came from the sapphire directly into her chest. What was that? Was the ring somehow responding to the power of the Reiki healer?

Jenna closed her eyes again and concentrated on the heat coursing through her. The nausea was starting to abate. The sick feeling never truly went away, but usually by around mid-afternoon it was manageable, allowing her to get small amounts of food into her body.

This healer had strong powers. Jenna's own gift, where she was able to communicate with certain animals was a subtle one. But now, it was as if Ebony's ability was calling to something deep inside Jenna. Something that wanted to answer her. What did it mean? Dan would know, she'd wait and talk to him.

Eyes closed, Jenna let her thoughts drift. Like Ebony suggested, she cleared her mind until only a bright, cloudy light filled the space. It was wonderful to just relax on the table, to have the warming glow of Ebony's energy gurgling through her like a welcome river of bliss.

It felt like only a few minutes later when Ebony's hand came to rest lightly on her shoulder. "We're all finished. You can get up when you're ready. But no rush."

Jenna shook the lethargy from her bones. Had she fallen asleep? She wasn't sure. Giving a huge yawn, she stretched out her arms and legs, then levered herself to a sitting position.

Wow. She felt better.

"Oh." Her hand came up to rest on her stomach. "You did it." She smiled at Ebony. "I feel almost human again. This is amazing."

"I'm glad." Ebony returned her smile, and again Jenna was struck by a certain familiarity. Ebony turned away and busied herself snuffing out the candles.

Just to fill the silence, Jenna said, "Maybe Dan and I will stay on a bit longer. Margaret River is a great little place. Lots of things to do, places to explore. It reminds me a little of my hometown of Berridale, up in the NSW highlands. Only Margaret River is even more touristy, if that's possible."

Ebony stopped what she was doing suddenly.

"Berridale? Did you say you grew up in Berridale?"

"Yes, my step-father had a small farm, just out of town." Pain speared through her at the thought of her dad, Joe. He was dead, murdered by Liam. The bastard.

"Oh." Ebony seemed to be floundering for something to say, and even through her pain at her father's memory, she could see the older woman was flustered.

"Why, have you been to Berridale?"

"I, um … No, I've never been there." Something about the way Ebony ducked her head when she said this had Jenna doubting her words. "I'm from around the Byron Bay area. Have you ever been there?" Ebony continued as a bright smile landed back on her face, whatever emotions the mention of Berridale had brought out were now firmly hidden behind a mask of congeniality.

"Yes, but I only spent a few nights there. I was traveling … a lot back then."

Ebony went on to expound the delights of Byron and Jenna listened to her prattle away, wondering what it was that'd upset her so much.

Dune, her dog, was nearby, she caught his sudden bright welcome in her mind. Dan and Dune were walking down the pathway toward the Reiki clinic. It was time for her to go. Jenna stood up from the sofa just as Dan opened the door and stuck his head inside. He looked gorgeous, as usual, curls from all that wayward blonde hair hanging over his eyes and that twinkle in his eye as he locked gazes with her.

"This is my husband, Dan," she said by way of an introduction. A small, furry face appeared around the bottom of the door. "And this is Dune."

"I won't come in," Dan replied, gesturing to the dog. But he held out his hand for Ebony to shake from the doorway. As he looked down, into Ebony's face, Jenna saw surprise flicker cross his gaze. When he looked back toward Jenna, a small troubled frown creased his forehead.

"Nice to meet you," Ebony replied, not noticing the byplay between them. "Is that a dingo?" Ebony asked, gesturing toward Dune, who still had his head around the bottom of the door, giving the place a good old sniff.

"Yes. Well he's at least half dingo,' replied Jenna proudly. She never tired of people asking about her beloved dog.

"He's gorgeous. Anyway, have a good stay here. Perhaps I might see you again?" she said to Jenna.

"Yes, yes, I'll be coming back. That was wonderful. What do you think, in a day or so?"

"Whenever you start to feel nauseous again." Ebony held the door for her to walk through and gave her a cheery wave as she closed the door with a click behind them.

As soon as she was alone with Dan out on the street, she asked him, "What's the problem?"

He cast a doubtful glance back up the street, toward the Reiki clinic. "Didn't you notice?"

"Notice what?" Exasperation tinged her voice, she didn't have time for his games.

"How much alike you and that woman look."

"What?" But she already knew what Dan was talking about. That'd been the thing niggling at her the whole time she'd been in the clinic. Ebony did look at lot like her. Or rather, Jenna looked a lot like Ebony.

CHAPTER FOURTEEN

Jay stared broodily out of the open door, elbows resting on the counter top. The surf shop was quiet this afternoon, only two customers since lunch time. But that was a good thing because the mood Jay was in today, he was likely to scare any customers out the door as soon as they saw his face. Doug was out the back, stocktaking, while Jay looked after the front of store.

His haggard reflection stared back up at him from the glass-topped bench beneath his elbows. Lack of sleep would do that to you. He should've stayed at home. But then he'd only be pacing around like a caged lion, with Axel watching him in confused silence.

Ebony's shop was just up the hill, at the other end of Main Street. A short five-minute walk if he cared to take it. She was in the clinic today, he'd seen the battered red Subaru parked down the side alley as he'd driven past earlier. They needed to talk. Well, he needed to apologize and she needed to listen. He shouldn't have let her leave the way she had last night. It was her face ... She'd looked at him as if he were the devil incarnate. It was only for a fleeting second, before she got her features back under control. But he'd seen the naked fear. And he'd been filled with total self-loathing. There wasn't a thing he could find to say in that moment which would've made it better. So he'd let her go.

He didn't blame her. It must've felt like he was trying to kill her. Imagine waking up to find a person you trusted—trusted enough to make love with just an hour or so earlier—had grabbed you by the throat and was trying to squeeze the life out of you. There was no way he blamed her for her reaction. It was all on him.

And perhaps she had a reason to blame him. That wicked scar on her lower belly wasn't something she would've put there herself. He hadn't said anything last night because he didn't want to dampen the mood. But when he put that together with the burn scars he'd seen on her back that first day he'd rescued her from the ocean, it hinted at Ebony being the victim of some evil son of a bitch. And if that were the case, the very last thing she wanted—or needed—was for another man to be violent toward her. Which made him even more of a monster.

"Fuck." He slammed his open palm down on the counter-top and it made a satisfying thump.

"You okay, boss?" A disembodied voice drifted from out in the back room.

"Yep, all good, Doug." Jay paced backward and forward behind the bench.

The surf shop was doing well, even better now he'd introduced the newer stock items he'd purchased on his last sales trip. In the next week or so, he and Doug and Stu were going to close the shop for a day and remodel the whole place. So many ideas of how to make better stock placement had been running around his head since he'd returned. But now all that took a back seat to his thoughts from last night. What should he do? How was he going to make it up to her? But then again, there was probably no way he was ever going to make this right again.

Professional help. He'd been avoiding it up until now, hoping these horrible nightmares would leave him alone eventually. But they weren't getting any better. If he told Ebony he was going to get some help, would that make it any better? Would she forgive him then?

There was a shrink right here in town, but he couldn't see himself letting everyone in Margaret River know his business. He'd find one further afield, in Bunbury or Busselton. Hell, he might even take the four-hour drive to Perth if it meant he found the right person.

Should he contact his old army CO? The army took this stuff very seriously and had offered him counseling on innumerable occasions. But he'd flatly refused. Maybe Christopher, his ex-army boss, could point him toward a shrink who knew about this kind of … problem he was having. Jay didn't want to put a name to it, because then it would gain even more power over him. After all, how could you put a name to the shame, guilt, sadness and anger that were all wrapped together in a heavy ball in his gut. It sat there all day long, like a black cloud, but came out to haunt him at night, when his normally strong defenses were down.

This kind of thing had only ever happened once before. With his ex-fiancée, Bryony. And look how well that'd ended.

The pacing to and fro wasn't enough to get rid of all this pent-up energy coursing through him. He was going crazy cooped up in the shop. If he didn't do something soon, he was going to find his feet walking him up to Ebony's clinic faster than he could say Jack Rabbit. Something to keep his hands busy, that's what he needed. He walked over to the shelves stacked with neatly folded surf-shirts and pulled them all down and made a pile on the bench. Then he started to fold them all over again, making sure every fold was military straight and sharp and each t-shirt was folded identically to the last one, all lined up along the bench with soldier-like precision.

Bryony hadn't taken his nightmares well, either. It'd been after he came home from his first tour in Afghanistan. After Tom had been killed. That's when the nightmares had first started. At first, they'd been much the same as most normal nightmares, lots of groaning and thrashing and calling out— or so Bryony told him in her condescending tone the next morning. But they'd soon escalated to him sleepwalking. Jay would often find himself walking down the corridor, or standing in the middle of the kitchen, unsure as to how he got there. Bryony became less and less tolerant of his night-time antics, and he'd often get up in the morning and find her sleeping in the spare bedroom.

One night, just after he'd signed up for a second tour of duty of Afghanistan, and he'd woken up to find himself standing over their bed, fists clenched and raised, adrenaline coursing through his body, the haze of blood lust turning his vision red.

Bryony was screaming, "You hit me, you hit me, you bastard," over and over again as she lay cowering in the bed.

That night he'd gone down on his knees and promised he'd make it right. That he'd get counseling, to tame the raging beast within. It seemed she'd been placated by his pledges and his pleading, and they'd agreed to work it out. She agreed to wait for him to come back from his second tour, and then everything would be fine.

But it hadn't been fine, because less than two weeks into his tour, Bryony phoned him and told him she couldn't keep doing this. Broke off the engagement, told him she'd already moved out of the house. And there wasn't a damn thing he could do about it. He was stuck in Afghanistan for the next six months, left to stew and fester in his own self-doubt and pity, while she moved on with her life.

He never did see a shrink. After that he didn't think there was a good enough reason. And in some sad twisted way he thought perhaps it was the punishment he deserved for not being able to help Tom. All he had to suffer was the occasional bad dream. Tom had an eternity of being dead. No comparison really.

Since then, he'd always made sure he stayed at the girl's place, so he could sneak home whenever he wanted to. Or on the infrequent occasion the girl ended up at his place, he made it clear she wasn't welcome to stay the night. Most girls didn't appreciate it, but then he wasn't after any major commitment, so it didn't matter. Axel was the only company he needed.

The dreams continued to haunt him, but they'd become a lot less frequent recently—who knew why—and Jay hadn't bothered about it. It was just something he had to live with. It never hurt anyone else.

Until last night.

Until he nearly throttled Ebony in her sleep.

"Boss, what're you doing?"

Jay jumped at the voice behind him. "These were all messed up." He pointed his chin at the growing pile of squared away shirts.

"Really?" The note of disbelief in that one word said it all.

"Yep. And now I'm finished, I'm off for a surf. You can handle the shop. There's been no one in for the last hour." The idea came to him in a lightbulb flash of brilliance. A surf, that's what he needed to clear away this God-awful melancholy mood.

"Sure, boss, I'm good here. Let me know if the waves are gnarly and I'll come down and join you later." Doug's words were civil enough, but the question mark in his eyes was evident, even to Jay.

Doug's gaze followed Jay as he went behind the counter and signed off on the register, gave the shop one quick perusal and then said, "Righto, have a good arvo." Jay managed to not quite meet Doug's eyes as he stalked out.

Redgate Beach, that's where he would surf. The waves were bound to be pumping over the sandbank today. A surf would help to clear his mind. He also needed to decide what to do about the possible break-in he'd had last night. The idea that his things had been touched—moved—still niggled at the back of his mind. But now, in the bright light of day, he was beginning to doubt himself. Had he just imagined it? But then he hadn't imagined that car parked on the street last night. Or was that just more of his over-active imagination? People were allowed to park their car in a street without having some kind of alternative reason. One thing was sure, he didn't have enough evidence to report anything to the police. They'd look at him like he was going slightly crazy. No, he'd just have to be ultra-alert for anything out of the ordinary. He was being paranoid. After all, nothing exciting happened in this sleepy little sea-side town.

Jay's feet took him through the alley and out the back of the shop, to where he'd parked his car. A surf. That was exactly what the doctor ordered. And then, when he'd worked off enough excess energy, and worked up enough courage, he'd drop into Ebony's place on the way home. Have that chat with her. He wanted to ask her about her past. They needed to share some of their secrets. But would she open up to him?

* * *

Now that she was here, Ebony suddenly found she didn't want to go in. She stood outside the hospital room, transferring her weight from one foot to the other, but not actually pushing the door open. Jesus, she was being silly. It was just Beau in there. He wasn't going to bite. Would he still be spouting all that strange nonsense from last night, or would he have forgotten everything he said? Both prospects unsettled her. At least he had a private room, so she could talk to him without anyone else overhearing.

Come on girl. She knocked on the white metal door and waited for an answer before she pushed it gently.

"Hi, Beau." All her apprehension was hidden beneath her bright smile. "I came to see how you're doing, I hope that's okay?"

"Yes, yes." He beckoned her in with his usual gusto. But it was only one-armed gusto today, his other arm tightly bound in a sling across his chest. "You're one of the people I hoped would come and visit me today." He patted the bed, indicating she should sit. Ebony eyed the visitor's chair, not sure she wanted to sit that close. "I wanted to say thank you. To you and Jay. Jay's not with you, is he?" He was still patting the bed, so Ebony carefully plonked herself on the very edge, trying to stay away from his other leg, which was in a large cast and propped up on a pillow. She shook her head to signal Jay wasn't with her—thank God—and ran an assessing glance over Beau's face. The two deep scratches running down his cheek had been stitched and didn't look half as ghoulish as they had last night.

"You'll have a couple of nice scars there," she said.

"Yeah, cool huh."

Ebony gave a surprised laugh. She should've known better. Of course, Peter-Pan here would think scars on his face were cool. "How about the rest of you? What did the doctors say?"

"Arm broken in two places and lower tibia fractured, but not too bad, all in all." Again, he gave her that look that said *cool huh*, as if broken bones were a badge of honor to be worn with pride. Men. She'd never truly understand them. Certainly not this kind of man.

"I can help with the pain if you like," Ebony offered.

"Thanks, but nah. The doctor has me on some great drugs. Maybe later, I'll take you up on that offer. They're not going to let me out yet for another day or two."

"I guess you'll be on crutches for a while. No surfing. How are you going to cope?"

"Heather is going to move in with me for a while. Only temporarily mind you. Then we can both help each other."

"How is Heather?"

"She's doing much better than me. Just a couple of broken ribs."

"That can still be very painful," Ebony warned, but Beau waved away her concern.

"What about the other two passengers," she queried.

A shadow fell over Beau's face. "Sandy's doing okay now. Heather told me they transferred her to Busselton Hospital for observation. She got a nasty bump on the head, but she woke up okay."

"Head injuries can be tricky, so I'm not surprised they're keeping her in for observation." Ebony gave him a relieved smile, but the unease was still there in the lines on Beau's face. "And what about your other mate, Bryce, was it?"

"Yeah, they transferred him to Busselton, too." A deep frown creased his brow, and he turned his gaze out the window. "But they're not sure exactly what's wrong with him."

"Oh?"

"He keeps telling the doctors that his back is broken, and he keeps yelling like he's in terrible pain, but the doctors, well they can't find anything much wrong with him."

"Ah." A line of ants marched up her spine at his words and the gooseflesh lifted on her arms and legs.

"How can that be?" He turned beseeching eyes toward her.

"I'm not a doctor," she said gently. "Sorry, I can't answer that question." But this was exactly what she'd been fearing.

Something abnormal was wrong with Bryce. Someone had tampered with his mind. But who? And why?

"Can I ask you a question, Beau?"

"Hmm?" He turned an out-of-focus gaze toward her, his mind still occupied by his friend's plight. But she had to know. Had to ask him this one question.

"You kept telling me the crash was your fault last night. You kept asking me to apologize to your friends. And then you told me a kangaroo jumped out in front of you." Beau's eyes quickly re-focussed and his head snapped around to look her full in the face. "But no one else saw a roo, Beau?"

"It was definitely there," Beau insisted. "It was there, right in front of the car, staring at me. It was instinct, I guess. I had to swerve around it." The fingers of Beau's good hand fisted in the hospital bed sheets. "Are you sure no one else saw it?" His eyes pleaded with her.

Ebony shook her head slowly. "The old lady in the car behind you said she never saw a thing, and she was looking straight at you. Heather also said she didn't know why you swerved. It was almost like you did it for no reason."

"But it was there." Beau's voice dropped to a whisper. "Wasn't it?"

"I don't know, Beau." This was going to sound like an odd question, but she had to ask it. "Heather said you talked to a couple of guys just after you finished fishing. Did they seem … Ah, I mean, did they say anything to you? Anything out of the ordinary?" She wasn't sure why, but these two fellows in the carpark seemed a little off to Ebony.

"Who?" His brow wrinkled as he tried to remember. "Oh them. Nah, they were just two tourists or something …" His voice drifted off as he seemed to think harder. "The older guy. Now I think about it … I did meet him a few days before. At the same beach. And he was with the same young guy, his son, I think. But I can't for the life of me really remember what the young guy looked like."

"What did they say to you the first time you met?"

"I can't remember," he replied, but as he did so he clicked his fingers in a very offhand way that had Ebony's hairs standing back up again. Beau should be able to remember at least something about his first conversation with the duo, even if he couldn't remember the details. But if he'd been hypnotized …

"Did either of them touch you?" she asked, doing an admirable job of keeping the worry out of her voice.

"What? Why would they … Actually, now you mention it, the young guy, he did shake my hand as they were saying goodbye last night, and I think he might've touched my neck at the same time. Which is a bit strange now I think about—"

"What about Bryce, did they shake hands with him?" she asked hurriedly.

"Oh, ah, I don't know, maybe. Why are you so interested in these guys?"

She wasn't about to tell him her theory, that these men had somehow hypnotized Beau and Bryce; that they meant to cause the accident. Because even she couldn't get her head around why someone would want to do that. Or who. It sounded too far-fetched, even for her paranoid mind.

"No reason," she replied lightly but her thoughts were racing.

"You do believe me? That I had to swerve to miss the roo, I had no choice." The look he sent her had the same beseeching intensity as the one he'd given her back when he'd brought his young son to her. But this time she had no ready answer. Not one that made any sense, anyway.

"Of course I do, Beau." Patting his free hand, she tried to stop the growing concern from showing in her face. There was one more question that needed an answer. About Beau's words just before he passed out last night. About him telling someone where someone else lived.

She opened her mouth to ask him, when the door popped open and a young nurse walked in.

"Time for your meds, Beau," she said in a bright professional voice. The shirt of her light blue uniform was almost busting at the seams, the buttons straining across her ample bosom. "Oh, there's no need to go, I'll only be a few minutes," she said as Ebony hopped off the bed and made for the door. The pretty nurse shook her perky ponytail as she looked down to grab Beau's chart from the end of the bed. Beau's eyes went wide in admiration.

"It's time I was going anyway," said Ebony, hand on the doorknob. There was no point in staying, Beau's attention was obviously elsewhere, and Ebony had more than enough information to keep her busy for a while. "I'll call in and see you tomorrow, if I can." She directed her words toward Beau, but his gaze remained fixed on the nurse.

"Sure thing, see you tomorrow," he replied, good hand already waving her out the door. Her shoes squeaked against the linoleum floor as she made her way down the corridor and out through the main reception. Who would want to hypnotize two strangers? And why would they want to cause a crash? But the thought that really had her heart racing was whose home address had Beau inadvertently given away? Her instincts were screaming at her that she needed to get out of Margaret River. Now.

Just as she stumbled into the hospital carpark, her phone rang. She pulled it out of her handbag and Jenna Simmonds' name popped up on the screen. Surely she wasn't phoning to make another appointment already. It was after six o'clock, technically Ebony's working day was over. Had something gone wrong after the Reiki this afternoon? Was she ringing to complain? Ebony kept the rising quiver at bay as she answered her phone with her most efficient voice.

"Hello, Ebony McAllister speaking."

"Hi, Ebony, it's Jenna here. You treated me this afternoon. For morning sickness." Jenna sounded hesitant. Ebony's heart rate spiked. Oh Jesus, she *was* ringing to make a complaint. Her mind went into overdrive, trying to remember the healing in detail. Nothing had gone wrong, she was sure of it.

"Ah, this is going to sound a little odd, but … Ah, my husband, Dan, and I …" Oh God, here it came. Ebony stopped walking, her shoulders hunched defensively. "That is … we wondered if you'd have dinner with us tonight." Jenna rushed on before Ebony could even form an answer. "As a kind of thank you for making me feel up to eating real food again. And also because, I have something I'd like to ask you. About the Reiki thing. I might be interested in learning more about it."

"Oh. Um …" What did Ebony say to that? She'd never been asked out by one of her patients before, and certainly not by a patient and her husband. It wasn't the most ethical thing to do. If Jenna wanted to learn more about Reiki, then Ebony would be more than happy to teach her at her clinic. Well, that's if she wasn't gone by tomorrow.

She was about to answer in that vein when Jenna broke in. She could probably hear Ebony working up toward a no. "We'd really like you to come. We'd pay for dinner and everything. And we could do with your recommendation on the best place to eat as well. Please."

Bother, now the girl was practically pleading with her. Perhaps it couldn't hurt. It had been a shit of a day for the most part. What with her night spent rescuing four young people from the car crash, then the … thing—for want of a better word—with Jay, she'd hardly slept last night. And now her very unnerving conversation with Beau, which made her feel decidedly edgy. Plus, there wasn't a thing prepared back at home, so she'd most likely be eating eggs on toast for dinner. Again. There was also that small niggling feeling whenever Jenna was around. Maybe she could sort out what it was about at the same time.

"Please come, Ebony," Jenna asked again.

"Okay," she replied. "There's a small Thai restaurant at the top of Main Street. They do the best Pad Thai in the whole of Western Australia. Do you think you can find it? I can meet you there in half an hour."

"Oh, that's great. Thank you so much." The gleeful relief in Jenna's words led Ebony to think she'd been expecting her to turn them down. "We both love Thai food. See you soon." Jenna rang off and Ebony continued her path across the carpark toward her car.

What the hell had she just let herself in for now?

CHAPTER FIFTEEN

"Oh, you're so right, this Pad Thai is to die for," groaned Jenna through a mouthful of noodles. "And it tastes so good after my decidedly bland diet recently."

"I'm glad you eat tofu. It's much better with the tofu," Ebony replied, through her own mouthful of food.

Jenna hadn't realized just how hungry she was until the food was placed on the table. The look on Ebony's face had been one of comical delight when she'd found out that Jenna was also vegetarian, just like her. It meant they could order more food to share.

They'd ordered the som tum, papaya salad, and the vegetarian laab, along with the gang jay, a vegetarian curry. Dan had ordered one of the hottest chicken green curries and was making appreciative slurping noises from across the table.

As soon as Ebony sat down with the couple, Jenna had assured her she felt fine. She knew Ebony might be harboring fears they were here about her Reiki treatment this afternoon. After that she'd watched as Ebony slowly relaxed in their company. The easy banter and talk about their trip were effortless topics of conversation. The older woman never broached the subject of why they asked her to dinner, and Jenna got the distinct impression she was prepared to wait them out. Jenna's palms began to sweat. This had seemed like a good idea at the time, but now Ebony was sitting here across the table from her, she was losing her nerve.

As Dan asked Ebony a question, Jenna studied her from over the rim of her water glass. She was so full of life, but there was also a reserve there, hidden behind her mask of friendly competence. Today she had on a pair of tan, hip-hugging capris and a bright embroidered red and cream flowing top. Jenna tried to guess her age. With the boho-chic style clothing, dark curls, and that smooth, rose-tinged skin, Jenna would've guessed she was in her early thirties. But something told her Ebony was older than that. Perhaps it was the tiny lines around her eyes, or the very few flecks of gray in her hair.

Her own mother would've turned forty this year.

Jenna started and nearly dropped her fork. What the hell? Where had that thought come from?

"You okay, babe?" Dan's deep voice soothed those vagabond thoughts and she looked up and smiled.

"Yep, sorry, was in too much of a hurry to help myself to more of this delicious food." Jenna grinned as she reached over and heaped some more gang jay onto her plate. It was good to be able to eat real food again. She'd lost a lot of weight over the past month, and her already slim frame was becoming decidedly angular. Even Dan commented on it, which was most unlike him. He always liked her any way she came.

Dan flicked a quick glance in her direction, brown eyes concerned. Not that anyone else would notice, he kept his emotions hidden under the facade of his easy-going swagger. For the millionth time, she thanked God Dan was here with her. That he'd come on this hair-brained scheme of a trip with her. That she'd married him. That she was having his child.

The last one was a big one. She was still coming to terms with the fact she was going to have a baby. But she'd get used to it. Such a sweetness enveloped her every time she thought about having Dan's baby. Nothing else in this world could compare.

Okay, it was time. Jenna sucked in a fortifying breath. Hopefully Ebony wouldn't completely freak out.

"So, Ebony. I wanted to say thank you again for your healing today."

"I'm glad I could help. Reiki doesn't always work so well on everyone. You must be very receptive." She gave Jenna a seasoned smile.

"Yes, maybe I am." Jenna hesitated, wanting to find the exact right words. Dan stopped shoveling food into his mouth to watch them. "And that's kind of what I wanted to talk to you about." Ebony picked up her napkin and dabbed delicately at her mouth and waited for Jenna to continue. "On the phone I said I wanted to learn Reiki. I might even be quite good at it. That's because I believe I may have some of the same, ah … power that you have."

"Hmm?" Ebony was only half-listening, her gaze had wandered toward the restaurant's large main window, which looked out over the main street.

"I was aware of the power you were using on me. Aware how you directed it through my body," Jenna continued, willing Ebony's gaze back onto her.

"Like I said, some people are more responsive to it. You must be one of those people." Ebony brought her focus back to Jenna, gray eyes the color of granite fixed on her, a little bemused, still fidgeting with the napkin.

"Yes, but I think I'm more than just perceptive." Jenna stopped and gave Dan a look. He nodded, to tell her it was okay, to keep going. Jenna laid her fork carefully down on the table and looked up. "Not many people know this about me.

I have a certain … ah, gift I guess you could call it." Ebony stilled as she spoke, perhaps finally realizing the relevance of what Jenna was trying to say. Jenna's vocal cords froze up. It was always difficult to explain what it was she could do. And not many people knew about her talent. Only the people she could trust. Could she trust Ebony? Yes, her heart was saying yes, even though she'd known the woman less than half a day. Besides, if anyone was going to believe what Jenna could do, it would be Ebony. If Jenna wasn't way off base here, she had similar talents, they just manifested in a different way.

"I have an empathy with animals." Ebony just nodded but didn't say anything. Lots of people had an empathy with animals, and Ebony's eyes were telling her this wasn't something to get all excited about. "Actually, it's more than an empathy. I can kind of talk to them. Well, not talk exactly. I get impressions from them. Images, emotions, that kind of thing. And they respond to me as well." Ebony's hands tightened on her napkin, which was now twisted into a messy ball of fabric.

"Okaaaaaay?" Ebony drew the syllables out as she considered what Jenna had just said. "That's um … very interesting. This world is full of wonders, amazing things we know very little about. But I'm not sure it's got anything to do with what I do. Reiki uses the energy we find in all beings and helps individuals to harness it and focus it on an area, to get the chi flowing again."

Jenna was a little confused. Ebony was telling them how Reiki worked, but completely ignoring the fact that what she did was a whole lot more. With all the Reiki she'd experienced before, never had she come across the extreme potency of the force of Ebony's healing. Ebony was doing something much more than just directing a life force, she was creating it, using her own innate power to enhance the healing one hundred-fold. Why wouldn't she own up to it?

Perhaps she needed a little more persuasion. They were comrades in arms after all. Or so she hoped.

"It's a lot more than merely being able to communicate with animals," Dan interrupted. "Jenna has a certain power as well. It emanates from her sometimes.'

"Yes," Jenna agreed. "And I think it's a lot like the power that you use to do your Reiki."

Ebony's shoulders had grown tense as she listened to Dan and Jenna. She sat up straighter in her chair, a frown creasing her brow.

"I'm sorry, I'm not really sure what you're getting at here?"

They'd obviously touched on a raw nerve. Was she denying she had the power? Perhaps she'd never told anyone else about it before. Perhaps this was the first time she'd ever met anyone with a similar aptitude.

Instinctively, Jenna reached out and touched Ebony's hand. The spark that flashed between them was almost visible. The same as when she'd first touched the older woman today.

Ebony snapped her hand back.

"Don't do that." If Jenna wasn't mistaken, that was naked fear in the woman's gaze as she stared at her, eyes wide, one hand clutched to the base of her throat.

"Sorry," she stuttered. "I didn't mean to offend you. I just wanted to show you how much of a connection we have. I've never felt that kind of thing before," she continued, desperate now as Ebony pushed her chair back. She was about to leave. Bloody hell, she'd gone about this all wrong. They didn't want to scare Ebony off. They wanted to talk to her, figure out if they were indeed as similar as Jenna predicted.

"Please don't go, Ebony. Let me explain." Jenna cast an urgent glance toward Dan.

"Look, thank you for inviting me to dinner, it was lovely." Ebony stood up and grappled for her purse under the table.

Dan stood up as well, hands outstretched toward her. "We didn't mean to scare you, it's just—"

Ebony cut him off. "And if you need more help with your morning sickness, please come and see me. But I have to go now." She stood there, purse in hand, dark hair tousled around her face and Jenna felt a sudden stab of empathy for her. She was scared. Scared witless. But of what?

"Thanks again for dinner, it was lovely. I'm sure I'll see you —" Ebony stopped mid-sentence and stared out the window. All the color drained from her face and she blinked rapidly three or four times, as if she couldn't believe what she was seeing. A tiny whimper escaped her lips. What the hell? Jenna turned to look out the window, to see what had rooted Ebony to the spot.

At first glance, nothing seemed out of place. The main street was full of people wandering up and down the footpath. It was still early evening after all. And a Friday night. People, tourists and locals alike, were heading out for dinner or a drink, or just a lazy stroll.

Then she spotted the man and the kid. They stood on the curb on the other side of the street to the restaurant. Were they father and son? The kid looked to be in his late teens with pockmarked skin and stooped shoulders. But it was the man who held Jenna's attention. He wore a black fedora hat, of all things, which made him stand out of the crowd. With a long dark coat wrapped around his tall torso. Surely it was way too hot to wear that? A long, gray beard covered the bottom of his face and his dark eyes appraised the passing crowd, almost like a king surveying his subjects. Heat prickled down Jenna's spine. There was something horribly familiar about this guy. Dan moved to stand next to her, also glancing out the window. His eyes fixed on the two men as they stood, waiting to cross the road.

Jenna glanced over at Ebony. Yep, it was definitely that duo holding her attention. Who were they to Ebony? And why did they instil such fear in her?

Then the man looked up, straight into the restaurant. His gaze locked onto Ebony, like a homing beacon.

"Oh no." The small sound left Ebony's bloodless lips and she dropped a trembling hand to the chair back for support. "I have to get out of here." Her head swiveled as if it were a spinning top. Then her eyes settled on a dark alcove and a corridor toward the back of the restaurant. A back door.

"Ebony, can we help you?" But Ebony either didn't hear her words or didn't care to answer as she fled toward the back door, leaving Jenna and Dan standing there, looking at each other.

"What the hell?" demanded Dan. "Who are those two guys?"

"I don't know, but I don't think I want to hang around and find out," Jenna replied. She hadn't liked the way the older man stared at Ebony, like he was a hunter and she his prey. And she also hadn't liked the way his gaze had shifted to her when Ebony fled, the light of comprehension seeming to grow in his eyes as he took her in. Why was this man familiar? An image of Liam flashed into her mind. Surely not. He was dead. So who was this guy then? She led the way to the counter to pay for their meal, Dan hot on her tail, and then they too left by the back door.

* * *

Ebony scuttled down the alleyway that ran behind the row of shops and restaurants. Her car was parked a block back, away from all the tourists and crowds, and her feet tapped out a fast tattoo as she strode through the murky dimness of the alley. *Walk, Ebony. No need to run. You're fine. Everything's going to be fine.* Her heartbeat was racing along with her echoing footsteps and a groan escaped her throat before she could stop it. Oh God, please. Please don't let it be him.

Her pace increased. Was that someone behind her?

No, it was her imagination gone haywire.

Think about something else. Anything else, so she made it to her car in one piece, without turning into a crumpled puddle of hysteria on the sidewalk.

Ebony had been enjoying the night. The food was good, she was delighted in the company of the young couple. She'd even managed to take the time when they'd all been consumed with eating to surreptitiously study Dan. He was tall and lean and had that general country air about him. With a mop of curly blond hair and square, strong shoulders. His style was laid back and easy, but those contemplative eyes of his never missed a thing. She could feel the connection Jenna had with Dan straight away. It was a strong one. An unbreakable bond. And now she knew why Jenna had married so early. She'd found her soul mate in that one.

But then it had all gone to hell in a hand-basket. Faster than Ebony could've ever thought possible. When Jenna started to tell her how she could talk to animals, Ebony's blood had almost frozen in her veins. It wasn't the fact she could communicate with other species that had Ebony's head spinning. It was her talk about the energy, the power she used to do it. The way she identified the power Ebony used to enhance her healing. No one had ever done that in her twenty years of practice. How could that be? In all her time wandering from town to town throughout the Australian continent, she'd never come in contact with anyone else who had similar powers to her own. When Jenna reached out and touched her, it'd confirmed everything in a blinding flash of reality. But by that stage Ebony was already planning her escape and gathering her things. Spooked by the girl's words, she'd needed to get out of there. Decide what to do next.

But that's when things got decidedly worse. When she'd seen him standing on the other side of the road.

They probably thought she was completely crazy or drunk, or on drugs, to have left the way she did. Without paying as well. But that wasn't her major concern right now. Her concern was the fact the man across the road had been Alexander Pallan.

Her ex-husband.

Oh fuck! Had he seen her? Did he know she was here? He had looked straight at her through the window. Gaze locked directly onto her. If she recognized him, then there was no doubt in her mind he'd recognized her.

She had to leave town. Right away. There was nothing else to do.

It was all making a kind of sick sense to her now. The long gray beard had thrown her off the scent for a while; hidden his true identity from her. Alexander used to have a dark goatee beard. He was normally well groomed and pedantic about his appearance. Perhaps the beard was there on purpose, as a disguise. She never would've guessed he would let himself look that scruffy. Not in a million years. It wasn't in Alexander's character. Except if he was hunting her, then perhaps he was prepared to do just about anything to get her back.

It had been him she'd seen walking down the street the other day. A week ago. If only she'd recognized him then, she could've been long gone by now. Jesus, let it not be too late. Let him not have found her hiding place. But then she remembered the break-in at her place, and the missing photo could only mean one thing.

A small part of her couldn't believe he was still looking for her after all this time. Was this a horrible kind of coincidence? Surely enough water had passed under the bridge by now. It'd been twenty-two years, for God's sake.

But Alexander was the worst kind of narcissist. He'd always thought of himself as being the *chosen one,* that he was destined to lead his little criminal gang to greatness, whatever that meant. If only Ebony had seen that in him right from the start. But she'd been blinded by his charm.

And he wanted her. At first because of her naivety, he loved that she was a virgin and he was the one man to deflower her. Because she was beautiful, a trophy for him to hold in his hand, to bring out and admire her sparkling beauty whenever the whim took him. But later it was also because of her ability.

Back then her healing power had only been in its fledgling stages, she was still learning how to control it and what it could do. But she'd made the mistake of telling Alexander. And he'd looked at her with open avarice in his eyes. She became part of his grand design, and ultimately more precious to him because he saw her ability as a tool he could use.

Alexander never hesitated to put other people's lives at risk if he thought they posed a threat to him or his ultimate goal. He was driven by his supreme arrogance, which culminated in rage if he thought he was being contradicted. Jesus, had Alexander caused Beau's crash? But why? He must've had something to do with the crash. The young man with him, it seemed he was the key. Had Alexander found himself another lackey, another vulnerable person, strong in hypnosis powers, who would do his bidding?

She'd been so wrong, thinking Alexander would've forgotten all about her. He obviously still hungered after her. How many times had he told her she was his property, she belonged to him, and no one and nothing would ever take that away from him. But there was no way she was going to spend the rest of her life chained to a madman. She'd rather die.

Ebony chanced a glance behind her. She was nearly to her car now, but the back street she'd parked on was much darker than the main street, only an occasional street lamp casting a hazy glow every now and then. A lone couple were the only other people walking down the street, hand in hand and way behind her. She was safe. For now.

Her car was there, parked next to the curb, only a few meters further on. Damn, she should've remembered to park it directly under a street lamp, because now it was in a dark patch between two of the lights. But she hadn't really thought anything of it before, Margaret River was normally a safe place.

Ebony stopped in her tracks. A lone shadow leaned up against the rear bumper of her car.

Without thinking, she turned on her heel, about to run, when she heard a familiar voice. "Ebony. Is that you?"

She stopped and let out a sharp breath before turning around. It was Jay. What in hell was he doing here?

* * *

"Hi, Jay," she replied brusquely. "Sorry, I'm in a bit of a rush, I can't stop now." He pushed away from the car bumper as she strode past him toward the driver side door.

Damn, it was just as he thought. She was really mad at him after last night. But she needed to hear his apology. Then if she decided she was never going to speak to him, fair enough. The key rattled in the car door as she unlocked it. A whiff of her fragrance reached his nostrils. A smell that was uniquely Ebony. A mixture of those essential oils she liked to use—lavender perhaps—with her coconut shampoo and something else that reminded him of the salt and the sand and a wild coastline. His guts tightened at the thought of that smell and how it'd wrapped around him last night. When they'd made love.

"Wait, Ebony. Please." She stopped fiddling with the door at his entreaty but didn't turn around to face him.

"I'm really sorry, Jay, but I can't do this right now." There was something in her voice. Something that brought him up short. Was it fear? And possibly resignation? Surely that fear wasn't because of him? Okay, he had tried to strangle her, but she knew he hadn't really meant it, right? There was something wrong with him. But he was going to fix it. Make sure this never happened again.

"Ebony, you need to let me apologize. This has been driving me crazy all day long."

Finally, she turned to face him. Even in the murky darkness her face was as pale as a ghost.

"It's fine, Jay, really. I'm fine." Was she going to fob him off and pretend nothing had happened? "Apology accepted."

"Bullshit," he almost shouted. Even he knew he didn't get away with it that easy. Why was she so determined to let this all go, without a fight, without a proper explanation? He'd admit he hadn't known her all that long, but the Ebony he'd discovered so far wasn't one to put up with this. This afternoon, after he'd left the shop, he'd spent a good three hours in the ocean, catching the occasional wave. But most of the time he'd just sat on his board, pondering. Pondering lots of things, but one thing kept returning over and over again to his consciousness. Ebony, and how she made him feel. Last night had been a first for him. He'd broken his golden rule. Allowing himself to become so enamored with a woman that he'd allowed her to stay the night. And look how that turned out. But the real question was, why had he let her stay in the first place? It'd taken a while for him to admit the answer. Because she was special. She meant more than just a one-night stand to him. Much, much more. More than anyone except for Bryony. But now he could hardly remember what it was about Bryony he'd been so besotted with. This thing with

Ebony seemed to eclipse anything he might've had with Bryony. Last night he hadn't wanted to break the intimacy they'd shared. Wanted to wake up with her, so she was the first thing he saw when he opened his eyes in the morning. He hadn't allowed himself to believe that might be possible again, until now.

"I'm sorry, but I need to go, Jay." Now he heard the desperation in her voice. With that she flung her purse in the car and scrambled into the driver's seat.

"What's the all-fire hurry?" he asked, leaning forward to grab the door before she could close it in his face. "I went out to your place tonight, to talk to you. But you never came home. So then I dropped past my shop to pick up a few things, and I spotted your car. I waited, because I needed to talk to you. To get this all out in the open." He knew this was getting into it's-none-of-your-goddamned-business area, asking her where she'd been, but for some reason his gut was churning, telling him something was way off.

"What's going on Ebony? Are you okay?" He'd relied on that gut instinct more than once in Afghanistan to get him out of sticky situations. Perhaps he was getting into stalker territory here, but something was telling him not to let her go. To get in this car with her and make sure she got home safely, even though it was obvious it was the absolute last thing she wanted him to do.

She huffed out a regretful sigh and her gaze drifted upwards to meet his. Her face was still terribly pale, her eyes reflecting the lamp-light from further up the street. Were those tears he saw forming? It was hard to tell in the semi-dark.

"Will you let me go if I promise I'll come and talk to you first thing tomorrow? If I promise that my leaving now has nothing to do with you?"

"I guess I don't really have a choice," he replied quietly. But something in the way her chin trembled made him sure she wasn't going to keep her promise. This was some kind of crazy roller-coaster of emotions she was riding tonight. When she'd first appeared, she'd seemed scared, as if the devil himself was on her tail, then she was desperate to get out of his sight, and now she was sad. Why was she sad? Sad because she couldn't forgive him for what he'd done to her? Or sad because she knew she was going to break her promise to him?

"Are you sure you won't tell me what's going on here? If you're in some kind of trouble, I can help."

She shook her head in denial, curls bobbing gently around her face. Then she did something completely unexpected. She leaned up and kissed him on the lips. A soft, sweet kiss. Full of longing and regret and passion. If he hadn't known any better, he would've sworn if felt like a goodbye kiss.

CHAPTER SIXTEEN

Jesus, why had she never got that security light installed like she'd been meaning to? It would've made her dash across the driveway and onto the front porch a whole lot easier. And perhaps she wouldn't be trembling quite as much if she could see to get the key in the door. It was too damn dark out here. And where the hell was Chili Dog? She always barked her welcome from the back yard whenever she heard Ebony come home.

Finally, the key slid into the lock, and she turned it, slipped inside and closed the door behind her. Then, leaning her back against the solidity of the door, she reached over and flicked on the light switch. A few deep, calming breaths had her heart rate almost returning to normal. Right, first things first. She needed to pack a bag and then gather up all her personal belongings. The pictures on the mantle-piece, the few bright scarves she'd draped around to pretty the place up, her tea pot and cups, the oil burners and candles she used for her Reiki practice. Not a lot really. But then she was used to packing her life up into a few boxes and moving on, she tended to travel light. Ten minutes, tops. That's how long she needed to pack up and go. Grab Chili Dog and stuff her in the car and just go. It was only a matter of time before Alexander arrived. He knew where she lived, of that she had no doubt. Her missing photo was all the proof she needed.

Jay's confused face hovering over her as she sat in the car appeared in her mind's eye. His handsome face had been twisted with concern and regret. He'd tried to apologize to her, but she'd fobbed him off. And now she was never going to see him again. The thought caught her like a knife to the ribs. An ache of longing coursed through her. She'd miss him. For the first time in a long time—and she'd been doing this a very long time now—there was someone she cared enough about to miss once she moved on. And Viv, she'd miss Viv too.

But it was more than just affection she felt for Jay. It went much deeper than that.

Perhaps it was a good thing she was moving on. There was no way a relationship with Jay would've ever worked. And when she did finally leave—because she always did—it would've made it that much harder.

Okay, now she really had to get packing. Where the hell was Chili?

"Good evening, Serena."

The deep male voice chilled her to the bone and she stopped dead in her tracks. The use of that name from long ago brought bile rushing to the back of her throat. A shadow detached itself from the kitchen doorway and moved forward into the light. Ebony's knees buckled beneath her and her world swam precariously.

"Oh, my dear, do I still have that much of an effect on you?" Alexander Pallan came forward and caught her neatly under the arms before she crumpled to the ground.

"No." Her voice came out hoarse and thin and she wasn't even sure it was she who'd spoken. Her limbs were like jelly, they wouldn't respond to her demands.

"Come, let me help you to the couch." He steered her toward the tired old sofa and she dropped down into it without complaint. Shock, she was in the throes of deep shock. Her eyes roamed over Alexander's face almost against her will. She didn't want to look at him, yet, inexplicably, she couldn't look away. He hadn't changed, not now she could see him up close. The beard was long, reaching well past the centre of his chest, scruffy, like an old fisherman's beard. Apart from that, he was the same man. Still carried himself erect and tall, stalked along in that disapproving way, looking down his nose at everyone. Eyes as sharp as a raven and nearly as black. There wasn't an ounce of fat on him, he'd always prided himself on staying trim and lean. But there were small changes she could discern, now she looked at him in detail. Tiny pouches of skin had formed along his sharp jawline, softening his features slightly. Deep creases ran down through each cheek, dragging his mouth down in even more of a sneer. And one eyelid sagged almost imperceptibly over those irascible eyes. Perhaps life hadn't been as good to him as he'd once hoped it would be.

Ebony dragged in a large breath of air. Even though so much time had passed, that effect he had on her, the way he could turn her into a mindless idiot with one twitch of an eyebrow, was still there. An instinctive fear, ingrained deep within her bones. It'd never gone away, never left her, just hidden inside like a big fat toad, waiting to come out and trap her again. She was useless, weak, not worth his spit. A woman who trembled beneath his gaze. He owned her now, just like he'd owned her twenty-two years ago. Ebony curled into herself, trying to get away from his menacing presence. Her fingers knotted into the edge of the couch, gripping it tight, as if trying to anchor herself to her surroundings. How had Alexander got here before her? She'd only spent ten minutes at the most talking to Jay in town before she left.

Alexander must've come straight here as soon as he'd seen her leave the restaurant. He knew exactly where she'd go. Smart enough to hide his car, so she wouldn't suspect a thing. It was probably parked out back, behind the dilapidated garage. How stupid could she be? There was no way she was going to leave Chili behind and he knew it. He'd played on her weakness.

"Oh, by the way, your little furry companion is fine. She's just having a nice nap in the back yard."

Oh Jesus, he'd poisoned Chili Dog. Something in her spine tightened.

He might be able to cow her down like the weak, stupid woman she was, but how dare he touch her beloved dog. Chili was an innocent animal, her one true companion, loyal and loving. Ebony's blood began to boil.

"I just gave her a sedative," Alexander snapped, when he saw the look of defiance on her face. "I know how touchy-feely you are about your bloody animal friends, Serena. Do you really think I would've killed your bloody dog?"

Yes, she knew he would without a second thought. But he was also a very intelligent man. He understood that if he killed her dog, she'd be less likely to do as he asked. This way he now had her dog as a bargaining chip.

He was a manipulative, arrogant bastard who thought he could get anything and everything he wanted. But that hit of adrenaline, when she thought he'd killed Chili, had done the trick. She sat up a little straighter. That gullible teenager Alexander once knew didn't exist anymore. She left her behind when she'd found the courage to escape him. Now she was an independent, determined, self-confident woman. She just needed to start acting like one. Squaring her shoulders, she dared to stare at Alexander, catching him directly in the eye. His gaze narrowed as he studied her.

Another shadow came through the darkened kitchen door and Ebony drew back into the couch. Alexander followed her panicked gaze.

"Ah, meet, Corey. I'm sure you'll like him." It was the young man Ebony had seen standing next to Alexander on the road this evening. Who was he to Alexander? Some kind of protégé. Minion, sycophant, were other words better used to explain this kid's association with Alexander. There was no doubt he was under Alexander's sway. And he was probably the one who was good at hypnosis. Alexander liked to surround himself with people with interesting abilities.

"Nice to finally meet you, Mrs Pallan." The use of that name had her rocking back against the pillows like she'd been punched.

"I'm not Mrs Pallan. Never have been, never will be," she ground out between clenched teeth. The young man just smiled blithely back at her, unperturbed by her outburst. The name Serena Pallan had been the very first thing she changed the day after she'd fled her old life. She could never go back to that old name, not in a million years. Her anger gave her renewed energy and she found strength returning to her muscles. Gave her renewed determination. She wasn't about to go down without a fight.

In the light of the living room Ebony could make out the boy's long thin nose and his broad shoulders, stringy black hair pulled up into one of those ridiculous man-buns all the young kids were wearing these days. She guessed he might be seventeen or eighteen. Ebony narrowed her eyes, noting the similarities between the two. Perhaps even Alexander's son? The boy was built like an ox, not at all like Alexander's tall, thin frame, but there was something familiar in his face. And Alexander did love sowing his wild oats.

So, Alexander had brought back-up with him. Obviously more determined than ever to force her to come back to

Byron Bay. After all, how was she going to escape two men. Her mind started running scenarios anyway, desperate for a plan. Any plan.

Headlights lit up the closed curtains, flashes of bright light bouncing off the walls, and then the crunch of wheels on gravel announced the arrival of a car.

A savior! But the thought disappeared as quickly as it'd come. One glance at Alexander and she knew whoever this was, they were more likely to end up a victim than a rescuer. Alexander's brows drew down in a deep frown, the fire of an all-too-familiar rage building in his eyes. Even though she hadn't seen Alexander in over twenty-two years, his body language was still bright in her mind and those warning signs were a bad omen. She needed to act now to stop whoever was here from ending up dead.

"I'll get rid of them. Whoever it is." She jumped up from the couch and was halfway to the door before Alexander reacted.

"Yes, you do that," he replied thoughtfully. "But make sure you do it quickly and do it well. Anything goes amiss, or they catch wind of what's going on and …" Alexander didn't need to finish his sentence, he just pulled a shiny silver gun out from behind his back. Ebony froze at the sight of the weapon, the implications of how serious this had become sinking in. Alexander shooed a smiling Corey backward into darkened kitchen and they both disappeared into the murky gloom.

Holy fuck. She could feel two pairs of eyes on her back as she went to the front door and opened it a crack.

Oh no.

It was Jay.

She had to get rid of him. Now.

Opening the door a little wider, she plastered on a fake smile and kept her body wedged tightly in the gap between the doorjamb and door. There was no way he was getting past her. Jay slammed the door of his 4WD and stalked across the driveway, his figure sinuous in the near dark.

"Ebony, hello," he called as he looked up and spotted her waiting in the doorway. "Sorry to barge in on you like this, but we need to finish our conversation."

"Hi, Jay." She made her voice bright and unaffected. Had he heard that waver in her voice? God, she hoped not. "I was about to go to bed, can't this wait until tomorrow? I did promise I'd come and see you." She laced her voice with as much reproach as she could muster.

"I know, but the way you left tonight ... Something didn't feel right."

That's the last thing she wanted Alexander to hear. If he got any inkling Jay suspected there was something wrong ... Well, she'd just have to get rid of him, as fast as she could. The hand holding the door against her body trembled and she squeezed her fingers tighter.

Jay stepped onto the porch and into the light cast by the weak bulb. Stubble coated his square jaw. She hadn't noticed it earlier tonight, but now it made the fact he was tired and tousled more obvious. The lack of sleep showed clearly in the heavy lines on his face. As did the anguish evident in his tense lips and furrowed brow. Her heart twisted in her chest. She wanted to reach out and smooth the misery away from that sensuous mouth of his.

"I'm fine, Jay. Just tired," she said instead and covered her mouth to stifle a fake yawn.

"Are you going to let me in?"

She tried to smile sweetly, hoping it didn't look as wobbly as it felt, and said, "No. I don't think that's such a good idea."

"Look, Ebony. I'm sorry about what happened last night. But I promise you, I'm not a danger to you. It will never happen again." Her heart almost broke when she heard that. She hadn't had much time to digest everything that'd happened last night. He'd scared her, badly, but that didn't mean she couldn't forgive him. In time. To work with him on a solution. There was a strong physical attraction. And up until last night, there'd also been a much deeper connection as well. Right now, she didn't know how she felt about him. At the same time, it might be the opening she needed to get rid of him. If she drove him away by telling him she was afraid of him—if she could be convincing enough—perhaps he might believe her and actually go. His life depended on her being able to get rid of him. She needed to be horrid. Harsh enough to wound him. Then he'd leave. Resisting the urge to take a quick glance over her shoulder, she tensed her knees to stop them shaking.

"Well I'm not prepared to take that risk right now." His frown deepened at her words. She took a small step backward, closing the gap in the door slightly. "I'm not sure if I'll ever be prepared to take that risk."

"Ebony, please." His voice was a low growl and he took a step toward her.

"We should just end it right here and now. That's the best thing to do." Heinous, but she had to be despicable to him. Make him go away. What else could she say that'd hurt him so bad he'd never want to see her again? Her mind fumbled with different scenarios but couldn't come up with the perfect line.

Get rid of him. Just get rid of him. The words pounded like a hammer in her brain. That's when it happened. She lost focus for just a second. And her eyes automatically slid sideways, checking to see if Alexander was listening. As soon as she realized what she'd done, she snapped her eyes back front and centre but it was too late.

His frown of misery was replaced by one of thoughtful scrutiny.

"Are you sure you're okay, Ebony?" Tilting his head, he tried to see past her into the house.

Oh God. Oh Jesus. Get rid of him now. Or he was going to be shot and killed.

"I'm absolutely fine, Jay. Now will you just get off my property and stop harassing me before I call the police. Leave me alone. We're over. I never want to see you again. Do you understand?" With that she slammed the door in his face. *Please go. Please go. Please go.* Clasping her hands in front of her, prayer-like, she listened at the door. There was silence. She turned to face the kitchen doorway, the darkness glared at her, full of malice.

That's when she heard it. The slam of a car door and the engine starting. He was going. Thank God. She sagged back against the door. Headlights speared through the gaps in the curtains, as Jay backed the car out and turned around in the driveway, spinning the wheels in angry haste.

"Well done, Serena," Alexander's smooth voice said from the murky kitchen. "It would've been unpleasant to have to kill him. Bodies are always so damned hard to get rid of." His tall form appeared from the darkness, a greasy grin on his face.

She couldn't speak and made her way on wobbly legs back to the couch to sit down.

Jay was safe.

The words rolled around in her head, eclipsing everything else for now.

"That was an interesting little tête-à-tête you two were having. Very interesting."

The hairs on the back of Ebony's neck rose up. Alexander was nothing if not perceptive. He now knew Jay meant something to her. Was more than just a friend.

"What do you want, Alexander?" Ebony said, fatigue making her voice weak. Now that Jay was gone, her own precarious situation slammed back home.

"That's an interesting question," he replied. Stalking over to the single chair, he made himself comfortable, looking for all the world as if they were two old friends sitting down for a pleasant catch up. Corey lounged against the kitchen doorway, picking at a zit on his face. How could the boy be so blasé about this whole thing?

"Because I'm not really here for you. But you are a very nice bonus, I'll admit that, and I'll definitely take it."

What the hell did he mean by that? But she wouldn't give him the satisfaction of asking, so kept stubbornly quiet instead. He just chuckled and said, "It's actually your daughter who brought me here."

"What?" Ebony's mouth dropped open, unable to form words. Nothing made sense anymore. Her mind whirled like an out of control car and she couldn't fix on any one thought for longer than a second.

Alexander watched her like a hawk. Lapping up her response, getting high on her confusion and shock. Enjoying every second of her reaction. The fucking bastard.

"I got word she was traveling toward Margaret River, and I couldn't turn down such a great opportunity," he continued. "She's away from the protection of her home, much easier to grab that way. I never dreamed I'd actually get two for the price of one, but it's very fortuitous, wouldn't you agree?"

Then it hit her. That out of control car in her mind stopped spinning and instead shone bright headlights onto the truth.

"Jenna," she breathed.

It was Jenna he was after.

It all made such perfect sense now. Alexander hadn't been making his way to the restaurant tonight for her. He'd been coming for both of them. Jenna's talk about having special powers of her own. That niggling familiarity whenever she saw Jenna. Of course, she was her daughter. The baby she'd left behind all those long years ago. It was the name that'd stopped Ebony recognizing her. Her daughter had been christened Emily, but she must've changed her name at some stage. Possibly to escape the notice of her murderous father. Chills snaked down Ebony's spine.

"How did you find her?" Ebony was shattered that her ruse, her terrible sacrifice had all been for nothing. Running away, changing her name, abandoning her baby to a virtual stranger. All for nothing. It'd taken Alexander twenty years, but he'd still managed to track her daughter down.

"Ah, my dear, I have my spies everywhere. You should know that. Jenna came to my attention a year ago, and I've been keeping a close eye on her ever since. Waiting for her to make a mistake. And she did make a mistake by taking a little trip. Away from the safety of her friends and that blasted desert. I've been biding my time, waiting for the exact right moment to take back what is rightfully mine."

How in hell did Alexander think he was going to get past Dan? There was no way Dan was going to let anyone just up and abduct Jenna. He had a strong protective streak, that one. Her eyes slid to Corey. Ah, that's why Alexander had brought back up.

"Although I'm not sure if I want to welcome her into my arms as my long-lost daughter or teach her a lesson in manners first. She is a murdering bitch, after all. She murdered her half-brother, my son, Liam, and I need to take retribution for that. But it can wait. I'll have plenty of time once I get both of you back to Byron Bay to mete out my justice. You'll both need a little retraining, I can already tell from that uncooperative look in your eye, Serena."

What was he talking about? Ebony's mind was going to burst with all this overloading information, she didn't know where to start processing it.

"What do—"

There was a loud thump from the back door at the rear of the kitchen. Then Corey was thrown bodily forward and landed on the floor in front of her, emitting a single grunt of pain before he lay completely still. Ebony jumped to her feet.

And there was Jay, on top of him.

Jay had broken in through the back door and crash-tackled him to the ground. Alexander rose out of his chair as Jay disentangled himself from the inert form and levered himself off the ground, biceps bulging beneath his t-shirt. Fire and hate flashed in Jay's eyes, his face screwed up into an impressive grimace. If Ebony thought he'd been scary last night, it was nothing to how he looked now. Jay advanced toward Alexander. Ebony had to warn him. Jay might think he could take down the older man, but she knew better.

"Jay, watch out for—"

It was too late.

Alexander pulled out the gun and pointed it directly at Jay. The cords in Jay's neck stood out, thick as ropes. His eyes flickered toward her, but he kept the rest of his body completely still.

Ebony got up and took a step toward Jay before she stopped. A madman was pointing a gun at the man she cared for deeply. She couldn't risk him pulling the trigger. Oh God, this was going from bad to worse.

Corey gave a low groan and sat up, rubbing his head.

"Get up, you imbecile," Alexander growled.

"What happened?" the boy asked groggily.

"You didn't lock the back door after we came in, that's what happened." Alexander flicked a contemptuous gaze at the kid on the floor. "Now make up for some of that stupidity and go and get something to tie this guy up with."

Ebony still hadn't moved, only her eyes tracked between Alexander, Corey, and Jay. Why hadn't he just driven away, like she'd told him to? Why did he have to be such a goddamned hero? Alexander was going to kill him, he didn't like to leave loose ends. A small groan escaped her lips.

"Jay, I'm so sorry." Nothing she could say would ever make this up to him. Or let him know how deeply she regretted all this.

"You sure know how to pick them, my love. Fine looking specimen this one." The gray beard quivered as Alexander leered at her. "He'll do nicely as a hostage to keep you under control, though."

Corey came back into the room, a roll of duct tape in one hand, rubbing his head with the other.

"Hurry up, you great lump. Tie him up." Alexander waved the gun alarmingly at Jay. They both watched in silence as Corey tied Jay's hands, then dropped him pitilessly to the floor, where Jay landed with a loud thump, but still no sound came out of his mouth. Corey bound Jay's feet with the duct tape and then slathered a large bit over his mouth.

Jay lay completely helpless on the floor. Even though he strained against the bonds, his muscles bunching and tensing, he was completely vulnerable and exposed. It was up to her to protect him now.

Corey leant down and punched Jay straight in the face, eliciting a grunt of pain. Ebony gave a scream of shock.

"Sorry," he apologized. "An eye for an eye," the boy said, grinning. "No one gets the jump on me. You understand, don't you, mate?"

"Right, now you've had your fun, leave him alone." Alexander stared at Corey until he retreated to the doorway into the kitchen, where he once again took up his nonchalant position leaning against the doorjamb, his broad shoulders almost filling the doorway. Alexander sat back down carefully on the chair and motioned for Ebony to do the same. What else could she do, he still had the gun trained at Jay's head.

"So, let's come up with a little plan, shall we." Alexander leant back against the pillows in the chair and let his gaze rove over Ebony. Her skin crawled as his eyes touched her. "I wasn't expecting to get such a serendipitous gift when I came to Margaret River, but I do intend to take the utmost advantage of it." Those dark eyes softened ever so slightly as he looked at her. "You haven't changed a bit, Serena. Except for the haircut, which is easily fixed, you're the same woman who ran away from me twenty odd years ago."

She physically flinched every time he called her that name. It made her want to throw up.

"My name isn't Serena. It's Ebony," she said defiantly.

"Whatever, my dear." Alexander waved away her protest.

She cast a quick gaze down at Jay laying on the floor, trussed up tighter than a Christmas turkey. What must he think of all this? Wondering why he'd got himself mixed up with such a fruitcake. And her violent, egomaniacal ex-husband.

"Whatever you call yourself now, I'll look forward to having my wife back at my side." He grinned at her.

"I'm not your wife," she ground out between gritted teeth. "That sham of a wedding you conducted when I was too young to know any better wasn't legal in any way shape or form. I've never been your wife and never will be."

The ridges between Alexander's eyes deepened into a frown.

"I'm sorry to hear you think that way, Serena." He gave a sad nod of his head. "It was certainly legal in my eyes. Is that perhaps why you thought you could run away from me?

Because *you* didn't think we were legally wed? Hmm." Tapping a finger against his chin he stared at her for many seconds on end. Ebony watched, but the gun never wavered from its target, still trained on Jay. "Well I can certainly fix that little error of judgement." A gleam of perversity came into his eyes. "And what better time than the present to correct a mistake. Because I always admit when I've made a mistake."

Ebony had to stifle the snort that threatened to erupt at his words.

"Right, well it seems I have a plan now. Thank you so much for your insight," he said, giving a mock half-bow toward Ebony. "Corey, get over here."

Corey leapt forward from his spot in the kitchen doorway.

"Yep. What're we doing?"

It was almost pitiable, how eager this boy was to please Alexander. Especially after the appalling way he treated him. But then Alexander treated most people under his thumb appallingly.

"I'm going to go back into town. I'll be back by daybreak. I want you to look after these two while I'm gone. Are you capable of that small task?"

"You bet." The kid's spotty face was alight with the desire to please. "Whatcha doing in town?"

Alexander frowned and for a second Ebony thought he wasn't going to answer. But then he said, "I'm going to find a celebrant. Then I'm going to bring them out here, so they can marry Ebony and I legally, with all the pomp and ceremony she requires."

Ebony sat bolt upright in her chair. "I'm not going—"

"You're in no position to argue, my dear." All he had to do was smile slimily down at Jay's prone figure on the floor and Ebony knew she was trapped.

"Then we'll go and pick up your half-sister and be on our way back to Byron. How does that sound for a plan?"

"Brilliant, Dad, as usual." The kid smiled and Ebony groaned.

CHAPTER SEVENTEEN

"Dan? Are you awake?" Jenna rolled over in bed. Weak moonlight filtered in through the cabin window, creating unnatural shadows on the floor.

"Yeah, babe," Dan's muffled voice leaked out of the side of his pillow.

"We need to go and see Ebony. First thing tomorrow morning."

"Okay."

Dune lifted her head from the floor beside the bed at the sound of their voices. Normally they slept in a tent where ever they went. But they'd splashed out on a cabin while in Margaret River, to help Jenna through this terrible morning sickness. And for once she hadn't argued with him. The soft bed and the bathroom made it easier to bear the nausea. The caravan park didn't allow dogs in the cabins, but they'd smuggled Dune in anyway. Jenna never slept unless her dog was nearby.

"Something's wrong, I just know it."

This time it was Dan's turn to sit up and prop his head against the wall behind the bed.

"I can't get her expression out of my mind. You know when she saw that creepy guy out the window."

"Yep, I know." Dan rubbed his eyes and emitted a large yawn. "Have you actually had any sleep?" he queried. "Or have you been worrying yourself sick over this for the past …" he glanced at the digital alarm clock, "… Four hours?"

It was now three o'clock in the morning, but Jenna didn't allow the guilty twinge at waking Dan up keep her quiet for long.

Her mind was whirling with plans and schemes. They'd shocked Ebony with Jenna's declaration of her powers, but hadn't been able to convince her. Yet. She'd take Dune over to Ebony's house and then she'd see exactly what it was she could do. Jenna was starting to have an odd feeling about Ebony. A voice kept knocking at the door to her subconscious, wanting to be let in, but she couldn't quite hear what that voice was saying.

After the debacle of dinner at the restaurant, they'd wandered over to the gas station to talk to Jacko. When Jenna mentioned Ebony had done a fantastic job at healing her morning sickness with her Reiki, and she'd love to drop off a little thank you gift to her, Jacko had tapped his nose and bent in closer. Jacko said Ebony seemed to prefer her privacy and not many people knew where she lived, but he and Beau, a local surfer, had been talking because they'd been shocked to hear someone had agreed to rent that run-down heap of scrap metal that passed for a cottage out near Redgate Beach. Beau confided then he'd helped deliver an old table out there for Ebony a month or so ago. Jacko said he knew Jenna was the reliable type, and he didn't think Ebony would mind if he told her where she lived. Country people, sometimes they were too trusting for their own good. But Jenna wasn't about to look a gift horse in the mouth.

"Who do you think that guy was? The one across the road, with the gray beard?" Jenna had asked this at least a dozen times already, but it didn't stop her asking it again, because the answer remained just as elusive.

"Jenna," Dan sighed. Then he sucked in a fortifying lungful of air. "We'll ask around in town tomorrow. Okay?"

"I didn't like the way he looked at Ebony," she said.

"Yeah, well I didn't like the way he looked at you," Dan growled in reply. He rolled over onto his side and placed a hand on her stomach. "Don't forget what you've got growing inside you. This little baby is more important than anything else. I'm not going to let you get mixed up in other people's problems."

She baulked at his words. Even though he was right, it didn't sit well with her. She wasn't one to be told what to do. And she wasn't one to leave well enough alone, either.

"I need just to talk to her," she repeated stubbornly. "There's something more I need to ask her about, I just know it."

"I get it, really I do, Jenna. But could you please get a little sleep before we go hunting for bogeymen and saving lost souls."

She smiled at him in the weak moonlight. "I love you."

"And I you. With all my heart," he replied, gathering her up in his arms and kissing her gently on the lips.

But as Jenna lay down, her head pillowed on Dan's shoulder, she couldn't stop the memory of Dan's words surfacing. *"Didn't you notice how much you and her look alike,"* Now those words echoed in and out of the caverns of her mind, ringing bells that told her there was something she was missing.

Jenna's mother had abandoned her when she was only a year old. Jenna had never truly forgiven her for doing that and she'd never asked her adoptive father too many questions. And old Joe wasn't much of a talker anyway. Then, after she'd seen Liam kill Joe and she'd gone on the run to escape him, it became apparent she needed to know a lot more about her mother's past, so she could unravel her own situation. But by then she spent all her time and energy on the run, desperate to stay one step ahead of Liam, and she hadn't had the time or the resources to look for her.

But now? Was this what her subconscious had been trying to tell her? What this trip was all about? Had it led her here? To find her mother?

* * *

Stupid, stupid, stupid. He was so fucking stupid. Stupid to get caught. He'd allowed his fear for Ebony get in the way of clear, logical thinking.

And now look at him. Trussed and helpless. Fucking useless to Ebony or himself. He thought he'd taken enough time to survey the scene. Waited and watched and bided his time, like his military training had taught him. Taken stock of the two men before he made his move. But it'd never crossed his mind that either of these men held a weapon. Too long out of the military, he'd become too used to civilian life; had started to think like a civilian again. He'd been lulled into a false sense of security by the benign look of them. One of them was only a teenager—built like a brick shit house—but still only a kid. How was he to know the young kid was so bloody strong? And the other one, Alexander, hadn't looked the type to carry a gun.

Jay wriggled his hands beneath him experimentally. Nope, they were bound tighter than a gnat's ass. The tiles were cool beneath his arms, where he lay half on and half off the throw rug on the floor. The kid must know his stuff. And the kid manhandled him like Jay weighed practically nothing when he'd been strapping him up. Perhaps those muscles weren't all just for show.

Ebony sat slumped on the couch nearby, dejection written all over her pale face as she stared, unseeing, at the fireplace in the wall behind him. Both her hands had been bound with duct tape. At least they hadn't taped her mouth shut. He had to keep reminding himself to stay calm, breathe steadily in and out through his nose. He'd almost asphyxiated when the boy taped his mouth shut, couldn't seem to drag enough air in through his nostrils to feed his adrenaline-fueled heart and lungs. But now he was calmer, he was okay.

The kid sat over at the small kitchen table, shoveling food into his face, making disgusting slurping sounds. A loaf of bread lay on the table, along with a couple of tins of what looked to be tuna, a carton of milk and some fruit. Didn't the older guy feed his trained monkey? The gun rested on the table in front of him. But neither he nor Ebony were any threat to him at the moment. The other guy, Alexander, had left over half an hour ago. To get a celebrant from town, he'd said. There was only one celebrant in the small town of Margaret River, and Jay knew Paulette would be most displeased at being woken up at this late hour of the night, to be dragged out by some raving lunatic to perform a wedding ceremony. But there was no way Jay could get a warning to her. He hoped Alexander's search would prove fruitless. But something told him that man always got what he wanted.

He'd never felt so helpless in his whole life. Not even when Tom lay dying in his arms. This took the feeling of powerlessness to the next level.

Why did Alexander insist on calling Ebony Serena? It was a question only Ebony could answer.

Jay rolled over, so he was facing Ebony directly and made some muffled sounds to get her attention. Eventually, her glazed eyes wandered down to where he lay on the floor at her feet. He rolled his eyes at her in what he hoped was a suggestive way, and made more muffled sounds, indicating he wanted to talk to her. The light of understanding seemed to enter her eyes.

"Hey, Corey," she called.

The boy's head snapped up from the tin of tuna he was forking into his mouth.

"What?"

"Is it possible to take the gag off my friend here? I think he's suffocating." Jay picked up on Ebony's ruse and made groaning, snuffling noises.

"Nah, Alexander didn't tell me I could."

Jay took that to imply Corey never did anything unless Alexander told him to do it. Corey went back to slathering another slice of bread with butter.

"Corey, please." There was more strength in Ebony's voice this time. More pleading. And a slight hint of a sensuous undertone. Was she going to flirt her way into getting what she wanted? "I really think he might be choking. What if I promise neither of us will call out. No one will hear us out here anyway. You've seen how isolated this cottage is. Please, Corey." Yep, definitely more seductive tones in there. Would the boy pick up on her subterfuge, or was he too young and too dumb to see it? "I know you're in charge here, now Alexander's gone. And we both know you've got a gun and won't hesitate to use it." Ah, clever girl. Flattery was often the best form of persuasion. "I don't think Alexander will like it if he comes back and finds a dead body instead of a live hostage."

"Hmph." The boy's face turned serious as he considered her statement.

Jay ramped up his efforts to sound like he was having trouble breathing, rolling around on the floor as well.

Corey flicked him a concerned gaze. "Alright. But no hollering, okay? Otherwise it'll go back on."

"No, he promises. We both promise," Ebony agreed in a hurry.

The boy got up from the table, strode over to Jay, ripped the tape off in one malicious move and went back to sit at the table.

"Jesus Christ," Jay hissed. That hurt.

"Are you okay?" Ebony leaned forward in her chair, trying to get a little closer to him.

"No touching or anything like that," Corey warned.

"I'm not hurt, if that's what you mean. Well, not physically anyway. My ego is a little battered though. I thought these guys would be easy to take down, but I was wrong." It wouldn't hurt to keep playing Ebony's little game of stroking the lad's self-importance. He heard a muffled grunt of satisfaction from the table.

"How did you know something was wrong?" Ebony asked quietly. Corey stopped eating and cocked his head toward them, obviously interested in his answer, wondering what they'd done to tip him off. But it wasn't anything either Corey or Alexander had done, it was Ebony herself.

"I'm not sure I can explain it," he replied slowly. "Call it gut instinct. I just knew you were in trouble. I put two and two together." He was trying to tell her the way she'd acted earlier when he'd seen her in town, agitated and scared, had planted the first seeds of doubt in his brain. "So, I pretended to drive away, then I stopped a few hundred meters down the road, parked the car and came back on foot. When I peered in through the window, I couldn't see exactly what was going on, but I could see you talking to two men, and you didn't look happy. I thought I could take them both. But I didn't count on them having a gun—"

"Huh, you thought we were just stupid hicks, didn't ya?" Jay started as the boy's voice cut through his. "Well, Alexander's smart. He's the smartest man I know. And the most powerful. And soon he's going to have the two things he cherishes the most." Corey grinned then, and Jay saw just how young the kid was. Young and gullible. It was obvious, even to Jay, this boy had been indoctrinated by Alexander's rhetoric. Brainwashed into believing he was doing the right thing. "And I'll have helped him get that." The hero-worship shone from the boy's face. "He's going to love that I helped him."

"Alexander is your father?" Ebony asked gently.

"Yep," Corey answered with pride. "My mum's one of his favorites, you know. And so am I. All the rest of his kids are just losers." Corey beamed as if he'd been handed a precious jewel. This all sounded a little odd, cultish even. How many children did Alexander have? What the hell had Ebony been mixed up in back then?

"Oh, right. And do you still live on the farm outside Byron?" Ebony continued to probe.

"Yep, that's right. We even had to build another house last year. Our family's growing, big time."

"That's good to know." There was resignation in Ebony's voice.

She didn't really think this arsehole was going to drag her back to his place. Did she? What kind of sicko would chase after a woman for twenty-two years? Jay wished he'd had a chance to talk to Ebony about her past, and find out who or what this guy really was. One thing was for sure, if this dickhead had been the one to put those scars on Ebony's body—and he was pretty sure he was—then Jay wanted to hurt him. Badly.

Something occurred to Jay. No, it couldn't have been them? Could it? But then it would make a sick kind of sense.

"Hey, kid?" Jay called out. Corey turned his head to look at him, a bored expression on his face. "You wouldn't happen to have been rifling through my house the other night, would you?" The boy's face split into a baleful grin.

"How did you know?"

Jay shrugged, a move hampered by the ropes around his wrists. Ebony shot him a sharp glance, but he avoided her eyes. "I like to keep my stuff shipshape. I could tell a few things had been moved."

"Me and Alexander were real careful in your place. Not like when we came in here the first time. Alexander didn't want you to know. He was pretty riled up when he found out Ebony was hanging around with you. Wanted to find something incriminating on you. Wanted to keep an eye on you. But that bloody dog of yours wouldn't shut up, barking in the back yard all the time. We scampered before someone called the cops. Alexander didn't find anything *interesting*."

"Right." Well, at least he'd solved that little problem. At least he wasn't going crazy after all. Thank God for Axel. Who knows what he and Ebony might've come home to after the accident if Axel hadn't scared these two fruitcakes off.

Corey just sniggered and went back to stuffing his face.

* * *

Ebony wanted to groan with despair. It sounded like nothing had changed. If anything, Alexander had gotten more powerful, not less. Alexander was a rich man. Rich from money left to him by a grandfather involved in property development. But also rich from the funds of illegal dealings and criminal pursuits. He farmed marijuana on the large acreage he owned near Byron Bay, as well as being involved in other prohibited drug trading, and had connections to a couple of the local biker gangs. Ebony always suspected he had something to do with the black-market gun trade as well. Why he'd never been arrested by the police, Ebony would never know. But every year that went by made Alexander feel even more invincible. He lived life like some kind of middle-eastern sheik, with a harem of women at his beck and call, surrounded by people he could trust, all with equally disreputable pasts. He was a megalomaniac. Why was she the only person who could see that?

Her fingers were going numb, the tape around her wrists too tight. Wriggling them surreptitiously, she tried to ease them into a less awkward position. It was uncomfortable to have her hands tied behind her back, it pulled on her shoulders and the muscles in her back threatened to spasm every time she readjusted her arms. Her head also ached where she'd been hit by the surfboard the other day. But at least she was sitting up, her discomfort was nothing compared to Jay. He lay on the ground, tilted slightly to one side because he couldn't lie on his back. He grimaced every time he moved, as his weight added to the strain the bonds must've been putting on his shoulders. She needed to escape. They needed to escape. Before Alexander came back, it was their only chance.

Ebony studied Corey as he went back to eating his sandwich. He was certainly large and overly muscled, as if he spent every waking hour in a gym, lifting weights. How Jay had managed to overpower the kid was a wonder. Ebony had never seen Jay in a fight, but she suspected he could handle himself well, especially if you took in his years in the military. But even so, if he hadn't bashed Corey's head against the tiled floor, Ebony speculated whether Jay would've been able to defeat him. Each of Corey's biceps were thicker than one of her thighs. His neck was like a tree trunk. The baby face that sat atop the body of a man was more than a little incongruous.

The boy talked the talk. But did he believe everything he said? If there was even a grain of doubt in the kid's mind, Ebony might be able to manipulate it to her own advantage. Not that she ever liked to pass judgment on anyone, but Corey didn't seem the brightest card in the deck. Full of young bravado and brute strength, but also naive. She'd like to bet he struggled academically. He was still young. Even though he'd lived most of his life inside the walls of Alexander's house, being indoctrinated with his lavish lifestyle, perhaps he was fresh enough to have doubts. After all, what teenager didn't second-guess their parents, want to rebel against authority? She'd been able to see through Alexander's lies and deceit, so perhaps he could too.

It was his power of hypnosis that made him so special in Alexander's eyes.

The bones of an idea were forming in her head.

Her gaze rested on Jay for a long second. The bruise was darkening along his left cheekbone where Corey had punched him in retaliation. His square jaw jutted forward in a tense line and his eyes, almost indigo in the dim light of the living room, seemed to flash sparks of defiance. A tight lump formed at the back of her throat as she looked at him. So fierce and honorable, ready to leap to her defense, put his own life on the line to protect her from two madmen. And look where that'd got him. She sucked in a breath, suddenly filled with determination. She needed to do this. For him.

"I was thinking ..." she said and bobbed her head meditatively. "What will happen when we get back to Byron, and you're no longer Alexander's favorite?" She put on her most sweet, saccharine smile. Corey gave a loud snort, as if the idea was ludicrous. "Well, you are hunting his long-lost daughter, aren't you? The one he's been seeking for over twenty years. What if Jenna becomes his favorite instead?" Another derisive snort was all she got by way of an answer, but she wasn't finished yet, not by a long shot. How much did Corey know about her? Did he know she'd had no contact with her daughter since she'd left her as a baby; that she'd never set eyes on her until just the other day? She hadn't known until less than half an hour ago what a wonderful, bright, spirited woman her daughter was. It was a gamble, but she was betting the answer was no.

"Before, you said all Alexander's other children are weak and losers, is that right?"

"Yep. All useless as tits on a bull," he said with a happy smile, as if the fact was indisputable.

"Well, I happen to know Jenna is none of those things. She's an independent, strong-willed woman, who leads a successful life running a cattle station. She's definitely going to become his favorite." Should she mention Jenna's gift? Her ability with animals. Would that scare Corey, or not?

"Don't matter. Alexander's not going to change his mind about me," Corey replied, full of youthful certainty. But was that a flicker of unease she saw at the back of his eyes?

"Okay, if you say so." She gave a shrug, as much as her bonds would allow. "I was also wondering," she said, pausing as if to gather her thoughts. "If I'm going to marry Alexander, become his lawfully wedded wife ..." just the idea of if made her shudder uncontrollably, "... then will that make me his favorite, too? I mean, I'd hate to push your mum aside, if she is really his favorite. But you know how Alexander can get. He is very selective." It was hard, given how much she despised Alexander and what he stood for, but she managed to pour enough sympathy and compassion into her voice so she sounded relatively believable, as if she really didn't want to de-throne his mother. Would he understand what she was hinting at? Alexander could be most fickle when it came to his *favorites*, as Corey liked to call them. When your usefulness was up, Alexander was very quick to discard you.

Ebony had seen it time and time again in the two years she'd been with him. But even after he'd used and abused them, very few people—if any—left the farm. Alexander's biker contacts probably took care of that. In the whole time she'd been with Alexander, no one had dared leave. She'd heard rumors of one person who'd absconded. Stories told of another young woman who'd finally come to her senses, leaving in the dead of night, telling no one where she was going. And then she'd never been heard of since. There were plenty of rumors of what'd happened to the girl, but none of them had been proven, and at that stage, Ebony was still sure she loved Alexander. And he loved her. He would never do anything to hurt her.

Corey narrowed his eyes and she could almost see the cogs grinding in his head. It was obvious he hadn't thought that far ahead.

"Hmm," was all he said in reply. But he stopped eating to stare into space.

Jay rolled over on the floor at her feet and gave her a quick wink. She had to keep the conversation going. If he started to doubt Alexander enough, she may even be able to convince him to let them both go. Time to up the ante.

"Do you think Alexander will let my friend here go, once I agree to marry him?" This time she didn't have to fake the fearful wobble in her voice. "I can promise you, Jay won't say a word to anyone. He's very trustworthy. Isn't that true, Jay?" She glanced down at him and he gave an emphatic nod of his head, playing along with her little game.

"I give you my promise. On my dead mother's grave." Jay sounded so sincere, Ebony almost believed him herself. Was his mother dead? She'd have to ask him once this was all over.

Corey gave a non-committal shrug. "Dunno." But he eyed Jay with uncertainty.

"Oh God. He's not going to make you kill him, is he?" There was a nice little hint of hysteria in her tone now. She sat forward in the couch and surveyed the boy fixedly. "Did he bring you along as his executioner? To do his dirty work for him? Is that why you're here?"

"Don't be stupid, I ain't gonna kill anyone." The panicky look in his eyes told Ebony he thought it was the truth. Little did he know exactly how manipulative Alexander could be. "He just brought me to be, like, his bodyguard and stuff. He never said anything about killing anyone."

"You almost killed those people in the car, when you made the driver crash," she said quietly.

Corey's head snapped up. "Whaddya mean? I don't know nothin about that."

Jay gave her a curious look. He wouldn't know anything about her theory that both Beau and Bryce had been hypnotized. By Corey. Because she hadn't mentioned it. She'd just have to run with her theory and hope he continued to play along.

"I know what you can do, Corey." This wasn't completely true, she had no idea what he was capable of. Her only knowledge about hypnosis and what it could achieve gained by watching bad TV programs. But she knew she was right. He'd had something to do with it.

Corey shrugged and took a large bite of his sandwich, staring at her with thoughtful eyes. So he wasn't going to confirm it. But his weak denial told her everything she needed to know.

Then he surprised her by saying, "I shoulda known you'd figure it out. Alexander told me you'd never know in a million years that I caused the accident. But I didn't kill anyone." The defensive note was there for them both to hear.

The poor kid, he still thought he wasn't doing anything wrong, that he wasn't just Alexander's lackey.

"You must be really good at it. Some kind of hypnosis, is that what you do?"

"Yeah." The kid's chest seemed to expand at Ebony's words. "I'm good at it. Real good."

"So why did you cause the accident," she asked casually.

"Because we knew they'd call him out to go and fix it." Corey jutted his chin in Jay's direction. "And then we could take a look around his house while he was out. We didn't know you were going to be there, but it meant you were out of the way too."

It made sense. She hadn't even known Jay had suspected a break-in until he confronted Corey. If only he'd told her. But it probably wouldn't have made a difference anyway.

"What's the gun for then?" asked Jay in a cool voice, returning the conversation back to the original agenda.

"To make sure you do as he says," the boy replied.

"Don't be fooled by Alexander, Corey." Ebony sat up straighter on the couch, putting on her most teacher-like voice. "Didn't you hear him say how he hated to get rid of bodies? Mark my word, he's killed before. And he'll kill again."

At her words, Corey laid the sandwich down on his plate and pushed his chair away from the table. Then he got up and started pacing back and forth over the tiled floor.

"You're lying," he spat toward Ebony.

"I wish I were, Corey," she replied sadly. "Why else do you think I ran away from him?" When he turned to stare at her, she said, "Because I learned the truth about him. He's an abuser, a user of people to get what he wants. He's violent and unpredictable. A bully who thinks his money gives him immunity. And I couldn't live with that truth anymore."

"You're lying," he said again, but with much less force this time.

"Please, Corey, you have to believe me. Alexander is a liar and a cheat and a murderer. He'll use you to do his bidding, then throw you away when you're of no more use to him."

"Who do you think will go to jail if I turn up dead? It won't be Alexander," said Jay, matter-of-factly.

Were they getting through? Ebony wasn't sure. And even if they were, would they be able to convince him to let them go? His fear and worship of his father was deeply entrenched. It wasn't going to be easy to break through that wall. But she could see cracks forming.

An engine rumbled outside and the grinding of wheels on gravel announced a car had returned. Ebony's mouth went dry. It was Alexander. They were too late.

CHAPTER EIGHTEEN

"I'm going to cut off your fucking nuts off when I get free, you asshole."

Alexander scowled and pushed the swearing woman in the back to get her to move. "Just keep walking."

Paulette Charmers was the celebrant Alexander had *appropriated* to perform this sham of a wedding and she was one *very* unhappy woman.

Ebony almost smiled at the venom and sincerity in Paulette's voice. She believed the other woman would do what she threatened, if she ever got a chance. And Ebony would gladly help her do it.

Paulette had sworn at Alexander throughout the whole walk along the bush track up to the top of the headland until Ebony decided she really, really liked this woman.

Perhaps Alexander had bitten off more than he could handle when he'd kidnapped her. Tall and willowy, Paulette would've been maybe ten years older than Ebony, but she wore her age well. Her short, bobbed hair was modern and edgy, dyed a deep blue, which set off her dark kohl-ringed eyes. Three or four earrings sparkled in each ear, along with a diamond nose stud. A crisp white shirt and black dress pants completed her professional ensemble. Margaret River sure did attract some different types of people.

But it seemed Alexander had finally had enough of the noise when she continued her diatribe.

"Shut up, woman." He waved a hand in her direction. "Do something about that noise, Corey."

The kid walked forward to where Paulette was standing in the middle of the track and touched her neck, mouthing some words as he did so. Her mouth slammed shut with a click, then her eyes went wide with shock and confusion. Corey gave a low snigger at the surprise on the older woman's face, but then lowered his head and averted his eyes at the quelling glance Alexander sent him.

So that was how he did it. Ebony was suitably impressed at the boy's hypnosis abilities. He was really good. Which meant perhaps he had a gift for it. Much in the same way she had a gift for healing and Jenna had a gift with animals.

At least Jay was safe. For now. Alexander had left him trussed up and helpless, back at her cottage, saying he'd decide what to do with that little bit of aggravation later.

"This will do nicely," Alexander said as he turned in a slow circle to survey their surroundings. They were on top of a small headland, just south of Redgate Beach, around a fifteen-minute walk from Ebony's cottage. They stood in a small clearing, surrounded by low scrubby bushland. Below them, waves crashed noisily at the bottom of a cliff face. This was a rudimentary lookout, made by the many feet of the people who trekked the popular Cape to Cape walking trail. Alexander strolled to the edge of the cliff and peered down. It was a ten-or-twelve-meter drop; the height of a three story building straight down into the swirling water. Pity there were no walkers out this early in the morning. But even if there were, Alexander could get Corey to easily take care of any unwary hiker passing by. After he hypnotized them, they'd just keep right on walking, with no memory left behind of anyone standing on this tiny lookout.

"And just look at that sunrise. Spectacular." He breathed in deeply, his chest puffed out in arrogant delight.

Ebony's gaze wandered to the orb of molten light peeking over the edge of the scrubby headland. Then she turned back to the water. There was very little swell, the sea flat and calm, almost peaceful. At odds with her inner churning emotions. Not a good day for surfing. Normally there'd be a few surfers hanging around in the breaking waves, waiting for that perfect set. Not this morning, however. They were the only people around for miles and miles.

Up till now, she hadn't noticed her surroundings, instead completely focused on Alexander and his crazy demands that she take them to a pretty place where they could be married at sunrise. The fate of Jay, and now Paulette rested in her hands.

"Sunrise, the start of a new day," she said absentmindedly.

"That's exactly right, my dear," he replied in surprise. "Thank you for finding this most perfect spot for our wedding." He came up and laid a hand on her shoulder, which she tried to shrug off, without success. "Right, Corey, get over here, and bring that celebrant. We need to get this ceremony under way, before we lose this wonderful morning light."

Corey took Paulette by the shoulders and steered her to a spot in the middle of the clearing. She fought him and he almost had to push her into position, but she could still only make muffled sounds through her clamped lips. Then Corey dumped a backpack off his shoulders and pulled out a tiny folding camp table Ebony used as a side table in her cottage, draping it with one of her bright orange scarves that'd hung over the mantle-piece. The celebrant's book and pieces of paper and a pen were also placed on top of the table. Corey took a few steps back until he stood on the outer ring of the clearing. What was going through the kid's mind? Had any of what she and Jay said to him earlier sunk in? It was impossible to tell. As soon as Alexander appeared back at the house any sign of uncertainty or rebellion had disappeared behind his dark eyes and spotty features. And now Corey stood off to one side, watching the proceedings.

Panic clawed its way up her throat. There was no way she was going to do this without a fight. But Alexander held Paulette as leverage against her. If she didn't do what Alexander wanted, all he had to do was threaten to kill her. Plus, Jay was still in the cottage. What would he do to him if she didn't comply?

There must be a way out of this. She couldn't let Alexander claim dominion over her again. She wasn't going back with him. Not as long as there was breath in her body. But she couldn't allow other people to be hurt. Ebony's mind raced from scenario to scenario, trying to find an answer to her dilemma.

A tiny flicker of something, a memory, flared at the back of her mind. She'd only ever used her power, the energy running through her, to heal. But could she use it to hurt as well? It was an intriguing thought and one Ebony had never considered before today. Was there any way she could turn Reiki to her advantage? Her fingers wanted to stray up to her Kyanite stone necklace, but her hands were bound, so she touched it with her mind instead. The smooth stone always sat snug and warm in the hollow of her throat.

No, she wouldn't do that. She could never taint her ability to heal by using it in a dishonorable way. No matter how much she despised Alexander. No matter how much she wanted to save herself. Could she?

"Look, my dear. I picked these for you on the way here." Alexander produced a posy of wildflowers from beneath his long coat with a theatrical flourish. "Your wedding flowers. How appropriate they come from the very bush that surrounds your little cottage. I'm sorry I couldn't do any better, but under the circumstances …"

It was quite a pretty bunch of flowers, with bright yellow balls of wattle, clusters of the little pink pimeleas, mixed in with some paler pink, almost white, verticordias, or featherflowers. The flowers were beautiful, and if they'd come from anyone else—Jay perhaps—she would've accepted them with delight, but it was what they represented that made her want to vomit.

"Picking wildflowers is illegal here," she said coldly. Not that a minor detail like that would ever worry Alexander. "You'll have to untie my hands if you want me to hold them."

"Certainly." Ebony saw the quick look he flashed at Corey, warning the boy to beware if she tried to flee. But she knew she wasn't going anywhere, not with two other people relying on her. "Shall we make Ms Charmers more comfortable too?"

Alexander flashed a small knife from a pocket deep inside his cloak and cut the tape around Ebony's wrists, quickly moving to free the celebrant's hands as well.

"There, isn't that better?" He smiled benignly at them both. Paulette shot daggers at him with her eyes, her mouth still locked up tight. "And just in case either of you get any silly ideas …" Alexander patted the bulge in his pocket with a smile. The gun. He'd made a show of putting it in his pocket back at the cottage, letting them know it was there. He waved a hand at Corey, and the kid went over to the celebrant and whispered something in her ear. Paulette sucked in a few deep breaths as the sway of his hypnotism left her, but she didn't speak, just pushed the hair away from her face and glared at the boy.

Alexander handed the posy of wildflowers to Ebony and indicated she stand off to one side of the clearing, nearer the cliff edge, and went over and offered Paulette her ceremonial book.

"Now this is going to be a nice, pleasant ceremony, with no angst or trouble. Ms Charmers will read the short civil ceremony I've chosen. Corey, have you got the rings?" Alexander didn't bother to look at Corey as he spoke, but perhaps if he had, he might've seen the look of sullen dissatisfaction Corey flashed in Ebony's direction. Was he finally coming to understand the ramifications of what was about to happen? Alexander had pilfered the rings from her jewelry collection, telling her he'd buy them both matching rings—rings befitting their union—when they got back to Byron Bay. "Serena, you will say nothing else, beside the words the celebrant gives you. Then I'll kiss my bride, and we'll head back to the cottage. Understand?" His dark eyes bored into her, then moved to Paulette's face. "The sooner we get this over and done with, the sooner you can get back to … well, whatever it is you normally do, Ms Charmers." Alexander waved a perfunctory hand in her direction and she glared back at him.

Was Alexander going to let Paulette go after the ceremony? Ebony's gut twisted with relief. She guessed he'd get Corey to do some of his magic and Paulette wouldn't remember a thing. The other woman's hands were clenched so tightly around her book it looked like she might crack it in two, but she did finally give him one curt nod. Poor woman. Ebony didn't blame her, she would've done exactly the same thing under the circumstances. Paulette had no choice but to obey.

Alexander faced Ebony, taking her hands in his. Every cell in her body screamed to snatch her hands back from him. The feel of his dry papery fingers on hers made her stomach roil. The smile on his face was horrible to see. He truly believed he was doing the right thing, that Ebony belonged to him and he was just reclaiming a lost possession. She swallowed hard.

Run. Run away, her mind screamed. She glanced at the celebrant, who was flicking through pages in her book. Then Jay's face came to focus in her mind. She couldn't run. For their sakes.

"Welcome one and all," Paulette began. She didn't lift her head as she spoke, just kept going in a monotone. "We gather here today to celebrate the wedding of Alexander and Serena."

Dear God. No. The word echoed in Ebony's head, but the rest of her body was numb with shock, no longer able to respond to her screaming mind.

"Marriage is perhaps the greatest and most challenging adventure of all human relationships. No ceremony can create your marriage. Only you can do that—through love and patience; through dedication and perseverance …"

Ebony's mind switched off, not wanting to hear the rest of what Paulette said. What was she going to do now? She couldn't possibly go ahead with this sham wedding.

* * *

Jenna was completely engrossed by the scene playing out in front of her. Hunkered down in the dense underbrush, she, Dan and Jay had crept the last few hundred meters on hands and knees through the spiky scrub. Ebony and the man she now knew as Alexander stood with the celebrant in a macabre tableau. She couldn't believe the gall of this man, forcing Ebony to marry him. Treating her like she was some sort of possession.

She focussed sharply in on Alexander—her biological father—sketching his profile, embedding it in her synapses. The long beard, the hawk nose, the terribly intense black eyes. The second she'd heard his name slip from Jay's lips she knew who he was.

He was her father.

Which meant that Ebony *was* her mother. The fact they looked so alike, that they both had similar powers, and that Alexander was claiming her back as his wife.

Thank God Jenna couldn't sleep this morning. Thank God she'd dragged Dan out of bed even before the sun had risen, with a premonition something was wrong.

"I need to see her," she'd told Dan urgently. "Something's wrong. Don't ask me how I know, I just do." Thankfully he knew her well enough not to argue. He was familiar with her quirks and foibles.

It was only a twenty-minute drive, taking in the few wrong turns they made down the maze of dirt roads running off Caves Road, before they pulled up outside the hut. Dune had whined from the back of the car, telling her she smelled something foreign and wrong.

"I hope she's an early riser," Dan had commented drily. "Or she's going to get a hell of a shock when we knock on her door this early in the morning." But there'd been no answer to their rapping on the front door. It remained quiet and still, as if no one was home. Dan wanted to leave, but Jenna followed Dune around to the back of the house and that's when they'd found the hire car, a brand new SUV parked out of sight behind the old garage at the back of the house. And then Dune's sharp bark of alarm had Jenna running toward what looked to be a dog kennel in the overgrown back yard. A dog lay chained up and motionless on the ground, Dune standing guard over her body. Her breath hitched in her throat. Was the dog dead? Had someone killed Ebony's dog? But no, she was warm to the touch and Dune assured Jenna she was just asleep.

Jenna's guts churned, and she took one look at Dan's worried face, then they both raced to bang on the back door. When there was still no answer, Dan stepped off the back porch and peered through a window and saw a man trussed up like a pig awaiting slaughter, lying on the kitchen floor. Dan broke through the door, shoving against it with his broad shoulders until it gave way.

As soon as Dan ripped the tape from the man's mouth, he started talking, imploring them to cut him loose. He kept saying he needed to save her, and he was going to enjoy killing that mother-fucker. Dune wouldn't leave the man alone, kept licking his face with delight. Jenna got the impression this man was a lover of dogs and a friend of Ebony's, so he must be okay.

"Calm down, Dune," Dan finally commanded as he struggled to cut the man's bonds. "You're making this impossible."

"What's your name?" Jenna asked.

"Jay, I'm a ... good friend of Ebony's."

The way he hesitated over that word had Jenna wondering, but she let the thought drop when his next words struck her right in the solar plexus.

"Wait till I get my hands on that fucking bastard, Alexander and his lackey kid, I'm gonna—"

"Wait, what did you say?" Jenna had an urgent need to sit down.

"He was taking them up to some headland. He thinks it's okay to abduct a woman against her will and—"

"Stop!" Jenna commanded. "What name did you say before?"

"Alexander? That fucker."

Her breath froze in her throat.

Dan's face blanched as he picked up on the significance of the name. "It couldn't be, could it?" he asked.

Jenna just nodded. This was too much of a coincidence. The name of the man who'd sent Liam to hunt her down had been Alexander. The name of her biological father.

Dan worked quickly to free Jay's hands and feet and the man sprung up as soon as he was cut loose. Even through her fog of confusion, Jenna couldn't help but notice he was good-looking. Tall, broad shouldered with a square jaw, and piercing blue eyes.

"I have to stop them," he said, but then stumbled and nearly fell against Dan.

"Your circulation was cut off by the tight bonds," Dan said, taking hold of his elbow. "Give it a few seconds to get the blood flowing again."

"Yeah, yeah," Jay answered impatiently. He cast them a sideways look. "Who are you guys anyway?"

"Ah ..." How did she answer that one? "It's complicated," she replied. "Let's just say we're Ebony's friends, too. Friends who want to help."

Jay stared at them both for many long seconds, that penetrating gaze seeming to cut right through her, before he finally said, "I'm gonna need all the help I can get, so I'll let you help. For now."

That got Jenna's blood flowing and a flush of anger rose up her face. "I beg your pardon? You'll *let* us help?"

Dan stepped in. "No time to argue now, kids. Do you know where they went?" he asked even as he headed toward the door.

"I've got a pretty good idea," Jay replied.

"Dune can show us," Jenna hissed at Dan's back as she followed him out the door.

Then he stopped and turned to face her, both hands coming up to grasp her by the shoulders.

"I don't suppose there's any way I can talk you out of coming with us, is there?" His blue eyes bored into hers, concern etched into the tiny lines around his mouth.

"I promise I'll be careful," she replied. "But this is our chance. You know if we don't do something about him … Alexander, then we might never be free of him."

"Yes, I realize that. But what about our baby?"

"If I'm right, then that's my mother out there," she said in a small voice. "Do you honestly think I'd let a chance to know my mother after all these years—to save her from that madman—just slip through my fingers?"

"No, I guess not," he sighed. "But, please, please be careful." He pulled her into a tight embrace. It only lasted a second, but it was enough to show her he was shaking. Not with fear for himself, but fear for her. And their baby.

"I love you." She gave him a quick, fierce kiss.

"I love you too, babe."

"Ah hum." Jay cleared his throat behind them, interrupting their intimate moment. "Alexander has a gun, so we need to be careful," Jay said as he led the way out through Ebony's back yard and onto a small track leading out through the dunes. "The kid, Corey also has some kind of … I'm not sure what to call it. Power of hypnosis or something like that. Whatever it is he can do, it didn't seem to come as any surprise to Ebony."

"Thanks for the heads-up," Dan replied.

They'd jogged quickly and silently up the bust track. And now, here she was staring at her nemesis through the branches of the thick coastal scrub.

And her mother. It seemed impossible she'd found her mother. The idea just wouldn't sink into her mind properly. But there she was, standing in the flesh and blood. Very, very real. Up until now, the idea of her mother had been an ethereal one at best. She had no real clue as to what she looked like, her personality, her favorite color, any of those things. Ebony had left no photos, nothing that would identify her when she'd left Jenna in Joe's hands. So Jenna made up a fantasy mother—who was by no means perfect, because what kind of mother abandons her baby after all—but she was still there in her mind. Would Ebony match that person she'd created in her head?

Only one way to find out.

Dune was off to her left, laying low in the bushes, panting softly, a growl rumbling deep in his throat. Jenna told him to stay out of the way, unless she specifically called for him. She didn't want him getting shot by Alexander. Dune didn't like her orders, but had agreed to obey, for now.

Jay said he'd lead the charge on this mission. He'd filled them in on his army experience on the way up here, and Jenna was happy to let him use his considerable knowledge of the art of warfare and taking down an armed opponent. Jay wanted Dan to concentrate on immobilizing Corey, while he concentrated on Alexander. They were all armed with makeshift weapons. She had a hammer, Dan was wielding a crowbar and Jay a metal bar he'd found lying in the back yard.

Jenna touched the pink sapphire ring hanging around her neck. Jenna's encounter with Liam had shown her how terribly wrong things could go in the space of a heartbeat. She'd nearly lost everything and everyone she cared about to Liam. And now a similar scene was about to play out again, right in front of her.

But they had the weapon of surprise on their side, Alexander wouldn't be expecting. Alexander had a gun. But Liam's gang also had guns, so it wasn't a new prospect to Jenna. And she and Dan managed to prevail that time. She'd just have to let things play out.

Casting her gaze through the shrubbery, she found Dan a couple of meters off to her right. His brow was clenched in deep frown lines of concentration, shoulders hunched beneath his chambray shirt, ready to spring up at the first signal from Jay. As if he felt her gaze on him, he turned his worried frown toward her, blue eyes dark with agitation. He would undoubtedly make sure he was first into the fray if anything happened. To make sure he protected her. But at the moment it was all a stalemate as they watched and waited.

The celebrant was reading aloud from her book, reciting the beginnings of a wedding vow. If they didn't stop this soon, Ebony would be married to this monster.

CHAPTER NINETEEN

Jay's heart was beating so loud, he was sure the four people standing in the clearing ahead of him could hear it. Paulette was closest, the back of the celebrant's legs were only a few meters in front of him. Thank God they hadn't heard them creeping through the bushes. The sound of the waves smashing themselves against the rocks below was loud in the still morning air, which helped cover any noise they'd made.

Paulette had already started reading the ceremony. Jay could only see her back, but even from that little piece he could tell she was really, really pissed off. Jay knew Paulette from the VFRS, and she was a formidable woman, independent and stubborn, who didn't take kindly to anyone telling her what to do. He was surprised she was even giving in to Alexander's demands. There was no way the Paulette he knew would've gone along with this. There was little doubt Paulette was being manipulated by Corey in some way. How did the ... hypnosis work? Could he only control one person at a time? Did he have to touch you to make it take? There was only one way to find out.

His military brain assessed the situation, even as he weighed up Paulette's predicament. But he knew he wasn't looking at this as objectively as he should. How could he, when it was Ebony's life at stake. Corey was going to be his biggest problem. If Dan could overpower him, then Jay would get the jump on Alexander. Why Corey was still going along with this sham wedding was anyone's guess. He was like an obedient puppy. This man, Alexander, exuded a certain type of charm, had an enticing aura around him, much like a cult leader. In Corey's eyes, his father could do no wrong. He'd seen this kind of blind loyalty many times while he'd been in the army. Mainly by the Taliban followers.

The biggest risk was Ebony herself. If Alexander saw them coming, there was a high probability he'd use Ebony as a hostage or shield, or both. How was he going to protect her? If only he could let her know he was here, to be ready for an intervention.

Dan looked strong, capable, and dependable. He wasn't so sure about the girl, Jenna. She was petite and willowy. But Jay knew you couldn't always judge a book by its cover, and there was an inner determination, a glint in her eye that suggested she wouldn't give in easily. There was also an uncanny resemblance between her and Ebony. He'd noticed it for the first time when she'd turned in profile to stare out the window, just after they'd released him from his bonds. Now, as he looked over to where she hunkered low in the bushes, he could see it again. Ebony's hair was short and dark, while Jenna's was long and blonde. But there was something in her high cheekbones, and the tilt of her upturned nose, the shape of her large eyes.

Jay switched his attention back to the people in the clearing. It needed to be now or never. If they waited much longer the ceremony would be over. Then Alexander would be married to Ebony. A strange wave of jealousy rippled through him. It made his gut burn with a loathing for Alexander as well as a desperate need to rescue Ebony from his odious clutches.

Ebony and Alexander stood facing each other near the cliff edge, her face in profile. She stood completely still, like a statue. But he could see she was as taut as a bowstring, every muscle clenched, as if ready to take flight at the slightest provocation. Her knuckles were white where she pulled back against Alexander's grip, gaze directed blankly over his shoulder. Jay's heart lurched as he watched her. He wanted to rescue her from marriage to a man she clearly despised. But there was more to it than that. Not only did he want to rescue her for herself; he wanted to rescue her for him as well. He wanted to be the man standing up there with her.

It was time to do this. A quiet calm filled him, a strange phenomenon he'd noticed when he'd been in the army, right before they commenced a raid, or were expecting an ambush. He'd formulated a plan of sorts, now they all just had to stick to it. He raised a hand quietly above his head, three fingers held in the air and waited until Jenna and Dan were looking at him. They both nodded to show they understood. He counted down with his fingers. Three. Two. One. Go.

Jay sprang to his feet and shoved his way through the last few feet of coastal scrub. Branches and spiky leaves scratched and tore at the bare skin on his arms and face, but he paid the burning pain no mind. He grunted with the effort of breaking through the thick tangle of bush, intent on making it to the clearing. The noise of his charge broke through the calm morning air like a knife slicing through butter. Jay could hear Dan doing the same thing further around the small clearing, heading for the hulking teenager, Corey.

Alexander glanced towards Jay when he heard the noise. He took precious seconds to comprehend what was happening. Jay was counting on his huge ego and vast arrogance to slow down his reactions. Alexander would never have dreamed anyone would dare attack him, certainly not in his moment of triumph. His black gaze zeroed in on Jay, pure hatred spearing through those dark depths.

Out of the corner of his eye, Jay saw Dan crash-tackle Corey to the ground, where the two men scrabbled and fought in the dirt. Paulette stopped reading and stared at him, mouth agape.

And then Jay stopped in his tracks, just as his feet hit the gravel of the clearing. Alexander had pulled his gun, as Jay suspected he might. Jay had been prepared for that, knew he might have to duck and weave, counting on a civilian not being a very good shot. Having surprise on his side, Jay was sure he could cross that distance and take him down, no matter what. Even if it meant he took a bullet.

But Alexander wasn't pointing the gun at Jay.

He had the gun to Ebony's temple instead.

Jay had underestimated him.

Fuck. No, no, no.

Ebony gasped, but said nothing. She didn't need to. The expression on her face said it all. She was terrified.

Alexander's face split into an odious grin. The sound of the other two men fighting reached Jay's ears, but he couldn't tell who was winning. The flash of a blue shirt caught the corner of his eye and then Jenna was there, going to Dan's aid.

Alexander's grin got even wider. "Well, well, well. It seems the whole family has turned up. Thank you, Jenna, for doing me a favor. Now I don't have to come and find you. Most accommodating of you."

Jay took a stealthy step forward while the madman's attention was on Jenna.

"Give it a rest, hero," Alexander said scathingly. "It'll take someone with a lot more intelligence than you to beat me."

Jay could still hear scuffling and grunting from the other side of the clearing, and then Alexander said, "Come on,

Corey, I'm waiting. I didn't bring you along just for your witty conversation."

"Got him," said Corey, his breath coming in raspy gasps.

Dan was lying on the ground on his stomach, with Corey twisting one of his arms painfully up his back, holding him immobile. Jay could only watch it all unfold like a spectator in a movie theatre. Corey must've used his hypnosis thing, because Dan suddenly stopped struggling and lay deathly still. Paulette froze, watching. Either unable or, unwilling to move.

"Dan!" Jenna surged forward, almost on top of Corey now.

"Stay right where you are, young lady," sneered Alexander, "or your mother dies."

"You bloody well let my husband go, you great oaf," Jenna snarled, but stayed where she was.

"So feisty," mumbled Alexander. Was that admiration in the lift of his eyebrows? "I love that a daughter of mine has such gumption. Even if you did murder my son. Your half-brother. Did Liam tell you that before you killed him?"

Jenna didn't answer.

"Ah well, I think I might forgive your transgression, now I've seen what an amazing woman you've turned out to be. I can't wait to get you back to Byron Bay."

The man was practically crooning, and it sent shivers of nausea through Jay. Just what did Alexander plan to do with his wife and daughter if he managed to follow through on his plan?

"No." The word fell so softly from Ebony's lips, Jay almost didn't hear it. She swiveled to look at Alexander, then Jenna, and finally Jay.

"Don't you dare." This time her voice was stronger. "Don't you dare destroy everything that's precious to me."

"Just watch me," Alexander sneered. "I own you, Serena Pallan. Always have, always will. I'm just taking back what's rightfully mine. You and your feisty daughter here will do exactly what I say."

* * *

Jenna yelled something at Ebony.

"What?" Ebony didn't understand. There was too much going on, her mind was a hurricane. What was she talking about? Oh God, Jenna was her daughter. That thought threatened to eclipse all others.

And Jay was here. He was in terrible jeopardy. Again. Had come to her rescue. Again. Stupid man. Wonderful man. Gorgeous man. She was more worried about him than she was about herself. And she was the one with the gun at her head. Would Alexander actually kill her? The answer sent shivers down her spine. Yes, he would, if she didn't give him what he wanted.

Then Jenna held something up in one hand. It glinted and flashed in the early morning light, sending out shards of pink luminescence. Something twigged in the back of Ebony's mind. A pink sapphire. She'd given that ring to Jenna. Left it tucked away in the blankets of her cot when she was only a tiny baby, on the day she'd run away. This ring was priceless, given to Ebony by her own mother. For some reason, it called to her, felt like it belonged to her. To her daughter.

Automatically, Ebony reached up to touch her own Kyanite gem.

Alexander must've seen Jenna's ring and his breath hissed in sharp and dangerous over his teeth.

"You bitch. You give that back to me." He took a menacing step toward her daughter, before he remembered he had the gun to Ebony's temple. "That was stolen from *me*. By her." He jammed the gun barrel against her head, hard, and Ebony gave an involuntary whimper.

It wasn't true, the ring had belonged to her when she met him. But Alexander always had an eye for anything of value, and after the first few months with him, Alexander had taken the ring away from her *for safekeeping*. It was the one thing she'd been determined to retrieve when she escaped his clutches. And now she had the answer to one of her many questions regarding her daughter. Yes, Jenna wore her ring. The thought that Jenna had kept it safe after all these years lifted Ebony's shattered heart.

"Give that to me, this instant." Like lightening, he swiveled the gun and pointed it at Jenna. Oh God, Alexander was going to shoot her.

She lunged forward, shoving him and the gun went off. The gunshot so loud, so close, she was stunned for many seconds. Alexander stumbled in the direction of the cliff but regained his feet. At the same time, Jenna's dog, Dune, emerged from the bushes, snarling like a banshee, standing in front of Jenna, guarding her.

"What the fuck …?" Alexander's face was a mask of rage, eyes tight and tiny like a pig, mouth twisted into a grimace.

Jenna cried out. Her gaze was fixed on Jay. He was lying on the ground, blood spurting from his lower leg. The bullet. When she'd knocked Alexander off balance, the bullet had missed Jenna, but hit Jay instead.

Jay's face was contorted with pain, but he was trying to get up. Trying to come to her aid.

Alexander face twisted and he raised the gun again. "I've had enough of this shit."

The dog snarled and looked as if he were going to leap at Alexander's throat.

As if snapping out of a dream, Paulette ran over to where Jay lay, ignoring Alexander and his gun. She put pressure on the wound and told him to stay still or he'd make it worse.

"Corey, do something about your fucking sister, will you," said Alexander, and Corey gave a start, as if he'd been watching in a trance. He'd probably never seen anything like this before in his life.

Dune raced across the clearing and landed on Corey's chest, knocking him to the ground. The kid went down like a sack of potatoes. He hit the ground with a small puff of dust the dog on top of him, mauling him. Corey's screams where terrible to hear. Finally, Jenna uttered a few words and Dune stopped ripping into him, instead staring down at the boy on the ground, snarling as if daring him to move.

Jenna started toward her husband ignoring the gun Alexander was aiming at her. But Ebony knew him better, knew he wouldn't miss the second time. He was going to shoot her daughter.

She did the only thing she could think of and jabbed her elbow into Alexander's stomach. She had to stop him. Had to take his focus away from Jenna. He stumbled back a few steps, close to the brink of the cliff now, and grunted. Eyes like molten lava turned toward her. But when he raised the gun again, it was still pointed at Jenna.

"You fucking whore. You're just like your mother." He stared at Jenna. "If you won't obey me, then I will kill you." Black eyes pierced through Ebony, right to her very soul.

Her heart stopped beating in her chest. She was terrified of him. Terrified of the control he had over her. Terrified of what would happen to her if she went back to Bryon Bay with him. She'd been running away from him for over half her life. Had abandoned her baby so he'd never find her. But most of all, terrified he was going to hurt Jenna.

It was time for this to end.

But he was never going to stop until he got what he wanted.

So, she was going to finish it for him. For her. For her daughter.

She lunged at Alexander.

Jay yelled, but it was too late. She was doing this. And if she died, then it would be worth it to save them.

She crossed the space between them, hands held out in front of her and rammed Alexander like a bull at a stevedore. He was big, tall, strong and solid. Her palms collided with his chest and it was like hitting a brick wall. One of her hands slipped upwards and she raked the skin of his neck beneath her fingernails as he let out a grunt of surprise. He grabbed her arm, tight, and his grunt turned into a yell as they both careened backward.

Toward the cliff edge.

For a second, time stopped as they teetered, then his back foot slipped over the edge and they fell, entwined together.

* * *

Ebony was drowning.

There was no oxygen left in her lungs. All the air had been knocked out when she smashed into the water. Her nostrils filled with burning saline water as a wave broke over her head. The cliffs towered above, blocking out the sky, and she could hear the waves as they broke into a million pieces, shattering against the base. Her body hurt all over. It hurt to move. It hurt to try and gasp a breath, reach for the surface.

Frothing waves kept crashing into her, the ocean rising up against her, determined not to let her pass.

Alexander. Where was Alexander?

Another large wave broke over her head and this time she felt herself being driven down into the depths. Adrenaline coursed through her body as she floated deep beneath the iron-gray surface.

Ebony struggled upwards, but her flailing arms and legs made slow progress.

Something grabbed her by the ankle.

Alexander.

He was pulling her down.

238

She turned and kicked out at him. She could just make out his face through the murky water. It was a mask of fear. The heavy coat he loved to wear, the one he thought made him look so suave and sophisticated, was dragging him down.

Then he grabbed her other ankle with his other hand. Now they were both sinking like a stone. Slowly but surely going down. He was going to drown, and he was taking her with him. He was going to win.

No.

Contorting her body, she bent in half, reaching for her ankle to pry his fingers away. But his grip was like iron. His eyes locked onto hers, full of hatred and fear. That's when she punched him straight in the mouth. And kicked out with all her might. His terrible weight let go and she pointed her head toward the surface and swam for her life.

CHAPTER TWENTY

Ebony sank to the sand, unable to stand. Bits of shell dug into her knees but she ignored them. Dragging in great gulps of air she knelt at the edge of the waves unable to move a single step further up the beach.

But at least she was on the beach. She'd made it.

"Ebony … Mum?" A voice drifted to her over the morning breeze. "Bloody hell, are you okay?" A warm body landed next to her on the sand. It was Jenna.

"Mum." Jenna's voice was raw and filled with emotion that it finally forced her to look up, into her daughter's eyes.

"Jesus, I didn't think you were going to make it around those rocks. I can't believe you did that."

Thankfully the beach was only a short swim around the headland, but it'd still taken every ounce of Ebony's strength to struggle against the current. At least the day was calm and windless, so once she'd gotten away from the cliff-face the water was smooth. Not like the other day. When she'd nearly drowned.

"Is he gone?" she muttered under her breath. Breathing was impossible. Her chest constricted so tightly she couldn't drag any air in. Was he really gone? And had she killed him? She was a healer. She was supposed to give life, not take it.

"What? What did you say?"

"Is he gone? He's gone, isn't he? I saw him drown. Did I kill him?" she asked, making her voice loud enough for Jenna to hear.

"I'm not sure, I was too busy watching you. And of course you didn't *kill* him. Don't be silly, you only did what you had to survive. To protect the people you care about."

Ebony was about to reply when Dan's voice resounded over the sand. "Jenna, are you okay? Is Ebony okay?"

"Well she's alive at least," Jenna replied. "Not sure how okay she is just yet, though." Little puffs of sand flew up as Dan sprinted over the sand and stopped abruptly next to the kneeling pair.

"Can you make it up to the carpark, Ebony?" Dan's hand landed on her shoulder. "I can carry you if you like. Paulette's already called the police and the ambulance. And we've got Jay up there as well."

At the mention of Jay's name, Ebony looked up, trying to make out Dan's features in the bright morning sunshine. How could the sun be shining when her life was completely unraveling?

"I can make it," she replied and got slowly to her feet. Ebony didn't remember much about the walk up to the carpark, it was all she could do to put one foot in front of the other. Her feet were bare now, she'd kicked off her shoes in the water, so she could swim better, and the sand warmed her toes.

And then there was Jay, sitting on the gravel, back up against a small tree on the edge of the carpark, Paulette by his side, still putting pressure on his wound, and it all came rushing back to her.

"You're hurt," she said, the fog clearing enough for her to focus.

"I'll be okay. No major damage. But you scared the shit out of me when you went over the edge. I thought you were dead." He reached for her and Ebony knelt down and fell into his embrace. Strong arms encircling her back, making her want to cry with relief.

"Me too," she admitted weakly.

"Don't worry, this isn't the worst I've had," he said pragmatically.

She was reminded of the scars on his chest. He was right, but that didn't stop her from feeling like it was her fault.

"We left Corey back up there," said Dan. "I tied him up, so he couldn't get away, so I could help carry Jay down. But I might go back and check on him."

"Did you see him?" Ebony turned to look at Dan. "Did his …" She was going to say body but changed her mind. "… Did he ever resurface?"

"Not that we could see." Dan's face was hard and unwavering. "Me and Jenna both hung over the edge and we saw you finally pop up—"

"That was the scariest ten seconds of my life, waiting for you to reappear," Jenna added quickly.

"I kept watching, while Jenna followed you around the headland. But I never saw any sign of him," Dan reported.

So, Alexander was dead.

Jenna sat down in the dirt on the other side of Ebony. Without asking, she gently took hold of one of her hands.

"I think I can hear the ambulance," Paulette said loudly. "I'll go and meet them, show them where you are. Jenna can you keep the pressure on Jay's leg." She showed Jenna what to do and then stood up.

"Paulette, I'm so sorry you got mixed up in all of this," Ebony said, not sure how she was ever going to apologize to this woman.

"Don't worry yourself too much. I'm just glad it's all over. God, if you hadn't pushed that bastard …"

She didn't need to finish her sentence, Ebony understood she wasn't a person who liked to be messed with. She felt violated and degraded and very angry. And she had every right to.

"You know that marriage would never have been legal anyway," Paulette added. "There are rules about marriage made under compulsion, as well as all sorts of paperwork that freak never filled in." She gave a grim smile and took off at a jog toward the faint sound of a siren.

It was a small thing, but it made Ebony feel slightly better.

"What are we going to tell the police?" Ebony asked. Jesus, were they going to put her in jail?

"The truth. It was self-defense. You have three other witnesses who'll attest to that. He pulled you over the edge with him and then he drowned, Ebony," Jay declared. Then as if he could see the doubt in her eyes, he added, "You didn't kill him."

She gazed at him, looking deep into his blue eyes. His handsome face hovered so near, and she let her fingers lift up to stroke the stubble on his chin. He was pale beneath his stubble, in pain from the wound. Almost absent-mindedly her mind reached out to him, wanting to soothe that pain. Heal it. But then she drew back. She needed his permission to do that. And she didn't want to ask with Jenna right there. The paramedics would be here soon with their form of pain relief. With everything that'd just happened, it might not be the best thing for her to try right now anyway.

Her gaze slid to her daughter.

"Jenna, you need to know …" She paused. There were so many things she needed to say to her daughter. And to Jay. So many things she needed to apologize for. The lump at the back of her throat which had been threatening to choke her since she emerged from the water, got bigger and bigger. Then tears welled, completely unbidden. Suddenly she was surrounded by people who cared for her. After so long on her own, dealing with her problems alone, never letting anyone get close. It was all so overwhelming.

"It's okay, leave it for now. We'll have plenty of time later," Jenna soothed, stroking Ebony's hand as if she were a child, before she put weight back on Jay's leg.

Ebony still felt like her bones were going to shake apart from the inside out. Delayed reaction to her adrenaline. Shock. But it was nice to have her daughter here. Touching her.

"It's alright, Ebony. That bastard can't hurt you anymore." Jay's hand came up to squeeze her upper arm. He must be able to feel her trembling.

"I know," she replied. "It might just take a little while to sink in, that's all."

"I'd like to be there to help you through it. If you'll let me. You don't have to do this alone anymore."

"Thank you." It was so humbling he was prepared to stick with her, after all he'd just seen. Was she prepared to answer all the questions she knew he'd have? About Alexander. About Jenna. About her life on the run.

"I just hope I haven't pushed you away, by ... you know."

Oh wow, she'd been so caught up in her own dramas, she'd completely forgotten about his issues. All of a sudden, his bad dreams didn't seem all that daunting. Not when she took into account the way he was looking at her right now. The way her heart lodged in her throat when he turned those eyes, as blue as the ocean, on her. It was dangerous, this feeling. But perhaps dangerous in a good way. Something she could get used to.

There were things he could do, people he could see to help him overcome his demons. There were things she might even try, if he'd let her.

"No, you haven't," she said simply. "Not at all." And the smile he gave her was something to behold. It made her want to grab his face in both hands and kiss those fierce lips until they both ran out of air.

* * *

"We found the gun," the cop said. It was the same cop who'd attended the crash scene the other night. "It was on a ledge about half-way down the cliff. Don't know how it didn't end up at the bottom of the ocean. Just luck, I guess."

Jay let out a sigh of relief and leaned back against the tree trunk. At least it would put beyond a doubt that none of them had been lying.

"But no body. Yet."

"What?" Jenna and Ebony spoke in unison and Jay's head snapped up.

"Not yet, anyway. But it will appear sooner or later. Wash up on a beach or get picked up by a fisherman. They usually do in the end."

"What happens if you never find a body?" Ebony queried, the tremble in her voice evident. Shit. This was the last thing she needed. He'd just assured her she was safe now. Could finally start living a life unafraid and unhindered. But now, with no body? There would always be questions.

"There isn't much swell today." The young cop gazed out at the calm ocean as if searching for an answer. "Don't worry, it'll turn up. One day."

"The paramedics are here," Jenna called out, shielding her eyes as she gazed down through the scrub at the edge of the carpark.

From his position, sitting on the ground, Jay couldn't see them, but he was glad they were here. His leg hurt like the hell. Not that he'd admit it. Putting on a brave face was one of those things he did extremely well. But a shot from one of

245

those analgesic inhalers the paramedics carried would be more than welcome to ease the pain.

Damn, this injury would mean time spent in recovery and rehab. He'd been through it all before. This time wouldn't be nearly as bad, the wound was just a through and through, with hopefully no lasting damage to his calf, but he still wasn't looking forward to it.

But he'd do it again, and then some. There was no regretting what he'd done. If it meant saving Ebony, then it was worth it.

Even if she decided she was never going to talk to him again. It was all worth it. Just looking at her now, his heart did stupid things in his chest when she gave a tentative smile. He wanted to spend more time with her. Spend lots more time with her. For the first time in forever, he could see himself long term with this woman.

But would she see it the same way?

She was just as damaged as he was, in different ways. He couldn't imagine what her life had been like, running from that maniac. Constantly looking over her shoulder. In a sustained state of worry. Now he understood her hesitancy to form bonds. Especially with him. He was grateful she'd opened her heart enough to give him a chance. It was a wonder she was as sane as she was.

He understood now, that when he'd seen her in town last night, she'd been about to run again. About to leave him with no explanation and no goodbye. But having seen this nutcase at work first-hand, he couldn't blame her. This guy would've done well joining the Taliban. They were all fanatical egomaniacs, intent on running the world to their own personal agenda.

A flash of darker green against the lighter scrub heralded the arrival of the paramedics. A young man with dark hair that drooped over his forehead, and an older woman following in his wake. They dropped their equipment on the ground near Jay's feet and the woman knelt next to his leg, gently nudging Jenna out of the way.

"My name's Marion. Do you mind if I take a look?" She directed her question at Jay, her dark green eyes candid and competent. He nodded, then sucked in a gasp as she gently lifted the wadded shirt away from the bullet wound. "Would you like some pain relief for that?" she asked, while casting an expert eye over the injury.

"Yes please." He was quick to reply. Marion nodded, as if to acknowledge how much pain he was in.

"Anyone else hurt?" the younger guy asked.

"You might want to take a look at the guy on the headland up there." Jenna pointed toward the hill where Corey and Dan were. "He's got a few nasty dog bites." She said it matter-of-factly, but from what Jay had seen, that boy would need more than a few stitches in his face and neck where her dog had subdued him.

"Righto," the paramedic replied cheerily. "Can you show me the way?"

"I'll need your help to get him on the stretcher," Marion commanded Ebony. "But then I think the police have more questions for you." She indicated the raft of men in police uniforms standing in the shade of a large eucalyptus tree.

Jay heard Ebony sigh. This was the biggest thing to happen in this sleepy town for quite a while. Everyone would want to be in on it, especially the cops.

"I'll come and see you in the hospital, as soon as I can get away," Ebony said, to him. But he knew it might be hours before they were satisfied with her version of events. She might be here for a long while yet.

"Promise?"

"I promise," she replied.

He hoped he could believe her.

* * *

Jenna sat snuggled beneath Dan's arm as they both lounged on Ebony's old couch. She looked so happy and content and in love. Ebony's heart swelled as she watched her daughter. One hand rested protectively over her belly, the other was entwined with Dan's, propped on his jean-clad leg. Her dog, Dune, lay at her feet. That dog never left her side. And Chili Dog, the traitor, was curled up right next to Dune. After a few initial sniffs, the dogs had become firm friends.

Unable to sit still any longer, Ebony got up from her chair under the pretense of pouring herself another glass of red wine. She offered the bottle to Dan, but he shook his head. Eyes half-closed, he looked like he might fall asleep right there on her couch. It was nearly midnight, and it'd been a long day for all of them. They'd only returned from the police station a couple of hours ago. Had spent most of the day there, going over and over and over their statements to a different cop every time. But with all five of them, including Paulette—Jay had given his statement from his hospital bed —all giving the same account the police had little choice but to believe them.

"You promise you'll come and see us?" asked Jenna.

"Yes, yes, of course. I wouldn't miss coming to see my new grandchild." As the word slipped from her lips, Ebony raised her hand to cover her mouth. "Oh my God, I can't believe how easy that was to say. And I can't believe I'm going to have a grandchild."

"It's all happened very quickly," Jenna agreed. "But it's a good thing. A really good thing." Jenna looked up and her blue eyes were filled with unshed tears. But she blinked them back.

She and Ebony had spent quite a long time this evening already, blubbering in each other's arms. Ebony never thought it possible she could have such strong emotions surging through her. She felt protective and tender and affectionate and distraught and lionhearted and yearning all at the same time. Such a mixture of feelings she could never remember having before. Except for once. When Jenna was born and placed into her arms. This more than anything else confirmed to Ebony that Jenna was her daughter. Because her heart told her it was true.

"You will stay with me for a few more days, though, won't you?" Ebony could hardly believe there was a note of pleading in her voice. She hadn't meant to plead. Jenna was a grown woman, with an independent mind of her own, but Ebony was desperate to have her stay for just a while longer. Now she'd found her, she didn't want to let her go.

"Yep, we can stay for a few more days," Dan replied, at the same time disentangling himself from Jenna and standing up to stretch. His frame so tall, his fingers nearly touched the ceiling when he raised his arms overheard.

Chili Dog looked up, but quickly lay back down when it was obvious nothing exciting was happening. Thankfully, Alexander had indeed been truthful about what he'd done to Chili. Ebony found her tottering around the back yard on the end of her chain when she'd returned this morning, still groggy from whatever drug Alexander gave her, but at least whole and healthy.

"But I need to crash. I'm beat. Do you mind?" He shot a tender look down at Jenna, now snuggling her way deeper into the couch.

"Go for it, babe, I won't be far behind you."

Both women watched Dan trail through the living room and into the spare bedroom. Ebony had quickly made it up for them this evening, after they'd returned from the police station. The springs on the old bed creaked as he lowered himself down and gave a soft sigh of contentment. A wave of fondness for this young man poured through Ebony. She was so glad Jenna had found such a wonderful partner. Someone who cared so deeply for her. Would do anything for her.

"We'll stay at least until the police have cleared you of any charges. And I'm sure they'll have lots more questions for us over the next few days, too," said Jenna with a yawn.

"Yes. I do wonder what they're going to do with young Corey, though. Do you think he'll go to jail?" Ebony was conflicted when it came to Corey. In some ways she was sorry for him. After all, she'd been in almost the same position as him, back when she'd been a gullible teenager. Held enthralled by Alexander's charm and charisma. She wasn't sure how responsible he was for his own actions. The poor kid had given her such a look of confusion and regret as they led him away in handcuffs, she'd wanted to tell him she forgave him.

"I'm not sure. The cops said he'd broken all kind of laws, there's charges of deprivation of liberty, which can be a couple of years in jail. But they also agreed he was under the sway of Alexander, so they might well be lenient on him," Jenna mused.

"Hmm." Ebony wondered what would be better for Corey. If he did get time in jail, he'd have a chance to think about what he'd done, perhaps repent and see the error of his ways. But then again people often came out of jail more damaged and vengeful than when they went in.

She shook her head. Enough about Corey, she didn't want to think about his predicament any more.

"I need to hear more about Shiralee Station. It sounds wonderful." But as soon as Ebony said the words she was reminded painfully why Jenna had gone to Shiralee in the first place. To escape her crazy half-brother, Liam, who was hunting her down so he could get back into Alexander's good graces. Her daughter had been on the run from Liam for years, and Ebony never knew. The irony that both she and her daughter spent years running from Alexander or one of his cronies, didn't escape her. Could she have done things differently? Not abandoned Jenna? And if she could, would she have? At the time, leaving Jenna in the safe hands of kindly old Joe had seemed the best solution. The only solution.

She and Jenna had only touched briefly on what life was like for Jenna growing up. She was shocked and saddened to hear of wonderful old Joe's untimely death. They'd both shed tears over that story. And now Ebony had one more person's life to feel guilty about. But every time Ebony thought about leaving Jenna and what it had cost them both, painful spasms of grief grabbed her chest and squeezed. So for now, she was better off not thinking about it at all. They would talk about it. A lot. Soon. But not now. Now it was enough for Ebony just to stare at her marvelous daughter. Drink her in. Her long blonde hair, those sparkling blue eyes.

"You'll love Shiralee," said Jenna. "I'll take you to meet all the animals."

Jenna's gift was talking to animals. It was just one more thing Ebony learned about her daughter today.

"Would you mind showing me your ring?' Ebony went over and sat next to Jenna on the couch, having to push Chili Dog out of the way with her toe; that dog didn't want to move too far from her new best friend.

"My mother gave me that ring. Said it was a family heirloom. It's worth a lot of money. I think her mother, your great-grandmother, was given it by the lady who designed it back during the second world-war. My grandmother worked as her secretary. She was a well-known French jewelry designer at the time. It could be worth over fifty thousand dollars."

"Wow," Jenna breathed, holding the ring in the palm of her hand. "I mean, that's great it's worth so much. But you don't know how I've longed for this. These stories, about me. And about you. About our family."

"I know, honey. And that's why I couldn't let Alexander have it. Because it was my one link to you." Ebony reached out and stroked her daughter's hair. They needed to explore this more, but all in good time. Jenna needed to know her grandmother, Celine, had died when Ebony was only fifteen. That her father couldn't cope and turned to drinking when her mother died. And that was one of the reasons she'd become a rebel, left home, met Alexander and fallen under his spell, when she was only sixteen.

Still staring at the soft pink glow of the ring in front of them, Jenna said, "Are you going in to see Jay tomorrow?"

A shaft of guilt shot through Ebony. "Oh yes, definitely." There just hadn't been any time today to go and see him in hospital. She'd managed to make a three-minute phone call, to make sure he was okay, and promise to go see him tomorrow. But with all the time spent with the police, and now getting to know her daughter, she hadn't had the opportunity. But she'd wanted to. Wanted to lay her head on his chest, hear his strong heart beating beneath her ear. Wanted to feel the solidity of him surround her, that wall of muscle beneath her fingertips. To make sure he was there, was really okay.

It was still unbelievable to her that Jay had been willing to put himself—his life—on the line for her.

She had some decisions to make about Jay. Tomorrow. She'd think about it all tomorrow. Tonight, she just wanted to go and sleep the dreamless sleep of deliverance. Of someone who finally had nothing to fear.

CHAPTER TWENTY-ONE

Jenna pushed the door open and held it for Ebony and Jay to walk through, Jay using his cane. Dan entered last and gave her a wink as he passed through. Without thinking, she reached out and pinched his bum as he walked past.

"Hey," he grouched. But his smile was large.

"Ebony." A large, brightly dressed woman rushed up to hug her. Jenna assumed this was Viv, the lady who owned the cafe, and one of Ebony's good friends. "Shit, babe, you're the talk of the town. Kicked some badass guy's butt, from what I heard." She held Ebony at arm's length to study her face. "But you don't look any worse for wear. Are you okay?" Ebony nodded and was about to speak when Viv's gaze alighted on Jay.

"Holy … Now *you* do look worse for wear. There were rumors, but I wasn't sure. What the hell happened to you, man?" Jay gave her a sheepish look, but even as he opened his mouth to reply, Viv held up a hand and said, "No wait, I want to hear the whole story, from the beginning to end. Come and sit down first." Viv led them to a private table, tucked in the back corner and once she'd taken their orders, French toast all around, in honor of Ebony, left them to talk amongst themselves, vowing she'd be back to hear their whole story.

Jenna felt like she'd been hit by a mini tornado. Viv's cafe was bright and airy and happy, a powerful reflection of Viv's personality. Her stomach grumbled loudly at the thought of food. She couldn't wait to taste Viv's famous French toast. It was so nice to actually relish the thought of food. Ebony had been doing Reiki on her every day for the past week, and the morning sickness was almost non-existent.

"Do you still feel okay, no more nausea?"

It was as if Ebony could read her mind. And that was freaking Jenna out just a little. Even though it'd only been a week, they were becoming more attuned to each other every day. Dan was dubious when she'd mentioned it, but it was as if there was some kind of sixth sense thing going on between them.

"Yes, I'm fine, Mum." she mollified. "More than fine, I'm starving." They both laughed and Jenna wondered if she was going to get fat now she was eating for two.

"I can't believe you're leaving today," Ebony said softly. Jay and Dan were deep in a conversation about the best carburetor to put into Dan's Holden ute, and the two women could talk quietly between themselves.

"I know, the week has just flown by, hasn't it?" It was the truth. Jenna had felt so at home in Ebony's cottage, she almost didn't want to leave. Even Dune had made a friend for life in Ebony's dog, Chili. But Dan was getting restless, even though he tried to hide it. And Jenna missed the animals back on the station. Her horse, Chainsaw, most of all. It would be a long drive home, probably take them four or five days. They were going to take it easy, to make sure Jenna's morning sickness didn't come back.

"You'll let me know. If you hear anything more about … well you know … him."

"Sure will," Ebony agreed. But there was an edge to her voice.

Jenna felt it more than heard it. They both remained uneasy. Because the police still hadn't found Alexander's body. Jenna was sure he was dead. They'd never seen him surface. But still.

Jenna shook her head and placed a hand over her belly. Funny how that movement was fast becoming a habit. Now there was a little human being growing inside her, she was constantly covering it, protecting it, nurturing it. And she'd never let anything hurt her baby.

"What did Billy say about their enquiries over east?" Billy was the young cop who'd been their liaison for the whole week. He had lots of questions for them, but he'd also been a valuable source of information.

"Nothing concrete yet." Ebony's fingers sneaked down to play with one of the serviettes, a sure sign she was nervous. "But he assured me they'd leave no stone unturned. From what we told them, it seems Alexander was into lots of illegal stuff in Byron. More than enough for the police to raid his farm."

Which all sounded promising to Jenna. If there was no *farm* left, then really, there wasn't anything left to be frightened of.

"It looks like Corey is going to spend time in juvenile detention." Ebony couldn't keep the concern off her face.

"Don't you dare," warned Jenna. "Don't you feel sorry for him. He was prepared to do whatever Alexander told him to. And even if he wasn't the one wielding the gun, he was definitely an accessory." Jenna hoped her strong words had an effect on Ebony. The last thing her mother needed right now was more guilt. She already had more than enough to deal with. "Anyway, it might do him some good. To be out of Alexander's sphere of influence, I mean. If he really has been locked away on that farm—or whatever it was—for all his life, a dose of reality won't hurt."

She was about to lecture Ebony further, when Viv returned to the table with a tray laden full of goodies, halting their conversation. Jenna's stomach almost tied itself in knots when the smell of the warm, buttery toast drifted past her nose. She caught Dan's eye and he winked at her. Her hand found his knee beneath the table and she squeezed it gently. It'd be nice, just the two of them again, in the ute, driving back to the station. To have Dan all to herself for the next few days was something to look forward to.

Viv pulled a chair up right between Jenna and Ebony, pushing Ebony closer to Jay, but Viv didn't seem to notice. Jenna did, however. She caught the look that passed between them. A look that spoke of things unsaid, but also of a strong connection, an underlying respect and allure.

Were they in love? Perhaps it was a fledgling love. Jenna didn't know much about Jay—hell, she didn't really know that much about her own mother—but what she did know had shown him to be a man of courage, loyalty, and determination. A lot like Dan. All things a woman like Ebony needed. She found herself hoping the two would be able to find their way through the maze that was the complicated start to their relationship and fall in love. After all, she and Dan had managed to do it, why couldn't her mother and this wonderful man?

It was a good thing she was leaving her mother in Jay's indomitable hands. He would be good for her. And she would be good for him too, if the small hints Ebony had dropped, about some leftover mental trauma from his time in Afghanistan were true. Ebony's gentle soul would help him heal.

Jenna was satisfied she was leaving her mother in a safe place, where she might finally learn to blossom and grow. They would keep in touch, and Ebony would come and see her up at the station. For now, that was enough.

* * *

The gentle hum as the waves crashed lightly onto the shore filled the evening air. Axel rolled exuberantly in the sand a few feet away from Jay. This was the first time in weeks the poor dog had been to the beach and he was making the most of every second. He sat up and looked at Jay, long tongue lolling joyfully out of the side of his mouth, then went back to rolling, sand flying in every direction. It was the first time Jay had been back to the beach as well, and it felt good to be sitting in his board shorts and t-shirt, toes dug into the sand.

Jay grinned and stretched his injured leg out in front of him. The bright red scar pulled painfully and he bent his knee slightly to ease the strain on his calf. It'd only been two weeks since the shooting, and he wasn't doing too badly. Even the physio said so this morning at his daily rehab session. Jay was on the mend, would be walking without a cane in another two weeks or so and then on to jogging and running soon afterward.

One of his first questions to the physio had been how soon he could start surfing again. God, he missed it. There were a couple of guys out there right now. Even though the swell wasn't big, it would be peaceful and relaxing out there, catching a wave or two, or just floating like flotsam on the ocean current. He recognized Gazza and Panno, both of them regulars here at Redgate Beach. A small fizz of envy bubbled through him, but it was gone as fast as it arrived. He'd be back out there soon enough.

And he wouldn't change a thing. Wouldn't trade all the days of surfing for the rest of his life if it meant Ebony was now safe and free of her ex. It was all worth it. She was worth it.

Thinking about Ebony got him wondering where she was. She'd asked him to meet her here. Of course, he'd agreed, but she wouldn't tell him why.

His mind was still a mess when it came to Ebony. He still wasn't sure what it was they had together, if indeed they had anything. She'd come to see him every day while he was in hospital and they'd sat and talked everything over. In depth. He finally understood the horror her life had been with Alexander, why she left him and why she thought she had to abandon her baby. How she'd survived the mental torment and anguish. The day she'd nearly drowned, when he'd rescued her, took on extra significance for him now.

Then the day he'd been released from hospital, Ebony's daughter and her husband were leaving to go back to their cattle station up north. And she'd been taken up with the preparations for that, as well as feeling a bit lost after they left. But over the past week, he'd only seen her once, when she'd popped over with mounds of containers full of healthy food for him to eat while he recuperated. She'd called him to talk on the telephone a few times, but never seemed to have the time to meet up with him. He'd got the distinct impression she was fobbing him off. But with all his rehab, and then spending a few hours a day in his surf shop making sure everything was all up to speed and running smoothly after his unscheduled week away, he hadn't had a lot of opportunity to pursue the matter.

Suddenly Axel sat up, sharp ears pricked, and stared toward the back of the sand dune. The next instant a small red shape hurtled over the top of the dune and rushed up to Axel. Ebony's dog, Chili. This was the first time the two dogs had met, and Jay went to stand up in case there was an altercation, but he needn't have bothered. After a few seconds of stiff-legged sniffing, Axel gave a small playful "Moof" and the two were off, chasing each other over the sand and through the waves at the edge of the water.

Jay stared expectantly over the top of the dune and was rewarded by the sight of Ebony appearing, arms full of baskets and blankets. He limped over to take some of the items from her hands.

"Hiya, beautiful," he said, thinking she was exactly that. Beautiful. The evening air lent a softness to her sculptured features. A simple summer dress with a pattern of light pink and white flowers set off her dark hair and showed her curves to their best advantage. Bare feet finished off her ensemble and Jay didn't think he'd ever seen her look more ravishing or carefree.

"Thanks for coming," she replied, almost bashful, only lifting the corners of her mouth in a welcoming grin.

"Of course. You call, I come. How've you been?"

"I've been ... good. Well, getting better every day. Doing a lot of thinking." She still wouldn't really look at him, seemed serious and nervous.

"Me too," he agreed as he helped her spread out a bright patterned blanket for them both to sit on. "What have you got in here?" His nose told him there were delicious things hiding in the covered basket.

"I made us an asparagus and leek quiche, and I brought some of Viv's sensational brownies."

"A woman after my own heart," he said. That got him a smile. His first proper smile for the evening.

"How's your leg?" Glancing down, she winced as she saw the scar on his calf. "Looks sore."

"Nah, it's getting better every day. If Alexander was going to shoot me, he couldn't have picked a better spot, really. Went right through the calf muscle at the back. Didn't even nick the bone." While all that was true, Jay wasn't about to tell her that there may still be nerve damage; he may never recover full feeling in his lower leg. But it shouldn't affect his walking or running and was a small price to pay when all things were taken into account.

"Can you walk a little? Along the waterline with me?" Almost before the words were out of her mouth her voice wavered and a deep frown etched across her forehead. "I'm sorry, I shouldn't ask you to do that. Let's just sit here, you'll be a lot more comfortable."

"Don't you dare humor me. I'll decide whether I can walk or not." He didn't that she was treating him like an invalid. A small part of him understood it was because she felt responsible for his injury, but he wasn't going to have a bar of it. Taking her arm in his, he said, "I want to walk, so lead the way."

They walked slowly down to the waterline without any further comment. It was good to have her arm slipped through his, her hip softly jostling against his upper thigh as they walked. He took the higher ground, while she walked along with her feet splashing in the ocean. They walked slowly, accommodating his limp into their rhythm. The sun was setting over the rim of the ocean, the shimmering orange glow snaking back over the waves to bathe them in its light. The two dogs raced past them, kicking up the spray and yapping at a few stray seagulls. It was a perfect evening.

"Do you remember the first time we met?" she asked finally, eyes turned toward the horizon.

He snorted. "How could I forget? Even though you deny it, you were lucky I was there that day."

"I know," she said, voice small. "I've never told anyone this, but I almost didn't want to be rescued. I think I wanted to drown that day."

"What?" This wasn't what he'd been expecting. It was an admission of how depressed and miserable she'd been. Thank God he'd come along. What if he'd been a few minutes later. Found her floating, face down in the water instead. The thought was unbearable, and his mind shied away from it. A world without Ebony wasn't worth imagining.

"It was my fortieth birthday that day. I was thinking about all the dreams I had that'd turned to ashes, all the things I hadn't achieved in my life, would never achieve because of Alexander. About the daughter I thought I'd lost, that I'd never get to know."

If only he'd known back then, how much deep emotional pain she was in, perhaps he would've done more.

"But I'm so glad you saved me, Jay. In more ways than you know." The last part was almost a whisper. "And now I'm doubly in your debt." She glanced down at his leg.

"Oh no you don't. You don't owe me anything Ebony McAllister. You saved yourself that morning on the cliff. You finally stood up to him. In the best way possible."

She studied him without words for a few paces along the beach. "Perhaps I did. But I don't really like to think about it." Her voice was still small and far away.

"That was a big price to pay," he agreed. Even though Ebony had no choice, it was kill or be killed, there would always be that faint ghost of shame haunting the edges of her mind, asking if there might've been another way.

"I'm not going to placate you with false platitudes and tell you not to feel guilty, that he was just a scumbag who deserved to die. Because that won't ease your burden any." He stopped their stroll and turned her to face him, his hands on her shoulders. "But Ebony, I am going to tell you, you did the best thing you could at the time. The only thing in your power. You saved yourself, Jenna, Dan, and me with your actions." Her eyes filled with tears as she listened to him speak. "And I'm also going to tell you to seek help from a professional. Someone who can bring some understanding and closure to this whole sordid affair." He had the urge to let his gaze slide away from hers, but he kept it fixed on her beautiful gray eyes. She had to know, even if he was still embarrassed to tell her. "Just like me. I've started seeing a shrink. About my bad dreams. I put it off for way too long. I thought I could fix my own problems. But now I know, I need help. There are just some things even I can't do on my own." That comment brought the vestige of a smile to her lips.

"Will you promise me, you'll go and get some help?"

She nodded. Then gave a low laugh. "Fine pair we are. Both of us broken and battered."

He cupped her face in both of his hands. "Maybe that's why we'd be so good together." Her gray eyes darkened like a stormy sea at his words, flecks of silver flashing in their depths. He could drown in the ocean of her gaze. Go down and never resurface. Never be rescued. That's when he knew. Actually, he'd known all along, but this was the moment when he finally accepted his fate. He needed this woman in his life. Wanted her like he'd never wanted any other woman before. Damaged as she was. Enigmatic as she was. Even with some strange unnameable healing power coursing through her. Beautiful as she was. He wanted her forever.

"I've fallen in love with you, Ebony."

* * *

Ebony's heart lurched sideways in her chest, threatened to break out of her ribcage. Had he just said what she thought he had? What she'd been dreaming of hearing. Dreading to hear.

Her fingers came up to touch his stubble-roughened cheek. For the past week, she'd searched her soul every day, wanting to find a reason compelling enough to make her leave Margaret River. Leave Jay. She'd even stayed away from him so that his physical presence couldn't influence her decision. Even though her body ached for his. They would never work as a couple together. They were too different. He'd be so much better off without her. She was eight years older than him. She was a freak with odd powers. And he had his own demons to conquer. Could she even contemplate sleeping with him again? The fear of waking to find his fingers around her throat hanging cold and heavy inside her. But for some reason, she was still here. Couldn't force herself to pack her car and go.

Because even after all their complications, she wanted Jay.

"Oh God." They were the only words she could muster.

"I know. It took me by surprise as well." Those wonderful lips curved into a lopsided smile and she found herself wanting to stand up on tiptoe and kiss them. Feel the heat of him funnel through his mouth into her.

"You know how old I am, Jay?" Her fingers tightened into a fist in the material of her skirt and she bit her bottom lip with her teeth.

"Yes, you're forty. I'm thirty-two. Age doesn't bother me. We're both mature, consenting adults."

"I'm just warning you, I'm no young thing with a tight butt and pert breasts. So, if that's what you're looking for you'd better move on."

"Ebony, I'm well aware of your … assets." He let his eyes flick down to her chest and then back up to her face. "And I love your curves. You remind me of a sultry French actress. What's your next objection?" He said it with no hint of dismay, as if he was prepared to stand here all night and fight off all protestations.

It wasn't that easy, though, and her face remained serious. "Okay, what if I tell you I don't think I want any more children. Could you live with that?"

This time his gaze lifted from hers, as he stared out into the darkening ocean, contemplating. "Yes, I think I can. I've never been much of a family-oriented man. I think perhaps my time in the army cured me of that. I haven't told anyone this yet, you're the first to hear it, but I'm sponsoring a family in Afghanistan. A mother and her three small children. I'm hoping to bring them here to Australia in the near future.

Help them to make a new life here. They can be my surrogate kids. Besides, we have Jenna and Dan and their new grandchild. Won't that make me a grandfather?"

Wow, he was full of surprises tonight. She wanted to hug him for what he'd just said. The fact he was happy to accept Jenna and Dan, and the new baby, into his life amazed her. And it wasn't any real stretch of the imagination to hear he'd sponsored a family. His big heart and his need to protect the people who couldn't protect themselves made her believe him without a doubt.

"What about the ongoing police investigation? You know it's going to take a while to clear it all up?"

"Probably," he agreed a little morosely. "But I'm as much invested in making sure this is all laid to rest as you are. I'm not going to be scared off by some perceived threat hanging over your head. You're not going to go to jail, Ebony. And don't forget, I was the one held bound and gagged, kept captive for hours on your living room floor." He held a hand up as she went to speak. "And no, I don't blame you for any of it, so don't even go there. I blame Alexander, fair and square. And I want to see his body found, so we can both have some closure." He was still staring at her, dark indigo eyes fixed on her face and she dared not look away. "The way I see it, we may just as well work our way through this investigation together. Together we'll be stronger."

She knew she was scratching around for reasons now, but this last question had to be asked. After all, her powers were as much a part of her as the color of her eyes or her love of French toast, or her stubborn need for independence. It couldn't be denied, and it couldn't be brushed under the carpet.

"What about the freaky side of me? What about this Reiki ... well it's much more than just Reiki, you know that now ... the power I have? I don't—"

"Stop, Ebony. Stop trying to find excuses. I love you. Every last bit of you. Freaky or not, I wouldn't have you any other way."

He meant what he said. She could feel it in the slight tremble running through his body. Hear the passion in his voice. See the truth in his eyes. He accepted her for what she was. That tiny blue morsel of cold, dark fear, which had been sitting in the bottom of her gut for the last week, finally thawed.

His hand reached up to touch the kyanite pendant, sitting in the hollow of her throat. A pulse of warmth and adoration and purpose flowed through the stone into her chest at his touch. It told her all she needed to know.

"Do you love me, Ebony?"

The question caught her off-guard. She knew what her answer was. Should she admit it? There was no going back if she did.

"Because, really, that's all it comes down to in the end," he continued.

"Yes, Jay. I love you." It was the simple truth and now she'd said the words it was as if a great weight lifted from her shoulders. Without warning his lips came down and crushed against hers. Her arms snaked around the back of his neck, pulling him in closer. She wanted to leap up and wrap her legs around his waist, but the memory of his injured leg stopped her just in time. Instead, she pressed herself closer into his solid chest, reveling in the feel of all those hard muscles pressed up against her soft curves.

When she'd first crested the top of the sand dune this evening, and seen him standing, tall and dark against the setting sun, his powerful arms and shoulders obvious beneath the thin t-shirt fabric, her heart had stopped. He was a specimen of pure, unadulterated male and she knew he was hers for the taking. If she wanted him.

Something wet and cold bumped her leg and she jumped. "Chili," she squealed. The red kelpie leaped up and placed her front paws on her nice, clean dress. "Oh Chili. Look at Axel, he's such a well-mannered gentleman. Look, he's not jumping up," Ebony reprimanded. Chili just lolled her tongue out of the side of her mouth and looked for all the world like she was laughing at her.

"At least the dogs get along. I don't think we'll have any complaints in that quarter." Jay had released her when she squealed, but now he pulled her back in and tucked her under his shoulder. "I can hear some of that quiche calling my name," he said, cupping his other hand behind his ear to listen. "Shall we go and eat?"

His limp was slightly more pronounced as they made their way back toward their blanket and she mentally kicked herself for not thinking. It must be aching from all the walking and standing they'd been doing. But he hadn't complained.

"If you'll let me, I can do something about the pain. If you want to come back to my house."

"Oh, yes, I definitely want to come back to your house," he said with a throaty purr. "But not for what you had in mind."

Her cheeks heated suddenly at his innuendo. But just as quickly the heat pooled much lower down as a wave of desire struck her. Jay pulled her back around to face him, so he could kiss her some more, and let her know just how much he had *other things* on his mind. The evidence of his desire pressed into her belly as he devoured her lips. The thought of what he could do with those lips had her knees almost buckling beneath her.

"I'll sleep on the couch afterward if you like."

"No, you won't," she declared.

He kissed her again, the promise he'd made to her heart indisputable in every touch of his lips and in his skin against hers. His soul against her soul, his love lifted her. Above the sand, above the ocean. To a place she'd never experienced before. Unconditional love.

If you liked Shadows in Deep Blue, you'll love;

Shadows in the Dust

Her heart's been broken by tragedy, but will a cowboy's courage be enough to save her when there's a killer on the loose in the outback.

Shadows of Red Earth

What if the only thing you wanted in life was your freedom? What if the cost of that freedom was the lives of your family?

The books in this series can be read as stand-alone novels, but are enhanced if you read them together.

Also by Suzanne Cass
NEW
Clear Skies

Stargazer Ranch Mystery Romance Series
Combustion: Prequel Novella
Wildfire
Firelight
Snowbound: A Christmas Novella
Snowfall
Cloudburst

Island Bound Series
Books can be read as stand-alone
Bound by Truth
Bound by Silence
Bound by the Stars

Colors of the Earth Series
Books can be read as stand-alone
Shadows in the Dust
Shadows in Deep Blue
Shadows of Red Earth

Romantic Suspense
Single Title
Island Redemption
Glass Clouds
Chasing Bullets

Love in the Mountains Novella Series
Books can be read as stand-alone
Rain on a Tin Roof
Lost and Found
Rescue his Heart

Connect with the Author

I really hope you enjoyed reading Shadows in Deep Blue. For more action romance info, upcoming release dates, and access to free books join the exclusive Suzanne Cass reader club. As an added bonus, you'll get a copy of my FREE STORY.

Solar Flare

http://www.suzannecass.com/contact/

Or you can stay in touch via my website
www.suzannecass.com

Facebook: www.facebook.com/suzannecassauthor/
Instagram: www.instagram.com/suzanne.cass/
Pintrest: www.pinterest.com.au/suzanne_cass/
Twitter: twitter.com/SusieCass1

About the Author

Suzanne Cass is an Australian author who writes rural romance and romantic suspense abounding with passion and danger.

Her debut novel, Island Redemption, won the Romance Writers of Australia Emerald Award in 2016. Suzanne was also a finalist in the 2019 Romance Writers of Australia RUBY award.

She had always had a fascination with the tough resilience of people who live in our amazing red-dirt outback country. When not writing about the characters that inhabit her head, Suzanne can be found roaming the Perth beaches with her border collie, or encouraging from the sidelines as her two sons play sport.

Stay in touch via my website

www.suzannecass.com

Or

www.ingramcontent.com/pod-product-compliance
Lightning Source LLC
Chambersburg PA
CBHW030635110726
47901CB00002B/449